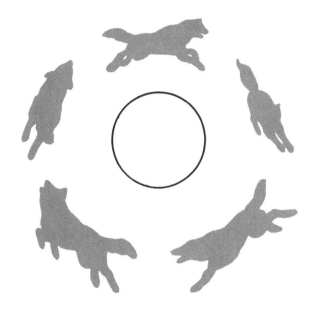

SUNDOGS

STORIES FROM SASKATCHEWAN

EDITED BY ROBERT KROETSCH

COTEAU BOOKS

Cover and title page design and inside artwork by William Johnson.

The publishers wish to thank the Saskatchewan Arts Board for assisting us with the publication of this book and in our general operations. We also thank the Canada Council, which provided assistance for the publication of this title.

Canadian Cataloguing in Publication Data

Main entry under title:
Sundogs

ISBN 0-919926-09-6

1. Short Stories, Canadian (English) — Saskatchewan.*   I. Kroetsch, Robert, 1927-
PS8329.5.S3S86   C813'.0108   C80-091046-X
PR9197.32.S86

coteau books

Thunder Creek Publishing Co-operative Limited
Box 239, Sub #1
Moose Jaw, Saskatchewan S6H 5V0

TABLE OF CONTENTS

AN INTRODUCTION

The short story combines, exquisitely, the personal vision with the sense of talk as something shared. The emergence of Ken Mitchell as a short story writer, in the early 70s, signalled to readers across Canada that the action in that literary form was moving West. Mitchell has a strong sense of both the public and the private dimensions of story; he spoke immediately out of his unique talent, but he spoke, from the beginning, for a place, a community, a history called Saskatchewan. Beyond that, in his mixing of the comic and the tragic, in his listening to our own speech, our unique as well as our shared language, he announced the revitalization of a form that had pretty much gone dead.

What struck me, in reading 70 stories by 34 Saskatchewan writers, was the *abundance*. An abundance of forms, of responses, of styles, of experience. To make of that abundance (that gift) a book, a table of contents from Alford to Vanderhaeghe, meant that I had to exclude numerous publishable stories that spoke both for Saskatchewan and for the renewed vitality of the short story form. I'd like to share a few of my thoughts on the stories that are, here, published.

Edna Alford, in "Barbed Wire and Balloons", tells a story about the telling of a story. She anticipates the sophistication that is characteristic of the stories that follow. Her heroine, like the reader, listens in on a particular telling, appreciates it, weighs it in her mind:

> She went to bed, but couldn't sleep for thinking about the whole thing. She got up and went to the window, which was long and high, two double panes of glass, one on top of the other. Her father already had the storm windows up, even on

the second storey. She levered the bottom window up and propped it open with a stick kept on the window sill.

Alford speaks for a place and an experience in Saskatchewan. But, beyond that, she shows us how a story gets told and how it gets *heard*.

The awareness of the art of storytelling is everywhere in the collection. Mick Burrs examines it almost directly through the activities of a photographer in his ambiguously titled story, "Composition in Black and White". Anne Campbell explores the art with subtle indirection in a story that is called, with an ambiguity equal to Burrs', "The Vocation". Robert Currie further develops the relationships among artwork and artist and audience (the lived or unlived life) in his story, "I Know What I Like".

A subject that used to occasion some of our most naturalistic fiction now inspires some of the most imaginative. Byrna Barclay introduces both the theme of ethnic experience and the tendency to treat it in new literary ways. Her story, "Testimony", is located equally in a Hutterite colony and in the concept of legal process, with all its dependence on language. And Gertrude Story, in *"Das Engelein Kommt"*, explores still another connection between language and the ethnic life when she has her heroine begin: "At our house people never spoke German. My mother would not allow it."

W. L. Riley, in "Pies", takes the encounter between two strong-willed women of ethnic background towards the comic, the tall tale, even the fable. Kristjana Gunnars, working with traditional memories of ethnic experience, makes those memories contemporary, joins Alford in her sophisticated setting of stories within stories.

Saskatchewan becomes a vividly contemporary place in the works of Pat Krause and Barbara Sapergia. Both writers are satiric, Krause in her treatment of go-getter males and their self-betraying monologues, Sapergia in her treatment of the tradition of women's fiction. Krause's new Saskatchewan hero begins: "Put 'er there, pal. I'm a Top Ten Man." Sapergia's "Sun" threatens an end to the tradition of sunrise and sundown endings.

The concern with contemporary life becomes a concern with contemporary form in the literary experiments of Brenda Riches and Reg Silvester. Both Silvester and Riches refuse the separation of imagination and reality that had come to mar traditional fiction. "My first true love gave me oranges to suck," a voice tells us in Riches' story, at once real and unreal. Silvester's fishing yarn is a tall tale unlike any told by your just-back-from-the-North fisherman.

Prose style itself, the way in which we traditionally write down our speech, is challenged by a number of the writers. William Klebeck, in "Pieces", finds a way to capture the lulling flow of experience and its eruption into violence. Eugene Stickland, in "How the West Was Won", translates the dream-world of television onto the page.

The hint of fable, of legend, of memory turning into mystery, is present in many of these stories. John V. Hicks has the fabulous occur on the Saskatchewan River after we are told, realistically:

> As you enter Ahab Grundl's tiny curio shop on River Street, wedged in between a furniture dealer's and a small cafe, you cannot fail to notice a carefully lettered sign, suspended from the ceiling by an almost invisible thread, which reads: You are Welcome to Browse.

And even as we read, the conventions of realism enter into conspiracy with other possibilities. The world's stock of stories begins to echo in our minds.

Lois Simmie, also, shows us how the literal Saskatchewan life begins to become its own legend: her heroine, Bethie, and the deaf and dumb girl of whom Bethie speaks, by the end of the story are "floating in the silence like a strange pair of sea creatures."

The children in Simmie's story are at the lake for the summer. Gertrude Story's characters come together and apart at a Christmas concert. "Speaking of playing," the narrator says in Campbell's "The Vocation". . . . Games and play are everywhere in these stories; the burden of work that characterized the fiction of an older generation is often absent. But the world of play, now, is fraught with overtones and implications. It informs the frightening and attractive portraits of childhood experience (consider, again, Riches' "Rites"). But it informs, also, the adult world in many of these stories.

Love, and her old accomplice, Death. Game turns into ritual in Terrence Heath's "A Proper Burial", as love and death become, explicitly, one. Freda Korber's story of childhood begins, "It was good to kill." But for most of the writers, death sends its surrogates. Death is a "young attractive physiotherapist" in Sorestad's "It Bodder Me". The man and woman in Anne Szumigalski's fable, aptly titled "Untitled", cannot locate their love, even in the act of love-making; that story, like others in the anthology, ends with the image of drowning.

Ritual turns to death-in-life, sex turns to surgery, in Geoffrey Ursell's "Fat". Past and present turn into future. Dieting and marketing become both reality and metaphor. Intimations of a science-fiction universe threaten old notions of the true. Ursell ends his story, appropriately, with thoughts (however ironic) on harvest. There are, again, whole books of stories to be told.

iii

The life-long dialectic of innocence and experience is, perhaps, the pattern, or the energy-source, that gives the stories in this book cohesion. On that movement, on that translation, that transformation, from one to the other, the stories often turn. Perhaps on that same translation the world turns, as in Guy Vanderhaeghe's powerfully realistic (and yet symbolic) story, "Dancing Bear".

To read *Sundogs* is both to enter and to transcend the world that is Saskatchewan. What surprises me, on looking at the list of authors, is my recognition that most of them have, at one time or another, been associated with the writing activities that *take place* at Fort San. There, in the Qu'Appelle Valley, solitude and community fuse into home. Home, in turn, translates itself into book.

This book, then, which in its title acknowledges our debt to weather, the weather of place, the weather of spirit, speaks also of the profound act of naming by which this mis-recorded Indian word, Saskatchewan, becomes Saskatchewan, becomes us.

Robert Kroetsch

SUNDOGS
STORIES FROM SASKATCHEWAN

BARBED WIRE AND BALLOONS

EDNA ALFORD

"What the hell did you do to yourself this time?" Jack was not a reticent man. But neither was August.

"I'm telling you, Jack, it feels like I got three bands of barbed wire cinched round my middle and some jackass is just a drawin' em tighter every time I take a breath."

Louella was upstairs in the back bedroom. She was only half awake but even so she recognized the voice right away. It belonged to August Pickard Moon, her mother's older brother. There wasn't another man between here and Battleford with that raunchy rhythm to his words, that molasses resonance. He was a great story teller if nothing else and Louella decided to get up and go downstairs.

Her favourite story so far was the one he told about the bull. When he was just a young buck, he said, he got himself a bull calf, a black one with a slobbering snout. He said his calf gained a pound a day. And every day, he'd lift the little bugger up over his head. Every single day. And because it gained only a pound a day and because he always figured he could lift one more pound with no trouble at all, he planned to lift the animal when it was fully grown. "And by jumping Jesus, that's exactly what I did," he said, "and the bastard fully growed weighed in at damn near a ton. And I lifted him, without a word of a lie, I lifted him right up over my head, right there at the Meadow Lake Stampede, right in front of the crowd.

1

Clap! You never heard the beat of it. Clapped till they bust out in blisters!" Louella loved it. She could see him clearly in her head, grunting and hoisting his big black bull, till finally she saw him pivot slowly for the crowd, so everyone could see.

"That's a lot of bull alright," her father had said. Later, after August had left, he said to her mother, "August never was a farmer, Iris, you know that as well as me. He don't know a damn thing about livestock. Your folks never had no cattle, only the grain, and he was no help with that either. Galavanting around to sports days was about all he was ever good for. That and drinking, of course. But he sure knows how to shovel shit. I'll give you that. Born in him."

Her father's case was solid. Louella knew that much, even then. But she loved the story and the way he told it and she had learned to keep certain things safe in the back of her mind where her father couldn't get at them. Things like Uncle August's bull. She grabbed her balding blue chenille kimono from the closet hook and shoved her feet into a pair of rabbit slippers, tufted and worn through to the hide where her feet rubbed together when she walked. Wrestling with the kimono all the way down the stairs, she flung herself headlong toward her uncle's voice.

Her father and mother were in the kitchen and both of them were in the process of examining August, who was for the moment silent. He revolved stiffly, all two hundred pounds of him weighted on the heels of his cowboy boots, setting up a linoleum creak which flattened the ears of the dog. Her mother already had the coffee pot ready to go on the stove. She was clutching a half-empty bag of Nabob coffee to her chest, like a stethoscope, looking at August as if she intended at the first appropriate moment to use it on him, to find out for herself once and for all what made the man tick. Her face was pale and serious under the bare light bulb hanging off-centre from the kitchen ceiling, and, from the look of her, Louella figured the situation must be pretty bad, whatever it was.

Uncle August, in one of his slow circles, stopped like the winning or losing number on a roulette wheel and faced her mother. Without speaking he stuck out one of his log-heavy arms toward Iris and nodded. Louella was by then standing beside her, and, without looking at the girl, her mother stuffed the coffee bag into her hands, which were already open, ready to receive something, like those of an altar boy.

Iris took the end of her brother's jacket sleeve and slid it off the arm with that particular gentleness usually reserved for undressing babies. August was wearing his lime green ball jacket, though he did not play ball. It had a red and yellow crest on the back that said "Hub City Sockets" in bumpy appliquéd letters with a matching bumpy black wrench underneath, though, as far as Louella knew, he had no particular affiliation with the Hub City Service Centre any more than he played ball. But August got around, she knew, and she supposed the jacket was just another one of the spoils of his fly-by-night way of life. Along with the peaked John Deere cap he wore, to the side, pulsing yellow with a small green deer, antlered and leaping on the crown at the front of the cap.

The first sleeve fell away and her mother began to peel off the other. Her father, who until then had been standing behind August, rubbing his whiskers and hitching up his pyjama bottoms, reached out and caught the jacket just before it hit the floor. He hung it over the back of a chair.

"Jesus H. Christ, August. What the hell kind of contraption you got on your back?" Jack spoke to the back of August's head. August had just rolled up the last of his tee-shirt and was preoccupied with the final unveiling of his most recently acquired burden.

Louella could see what her father meant. It was a contraption alright, a back brace. It was ribbed and looked a little like Grandma Moon's old flesh-coloured eyelet corset, but it was white and padded thick with foam, like the neck brace her mother had to wear after her whiplash a couple of years ago. Except this brace circled the massive circumference of Uncle August's chest and back. His belly button, which should have been buried like a winking eye in the folds of his belly, remained unfettered, a saucy protruding bump, exactly like the ones she had seen on the bellies of ten-month-old babies. Louella saw her mother's eyes scrape open another notch when she saw the brace and the button.

"Now let me see," August began slowly as if he weren't quite sure himself what had happened to him. "I guess I'd have to say it had something to do with the cows, and God almighty," he sighed, "I guess if I was pushed, I'd have to say it had something to do with the Indians, too." Louella picked out a chair directly opposite to the one with the lime green jacket hung over the back. She wanted a good seat so she wouldn't miss anything.

"Well, hell, it's a long story," he began again, "and of course it's late and if you folks got no time for listening—" This part was rhetorical. There was no question about their listening.

"You gonna tell the damn thing standing or sitting?" Jack said.

"Sitting, Jack. I been standing for a week. Help me get this goddamn contraption off." The request put them all at ease for they knew then that the brace was more like a theatrical prop than anything else, that, whatever had been the matter with August, it must be almost over. He wouldn't have to wear the contraption forever. They relaxed. Louella pulled another chair over close, put up her feet, and wrapped the flaps of the old blue chenille around her legs.

She looked as motheaten as her slippers, and hadn't even taken the time to run the brush through her hair, which was like her mother's, only redder. It looked a little like someone had set fire to a bramble bush. But she wasn't really worried about her hair. She knew Uncle August didn't care how she looked because she wasn't *on*. He was *on*. He played fiddle with the Rowdy Roses, played for all the dances for miles around, all the way from Battleford to Lloyd. He had a stage sense not everybody has. And a sense of timing. Louella was audience, and audience could look any way it liked so long as it was there.

While her father helped August unhitch himself from the brace, rolling his tee-shirt back down over the enormous liberated belly, her mother measured six teaspoons of coffee directly into the boiling water in the pot, set four cups on the table along with a jar of spoons, sugar bowl, creamer, and an ashtray. Uncle August smoked. "It'll be ready in a flash," she said and sat down.

"Maybe August don't want that kind of lightning, Iris," Jack said. "Maybe he needs a shot. Whadaya say, Aug?"

"Now you're talking, Jackie. I got a lot of pain in my condition. I tell you, if it were any closer to Easter, I'd think I was carrying the goddamn cross."

Jack poured two glasses half full of Three Feathers and set them on the table. August made his way to the chair with the jacket on the back and lowered himself slowly to the seat. He took off his cap, drawing the back of his right hand across his brow as he did so. Iris took the cap and put it on the arm of the sofa, which served as a barrier between the living room and kitchen of their farmhouse.

While she poured coffee for Louella and herself, August fidgeted in his chair, straightened, stuck his right hand behind his back, reached under his tee-shirt and rubbed so hard Louella thought he'd flay the skin right off. He took a long, sucking sip off the top of his drink, taking in more air than rye. Jack lifted his glass and drank half the amber liquid straight off.

"Get on with it, Aug," he said, rubbing the line of whiskey on his lips downward into his whiskers, like a salve which smelled more like Zambuck or Zinc to Louella, not rye.

August lifted his unoccupied hand to his broad forehead, splayed his fingers and ran them over the shiny skin on the top of his skull as if there were hair, handfuls of it. "Dammit," he said, "I'm just trying to recall here what time it was it happened. I know it was a Thursday — no, by God, it was a Friday — payday for the other

4

fellas. I don't worry about that no more, Jack, since I bought the truck. Now I'm my own boss. Anyway, I know the sun was about halfway down the other side of afternoon, three, maybe pushing four. I'd made seven trips already, up the Meadow Lake grid, up past the reservation there, thirty-five, maybe forty miles from here. Haulin' gravel. And every time I come back empty, well I had a scrap of time to think."

August had bought himself a gravel truck in the spring. "God knows where he got the money," Jack had said. "He never has two cents to rub together." But Louella thought August had always been very enterprising — in his way. He'd been in and out of more occupations than they could count, wheeling and dealing his way through farm machinery, the manufacture of rapeseed oil, grave digging and landscaping, the oil rigs, insurance, janitorial services, taxi driving, and bread delivery — these were only the few she could remember from the stories. Now he had bought himself a gravel truck and all the relatives hoped he could make a go of it this time. That was how her father had put it. Make a go of it.

Louella didn't judge August by whether or not he could make a go of it and she didn't think it was right that most of her relatives did, with the possible exception of her own mother. Louella was in grade ten and the threat of having to make it on her own hook was at least a year or two away. But once in awhile, usually late at night, the prospect of finally being responsible for all her own decisions worried her. Then all the vague and nameless future decisions buzzed her like the random, mindless threat of bees. And she saw herself, like Uncle August, turning every which way in life, trying to figure out the best or safest or most lucrative or most worthwhile way a person could live. And her worst fear was the never ever *knowing* what the right one was. The *right decision* rose like the ghost of Marley, every year more and more rarified, more remote, more guilt-laden, and especially more threatening. She had her dreams, but they gave her small comfort. For one thing, they had to do with painting pictures, an idea she got after she had been to the Imhoff Art Gallery near St. Walburg. This was not exactly what her mother and father thought of as a level-headed sort of plan. And dreams of any kind were under suspicion around this house since Uncle August was, above all, a dreamer.

"So I'm coming back empty the seventh time," August said, "and I'm listening to the radio and I'm lookin' around, seein' which crops is ready for threshin', here and there lookin' at the cows — that sort of thing. And I begin to think. And you won't believe what I'm thinkin' about, Iris."

Louella started involuntarily when her mother jerked and

opened her eyes. Iris began to fuss with the lace around the collar of her brightly quilted robe — this animation instantaneous, as if August had just pushed the "on" button of a machine. Louella noticed that her mother's hair was no more respectable than hers tonight. She had managed to find her new glasses with the amber plastic frames, squared off on their owlish edges, but they gave her no protection from August.

"I'm thinkin' about *cows*, Iris, the cows I been passing fourteen goddamn times already. Finally it registers — them poor bitches is dyin', I says to myself. The hides, I'm tellin' you Jack, them hides was hanging like gunny sacks. You could've hung your hat anywheres you wanted on the poor buggers. Their bones just stuck out like goddamn coathooks and their hair was all matted and the tufts was just a flyin' in the wind like puffs off an old dandelion."

"Now hold onto your horses a minute, August," Jack said. As Louella suspected, her father had definitely not been sleeping. "Where in hell are you talking about? You don't mean to tell me every bloody farmer between here and Meada Lake is starvin' his cows, because it ain't so."

"I was gettin' to that, Jackie." August raised his thick black eyebrows as if to let her father know he was nobody's fool. He tipped his head back and closed his eyes. The sausage fingers of his left hand cradled the remaining amber in his glass. Louella always wondered how a man with such thick fingers could play the fiddle like he could. His right hand was still behind his back and kept right on rubbing, as if pain were his lot — external or self-induced, it made no difference; he had to bear it. This constant rubbing had a great effect. She had to hand it to him.

"To get to your point, Jack," he began.

"I'd be grateful," Jack said, rolling his eyes away from the dark half-moons which had risen beneath them.

"The fact is," August continued, "them cows was on reservation pasture. And the goddamn government give them Indians the cows so's they could start a herd. You and me, Jack, the goddamn government don't give us a plug nickel, and we're scratching, ain't we, hard as we can, just to make a go of it. Not a nickel, let alone a herd of cows. In fact, they're suckin' us dry most of the time."

"I don't give a damn whose cows they were, August. They have to belong to somebody. And I ain't sittin' up all night talking politics, neither." Louella was afraid her father had decided to go to bed. And August would leave, knowing he had pushed him too far this time.

But Uncle August groaned and Louella was amazed at the speed with which her mother jumped up and grabbed him a cushion from

the sofa and tucked it behind his back. He said she shouldn't have —
she was a saint, he said, and she was too good to him, and he was no
good for nothin' anyway, and he should be moving along so they
could all get to bed.

"August Pickard Moon," said Iris, as if she were scolding a
small child, "what's a sister for?" Although, to look at them, Louella
couldn't tell they were related at all. A difference of night and day,
people always said. "You tell us your story, August," her mother
said softly, "we're all ears."

Jack stood up, raised his arms over his head, bent them crooked
and clasped his hands behind his head. Louella thought she heard
his knuckles crack. He left the table and she thought he was finally
fed up and was on his way upstairs, but he headed for the back door,
flapping his slippers on the linoleum as he went. He stood at the
screen door for a long time, looking up. Then he turned and flapped
back to his chair and sat down. "Full moon tonight, Aug," he said.

"I seen that, Jack," said August, smiling, "and I see your point."
His voice was feathery, like the pillow Louella knew her father
would rather have had. "It don't matter whose cows they were. The
fact is they was starvin'. That pasture was just about as bald as Jackie
here." Her father's hair was totally grey and was beginning to thin,
but Louella could see you'd have to be half blind not to notice he was
by no means as bald as August. "They even ate the goddamn twigs. I
mean there wasn't a leaf on a bush nor a blade of grass nor nothin'.
That's how poor it was. And the bastards were too goddamn lazy to
move them cows to decent grazing.

"The cows was all standing in a row along the west fence with
their heads bowed, stuck through the second and third rungs of
barbed wire. Twenty-five, maybe thirty head, black and white. All
with their tongues hangin' out, droolin' over a field of alfalfa on the
other side. And it was one of the finest alfalfa fields I ever seen, even
if I do say so, regardless who planted it, white men, Indians, or Jesus
Christ himself."

" 'Nough , August," Jack said, nodding toward Louella.

"Maybe so, maybe so, Jack, but the fact is them cows was
starvin'. They'd chewed a swath about two feet wide all along that
fence, picked her clean as a chicken bone. I bet you couldn't have
found a ounce of vegetation on that swath if I'd a paid you a hundred
dollars."

"For a hundred dollars, I'd a taken it out of my own hide," Jack
said.

"I bet you would, Jackie. I bet you would. Thing is the poor
bitches couldn't reach no further. And I mean, what the hell'd they
ever do to deserve that, I'm thinkin' to myself. Starvin' to goddamn

death right beside the best field of alfalfa on the face of the earth. I mean, they're innocent, the poor buggers; they may not be smart, but they're sure as hell innocent." August adjusted the pillow behind him, pulling it up higher so that one of the tassels tickled his right arm, just below the armpit. He reached around with his left arm, awkwardly, in a way Louella thought would've hurt his back, but he didn't flinch or groan. Just flicked the tassel up and tucked it under the pillow.

"Well," he said, "the point is I got to thinking about all this on my dry run. I get back to the pit and they load her up and I see that all the other trucks is through for the day. I'm the only one making the last run back. I cranks her up and away I go and pretty soon I come to the pasture, which was on reservation land, Jackie, whether you like it or whether you don't."

"This story don't seem to have a damn thing to do with Indians, August, if I ain't mistaken. Could'a been anybody. Fact is you don't really know for certain whose cows they was. Everybody around here rents pasture from the reserve, for Christ's sake."

"Maybe so, Jack. But it seems to me that it do have something to do with Indians. Problem is I ain't quite sure what yet. But why else do you think I brung em in?"

"I believe I need another drink, Aug. Throw me the bottle. I'm damned if I can make head nor tail of your goddamn cows, August. How about you, Iris?"

Louella could see her father was fairly near to being lit by this time, which was unusual for him, but her mother had never been one of those women whose greatest need in life is to ride herd on other people. She smiled like a young girl, her freckles like the spots on the photographic negative of a fawn's back Louella had seen in the science lab at school.

"Give him time, Jack. Maybe he's got something to say," she said.

"Thanks, Iris," said August, humble and nodding his head toward her. "But I believe I need a little lubercation too before I go on." He poured a drink. Then he pulled a slightly flattened pack of Player's cigarettes out of the back pocket of his pants and lit up. His fingers had grease in the creases at the joints, and his right index finger was yellowed from the top joint to the nail. The nail was completely yellow except for a thin ring of dark green grease around the cuticle.

"Them things are gonna kill you one of these days, August. Why don't you give em up before they put you under?"

"Now Jackie, why'd you have to go and say a thing like that? You should know by now the truth ain't always what a person wants to hear — or needs to. Though I ain't sayin' it's so in every case. Sometimes the truth is what you have to have, like it or not. I'm only sayin' it ain't always that way."

They had all but forgotten about his back, especially August, who had discarded his cushion altogether and now sat straight up in his chair, by turns moulding and poking and pinching the air with his hands as if it were made of bread dough. "As I say, I gets close to the pasture—"

"I thought you said you was there already," said Jack.

"And from a distance," August continued without pause, "I could see the pitiful creatures lined up like they was in a bread line for what I guess must a been their fair share of heaven, such as it would be for a cow. And I says to myself, 'No, goddammit! If he don't treat his creatures no better than that, the good old Lord don't deserve em. The old bastard's gonna have to wait.'

"So I shuts her down right then and there but she doesn't roll to a stop till about fifty feet past the fence. I opens up the glove compartment, takes out my pliers and away I go. I walks a ways back and as I'm goin' along I'm lookin' around. And there's not a soul anywheres, no machinery, no buildings, nothin'. I don't see or hear no cars. Just the wind and the sun and the high sweet smell of tall alfalfa. And the goddamn great blue sky. Not even a cloud.

"Pretty soon I come to the fence, so I straddle the ditch and spread the wires and I'm through. Took me a bit more time than I figured on account of not having snips, just my pliers. Fact, I caught my finger on one of them metal barbs — like thorns, Iris, only they don't give. Opened the sucker up about a half-inch deep. This here's the scar, Iris." He stuck his afflicted finger about six inches from her glasses so that momentarily Louella saw her eyes cross over to the bottom inside corners of her lenses. "And bleed," he said, "that sucker bled till I thought there'd be no stopping it. I damn near passed out."

Louella leaned forward to get a better look at the evidence, white scar tissue already starting to form a layer over the tiny red fissure in the sausage skin. Even she had a lot of trouble believing that so much blood had come from so small a wound. Her father just bowed his head and shook it back and forth slowly, like an aging buffalo.

"But I opened up that mothering fence in four places, about thirty or forty feet apart," August continued, more agitated now, his fiddle voice almost a half-octave higher. "And when I'm just about finished the last hole, I look back and —" He could hardly go on, he was laughing so hard, slapping his spread thighs and wiping the water from his eyes with the wide back of one hand. "— them

9

goddamn cows was all through the *first* hole. And I been working like a bugger for nothin'!" He made a whistle sound like the sound he made with his bow at the climax of the "Orange Blossom Special", high-pitched and thick and compressed. Then he doubled over and held himself in his own arms as if the pain had somehow wriggled from his back around to his belly.

He grew more serious as if a dark cloud had passed over the sun in his storybook sky. "That ain't the worst of it," he said, "that's the best. When I get back to the truck, I look up at her box and I see my load has shifted on the way out from the pit. I'd figured as much. I hit a pot hole about five miles back. Anyways, there was little turds of gravel rolling off already just like they do on the new mounds at the graveyard outside town." Then to Jack he said, "This job ain't much different from when I was grave digging, Jack. Same kinda thing. Just layin' down dirt and stones as far as the eye can see. Anyway, so I climb up to the cab and get my spade out from underneath the seat. Up I go because I have to skim the high part of the load over to the other side of the box or I'll lose most of it before I get up to the goddamn site if I haven't already.

"I no sooner get up there and I'm straddling the hump I have to clear and I look up at the sky and down at my little herd which is havin' a field day, fillin' their faces to their hearts' content. I can hear them from all the way up there. And you know, Iris," he said, looking deep into her bifocals as if he were trying to locate her under water, "I never felt better in my life. Just like August Pickard, the fella dad named me for, the guy in the balloon that climbed the highest of us all. I know what it musta been like. How he musta felt. Felt that way myself, Iris, on top a my truck."

Louella remembered the story of how Grandpa Moon had come to give August his name. In those days her grandfather spent his waiting time reading the Western Producer or the Farmer's Almanac — anything handy to take his mind off the back bedroom labour until the midwife brought out something more certain than herself. That particular occasion, the third of its kind in as many years, August said, Grandpa was just clipping the silver metal arms of his spectacles together when the midwife came out with a boy — the first Moon son.

According to August, Grandpa Moon rose from his chair like a king and solemnly declared that if that was the case, then the boy's name would be Auguste Piccard, only he pronounced it August Pickard, having had a hard enough time learning to read English, August said, let alone French. August Pickard, in honour of the man in the last article he had read — the man who had got him through the worst of the waiting. The man who that year, 1932, set the record for having flown the highest of any human being on the face of the earth — in a hot air balloon. And who would later set the record for having sunk the deepest, in a deep-sea diving bell. But Louella's father always maintained that August came ill-equipped. No balloon and no bell. And he didn't think much of Auguste Piccard in the first place.

"*That* poor son-of-a-bitch," Jack muttered now, "thinkin' he went so high. No more'n'a flea on a dog's back. About the same size hop in the general scheme of things."

But August didn't seem to hear him, and regardless of what her father said, Louella couldn't remember when she had ever seen her uncle's large brown eyes so bright. "No shit, Jack, I felt so good I stretched out my arms," he said, "like this, high as I could, to see if I could get ahold of the big blue bugger, give him a hug. Then, just as sure as I'm sitting here," he continued, bolting upright in his chair, "I slipped. And down I went, just like that." He raised his right hand high in the kitchen air toward the ceiling light bulb, straightened the thick index finger and dive-bombed it onto the yellow arborite. Louella heard the finger bones crack. "Just like a bloody bird, froze and fallin' through the winter sky," he said.

"Landed flat on my back. Right on a goddamn bed of gravel. Not your fine stuff neither — boulders, I tell you. Jack — you're always the one bitching about your boulder roadbeds — well this was one of em for sure." Louella imagined August on the boulder bed, his muscular arms stuck out perpendicular from his sides, his legs spread, his tee-shirt lifted a little, exposing his innocent belly button to the elements. "They say he sees the little sparrows fall, but to tell you the truth," said August, "I got the impression that if he saw me goin' down at all, he didn't give a damn."

"The goin' down was bad enough," he said. Louella's mother nodded and shook her head alternately, but always sympathetically. "But when I tried to get up," he continued, "I thought maybe I broke my back. The pain was way worse than when I got my foot caught under the stoneboat, Iris."

Louella could tell her mother remembered by the way she winced. Though Iris was forty-three, Louella knew she had better recall of the minute memories of her childhood than she had of last week. Her father sat like a stone, patiently, as if he were waiting for something, his eyes turned upward, inspecting the ceiling. Trying to figure out a way to straighten out that light fixture, Louella bet. He could never stand to leave a thing off-centre.

August continued anyway, undaunted, figuring part of an audience was better than none, Louella supposed. "The pain was so bad at first," he said, "that I figured I'd be better off not fighting it.

So I just lay back and look up at the sky. But all I can see is that great big blue bastard and finally I can't take it no more. So I looks him straight in the eye and I says, 'Jesus Christ, you would've done the same goddamn thing if you'd a been here, now wouldn't you, you son-of-a-bitch?' But I don't get no answer of course. Dead silence.

"By and by I think it could get a helluva lot worse if I don't get off the middle of the road. After what I said, I figured he'd probably send one of them big semis straight up from the city to do the job. And I'd be flatter than the bloody Province of Saskatchewan. So I worked at it and pretty soon I could get up. But I still got to wear *that* goddamn contraption," he sighed and pointed at the brace hanging harmless as a limp dishrag on the knob of a cupboard door. "Doc says maybe I gotta wear it the rest of my life, off and on. Ain't that a bugger? But by the Lord Harry, *it was worth it!*" He stretched, settled back, and smiled.

Louella wished she could clap, but now her father spoke. "August Pickard Moon. You are a goddamn fool." His speech was dangerous, precise, separating every word from every other word with a thin slice of silence.

"Now wait a minute, Jack," her mother interrupted gently. But Jack clenched his fist and thumped it on the table, not only making the spoons rattle, but causing them to hop around, clinking metallically, directionless on the yellow arborite table top.

"You stupid bastard," he said, "you killed them cows just as sure as puss is a cat, just as sure as if you put a shotgun to their heads and blew their brains out. Damn it, August, you should have known better. If you'd a gone back the next morning, all you'd a seen is thirty fuzzy black and white balloons, dead and rotting from the inside out. You might a seen them in the air in fact, they'd be so goddamn bloated." Jack straightened up, stiff and self-righteous in his chair, his back erect. "There's only one way they could a been saved, Aug," he said quietly. "And that's if somebody'd a gone out there with the sharpest knife he could find and drove it straight through the hides to the high point of the bloat. Saved em from their own hot air. But I don't suppose nobody done that."

From his sad, immobile, disbelieving face, Louella could tell that August had not known better, that the fact her father had just brought to his attention had never even crossed his mind. All the cups and glasses on the table were empty now, even the bottle. There was a terrible dry silence. Louella began to watch her rabbit slippers with the kind of intensity which suggested they might come to life, wriggle off her feet and run back upstairs to hide under the bed where she wished she had been right then. For a while she couldn't bring herself to look back at Uncle August's face. But after a respectable silence, she did. And when she did she saw that the MacIntosh flush on his fat apple cheeks had disappeared. She looked back at the Three Feathers bottle, half expecting it to have been restored.

Finally her father spoke," 'S'at it?"

" 'S'it," said August, suddenly heavy with his own weight. Louella thought he looked like any man would, just come down out of a storm in a hot air balloon, finding himself on earth again, forced to walk around on two legs like everybody else, at least until the weather cleared, always an indefinite period of time around here. He rose slowly, like the elderly, stood, and lifted his tee-shirt.

Iris already held the back brace positioned in air, spread and waiting for August's massive girth. He stuck out his arms and she laced him up quickly, the quicker the better, Louella felt. He rolled his tee-shirt down over the brace and Iris helped him into his lime green ball jacket. She plucked his cap from the sofa and handed it to him. He turned the yellow cap slowly with his sausage fingers till the peak was in its proper place and the miniature deer leapt above his forehead where it belonged. He pulled the peak down so that it shadowed his eyes. Louella had never seen her uncle's eyes so dark, that dark black-brown of limb holes on the skin of hard wintered poplar. Her mother was a good foot-and-a-half shorter and a good hundred pounds lighter than August, but she reached up and tried to circle his trunk with her arms anyway.

"It don't matter, August," she said. "You did what you thought was right. That's the important thing."

"Well, Iris, I don't know about that," he said sadly. "I got no way of knowing if I'm damned or blessed or nothin' at all. But I'll tell you one last thing. When I got up from that gravel bed it felt just as if I was giving birth to a goddamn roll of barbed wire."

"Sort of like your story, Aug." Jack's voice was softer. He had made his decision. "Take care of yourself," he said.

And Iris had made her decision. "Come again soon, August," she said. "Thanks for dropping in and letting us know how you're doing."

"Yee-uh, and thanks for the shot, Jack," August said. He turned and made a stiff, cumbersome exit through the door which Jack held open, formally, like a funeral attendant.

Louella was the only one who had not yet made up her mind. There seemed to be a lot of pitfalls in the business of making decisions. She couldn't even seem to figure out for herself whose cows they were, much less whether Uncle August had been right or wrong about what he had done. She went to bed, but couldn't sleep for thinking about the whole thing. She got up and went to the window, which was long and high, two double panes of glass, one on top of the other. Her father already had the storm windows up, even on the second storey. She levered the bottom window up and propped it open with a stick kept on the window sill. The bottom of the outside frame had a rectangular wooden flap which she now lifted back, revealing three small round holes of cold, clear air.

She stood there for a few minutes just breathing and watching the full moon, thinking maybe she might see it move one way or the other, up or down, if she just kept a careful eye on it. But it didn't. The sky was clear and the moon stood exactly centred in the upper pane, balancing a brilliant bull of stars.

TESTIMONY

BYRNA BARCLAY

I, Donna Claire Brown, of the City of Saskatoon, in the Province of Saskatchewan, freelance court reporter, MAKE OATH AND SAY THE FOLLOWING:

Yes, I understand the procedure, I'm a court reporter myself, it's just that I'm used to recording an affadavit, not making one. I must get my facts straight, but I'm not sure of anything now. Not after what happened.

I left Prince Albert for Saskatoon at five o'clock on Friday, with over ninety uncertain miles ahead, and with my own constant caution, not fear, of travelling at night.

I rarely drive on the highway at night. So often a jury won't come back with a verdict until after midnight and then it is much too late to set out for the next trial. So I never drive after dusk, not because I'm afraid of night travelling, but because of the problem I have with my eyes.

It isn't anything that can be corrected with glasses, and my eyes never bother me during the day. For some reason, my judgement or perception of things changes after dusk. On the road I can't tell which cars are coming towards me or which cars are moving away from me; and they all appear to be exactly the same distance from me. I'm fine on a divided highway where I can keep to the right lane and don't have to pass other cars, or if I'm travelling with His

Lordship. Then I stay close behind him, use his red tail-lights as a focal point to keep distances in perspective. His Lordship was the reason I decided to risk returning to Saskatoon at night and in a blizzard.

I never do anything on impulse — even my spontaneity is based on a well-thought-out course of action — and I chose to leave that Friday for reasons that had accumulated over a period of fifteen years. There were obvious reasons, of course, like the protection I must give His Lordship by not revealing his name. We were to have the entire weekend together.

There was no traffic ahead or behind me, but this road was always well-patrolled by the RCMP. I would make it. The road was clear, not even a patch of ice, and no signs of snow. It wasn't dark yet.

Static on the radio and a wavering announcer's voice: *degrees centigrade . . . below . . . last recorded . . . wind chill factor.* I switched it off.

The days were getting longer now. No, this light was — *strange* — dashing the word out of my mind, only to have it replaced by: *un-natural.* I was moving toward, into the storm.

It was the light. The whiteness of everything around me. It was like entering a new dimension. There was no horizon, no division between land and sky, only a wall of white looming ahead of me. On either side, the farmers' fields stretched away like endless burial grounds. In many places, barbed wire fences were downed and covered with snow. Shrouds of white willows. Mounds of humped white earth. Skeletal branches, like arms reaching out of graves. Sky was white. Air heavy and stilled. The looming wall ahead of me; and I was drawn, pulled, into the storm.

It was like breaking the sound barrier. Wind and snow hit at the same moment, and the car buffeted. It veered to the right, towards the ditch. I gripped the wheel, held it steady, kept the car on the disappearing road. Wind battered the car. A driving, slanting snow, like needles on the windshield. I switched on the wipers, but the glass was misting, small runs of water streaming into the corners of the window. I turned the heater off and opened the side window.

I don't know how many miles I put behind me, how long I battled through wind and flying snow. I hunched over the wheel, peered through the wedge of clear glass swept clean by rubber wipers, tried to will the car through the swirling whiteness. The car crawled slowly southward.

Gradually, the light dropped, falling from a blue white into a pale yellow, then shades of grey until it was dark all around me, wind and snow beating steadily all around me, the only sounds the grinding motor and my own shallow breathing. Wind blew snow in from the fields, banked drifts along curled edges of ditch, smothered the road. I was slowly plowing through snow, breaking a new trail. I missed yellow lights of scattered towns, yard lights of intermittent farms. I didn't know where I was, my only thought: *keep on going, and don't stop, no matter what, just keep on going.* I was losing all sense of place, of time, of direction, and finally of myself.

A dark shape leaped into the headlights' beam, round like the humped back of an angry animal. A car crossways on the road. I slammed on the brakes, swung the wheel to the left, swerved, and was stopped by a mound of snow. I shifted into reverse, back wheels spun, motor whirred angrily. I was stuck. Quickly, I shifted into drive, then reverse again, then drive; rocking the car, but it wouldn't move forward or backwards.

What to do? It would be a courting of death to leave the car and attempt to walk to safety; I'd soon be lost in the blizzard and downed like a farmer's snow-bound calf. I'd just have to wait out the storm until morning or a patrol car found me, whichever came first. I was afraid to leave the motor running, thought of carbon monoxide poisoning, but if I turned it off it might not start again. I compromised by rolling the window down just a fraction more and leaving the car in neutral.

My feet were freezing, my new black boots cracking with cold. I reached over the seat for the blanket and wrapped my legs and feet in it. I lit the candle and set it on the dashboard. I opened a new pack of cigarettes. Waiting for help, I don't know how long I was lost.

I'm a survivor, and the image I had of myself that night was one I've projected before me all my life. At thirty-nine and holding, I'm a professional woman, I run my own business. Of course, it's the governments, provincial and federal, that hire me, but I'm my own boss, and I cover the province, five days out of seven, when the courts are in session. Fifteen years on the road hasn't left much time for a personal life, there's only His Lordship, and I've followed him from courtroom to courtroom as far south as Swift Current and as far north as Prince Albert.

I've been on my own since I was seventeen. I never had a family and never wanted one; the only home I ever knew was Haultain House, an orphanage. After business college I landed a job in the steno pool in the Saskatoon Court House, and it was there that I met His Lordship.

I suppose we were people ahead of our times: in those days there were two choices open, either marry or break up, and we chose a fifteen-year-long affair. I remember the way he looked fifteen years ago: blonde boogie-cut with sides greased back, draped grey flannel pants, and tweed jacket with patches on the elbows. He was so thin I used to tell him to carry anvils in his pockets so the wind wouldn't blow him away. I remember the dramatic change when he put on his robes, the sudden ringing voice, the strong presence in the court room even before he became a judge. He helped me set up a business of my own.

An abrupt knocking of a flashlight on the side window.

"Hey! Hey, lady! You okay in there?"

It was an RCMP constable. I climbed out of the car, and he gripped my elbow and steered me through the whirling night. My feet sunk deep into snow, my legs began to burn with cold. In front of my snow-buried car, a municipal grader, its yellow lights blinking through blowing snow like eyes of a giant predator. Next to it, the patrol car, and I expected the constable to direct me toward, not away from, it. "Two miles down the road!" he yelled. The grader was backing up now, and roaring, the constable hollering, "Safe there!", words swallowed by the screaming wind.

Behind the patrol car, a two-ton cattle truck. The constable boosted me up, and leather hands hauled me over the side into the back of the truck.

"Sit down," someone said. A dark figure wrapped in blankets.

I crouched down, and two black woolen arms wrapped a blanket around my legs and feet.

"Lucky for us the Hutterites came by. Drink this."

It was whiskey, and it burned my mouth and throat.

The truck lurched forward, tires spinning; it shook, then rumbled slowly backwards, the front swinging to the right; and it seemed to dive forward again, plunge into the storm.

It was a dark shelter, the high sides of the wagonbox a protection from the wind. Inside, there were many dark and huddling people, blanket mounds that made them look like pot-bellied stoves, their breath white smoke. I couldn't tell if they were men or women until they began to sing.

I am still haunted by that sound: almost a keening, but ringing like many steeple bells. The first song was a German love song, the second began with, "Thank God I am a woman and I know where I belong," and the remaining many songs they sang were all hymns I had never heard before. Two women at the front of the wagonbox led the singers, choosing the songs and beginning each one only a syllable or two before the others joined in. I wanted to sing with them, but I didn't know any of the words.

I don't know how long we struggled through the storm towards the colony. Twice I felt the truck swerve, the people all leaning into the turns, and I guessed we had gone far west of the main highway.

We turned off the washboard road onto colony land, and suddenly, in one motion, the women grasped the railings and pulled themselves up, their voices slicing into the wind, the words, "I was lost but now I'm found," an answering call to the colony. The women faced the wind, points of their scarves lifted, and they sang us down a tree-lined lane.

I rose too, wanting to see ahead. The first sight I had was of many lights scattered over what looked to be equivalent to the area of a small town. The truck seemed to float towards the first yard light, which grew larger and stronger until it seemed like a beacon. Finally, we stopped before the first house.

A crowd of people immediately surrounded the truck. Again, hands lifted me out, and my feet touched down on a cement sidewalk. There was laughter and a calling out of names; older women seemed to be teasing younger ones scrambling down from the truck; but they spoke German and I couldn't understand them.

A black woolen hand patted my arm. "You be fine now." The accent wasn't German, as I would have expected, but closer to a southern drawl. Each word was pronounced slowly and deliberately, as if the speaker were trying out each sound for the first time. "I'm Ruth."

"My name is Donna," I said.

"Doooh-na," Ruth said.

"I like the way you say my name," I said.

"We talk funny here," Ruth said, ducking her shawled head towards me. "Not like Hutterites anywhere, so even people in other colonies make fun of us."

I was herded, with the man who gave me whiskey and another squat figure in a laminated parka, towards the house. Ruth beside me, taking long strides. "It's because of where we came from," she said. "Why we talk so slow. The first immigration was from a long way south I think. We speak only Low German until we are seven, then go to English teacher, but we write in High German. Many books my father writes, many sermons, but only in High German. His English is very good. But best I like to sing in German."

"Do you always sing?" I asked. "I mean, I've never heard anything so—", suddenly feeling foolish.

"We always sing," Ruth said. "When we work, if I don't sing I get lazy. Singing keeps my hands working fast."

"I hope we don't have to stay all night," the man in the brown tweed coat said. He turned down the raccoon collar and entered the house ahead of me.

19

"This house has full basement," Ruth said. "The only one on the colony. The moneyman lives here. I hope I go to the new colony and live in house with full basement."

The white house, the only single-family dwelling on the colony, was not unlike any bungalow in a middle-class urban district. Or so it appeared from the outside. The entrance was a large room similar to the men's wash-up rooms found in large farm houses outside the colony, but there were sheepskin coats and traditional black Hutterite hats hanging on wooden pegs. The inner door opened onto a long hallway with tile flooring.

"Welcome, welcome!" A thick-set man with a wind-burned face showed us into a room at the end of the hall.

Ruth was pulled aside by a dumpy woman with wire-rimmed glasses slipping over her wide flat nose. The women clustered at the door, beaming at the three guests, but they did not enter the room. They all wore Hutterite cloth, bright cotton blouses and skirts of different colours and patterns, but cut in the same style: bodices with tight long sleeves, high necks, buttons down the front. The scarves were black and white polka dot, but the skull caps holding back their waist-length hair were sewn from the same material as the bodices.

The inner room was warm, the walls polished oak. Four Hutterite men leaned forward on an oak bench that looked like a pew. They rested their elbows on knees, hands folded as if ready for prayer. A homemade cabinet held three shelves of books bound in black leather and I didn't know if they were accounting ledgers or Bibles. The only other furniture in the room was a kitchen table, the top arborite and legs chrome.

"Welcome, welcome," the Hutterite elder said again. "We are grateful our painting party has returned safely from North Dakota!"

The women shrank back from the doorway, hands smothering giggles.

"On such a night we have much to be thankful for! Our young women return with many barns painted. With many proposals for marriage!" The elder explained why the Hutterite truck held only women. They were a painting party returning from an intended, pre-arranged meeting of young people from many colonies. "But sit! Be comfortable! And we have rhubarb wine." He poured wine into kitchen glasses on the table. "Aged seven years!" he laughed, and handed around the glasses.

I sat, with the other two guests, on straight-backed, hard vinyl chairs. We sipped the wine.

"Good!" the elder said. "Better than Liebfraumilch!"

The Hutterites laughed. The elder remained standing before the kitchen table, glass raised as if he were toasting God. "We are thankful that you made your way here through the storm, and you are welcome to join with us this very special night. But forgive me, I do not know your names. I am Reverend Timothy!", reaching for my hand.

"Thank you for giving us refuge," I said.

The tall man in the tweed coat with raccoon collar jumped up and began to pace before the table. "We mustn't be kept waiting!" he said. "We must not be kept waiting!"

"Storm will soon pass over," Rev. Timothy said. "By morning, I am sure, and then you can leave."

"I'm a doctor!" the man said, as if he were another kind of missionary. "I can't be kept waiting here all night! Haven't you got a telephone? Can't we be driven somewhere?"

"Ohhhh, another one!" the squat figure in the laminated parka said. A gloved hand pushed the hood away from a face that was covered with hair. "Do you know, Doctor . . .", sentence trailing away into fragments of sighs and coughing.

"You keep people waiting," Rev. Timothy said, "so maybe it is good for you to wait now."

"We must not be kept waiting!" The doctor paced, feet shuffling, overshoes flapping, his hands folding and unfolding as if he were pleading with God and the Hutterites.

He reminded me of His Lordship, the doctor believing he was created in the image of God, the judge believing he sat higher than other people and much closer to God when he handed down decisions. I suddenly remembered him, the last weekend we were together, in the bathroom clipping his white side curls before the mirror, his hair curling on the ivory tile like a stunned and dying white worm. "Time must be deferred!" he said.

"Time is transitory," I said.

"Ah," Rev. Timothy said, "but time is eternal."

"It is God's will," the person in the parka said. A woman was emerging from it, breasts encased in a brown blouse thrust out first, then heavy arms; and she shed the parka like a cocoon. "My illness," she said. "It is God's will." On her right cheek, a swath of long black hair. Patches of hair on the left, like cat's fur. "My name is Lydia," she said, "and I'm going to Bible College, was supposed to do a workshop with children in Prince Albert. I want to work with children." Her hands fluttered around her face but didn't touch it.

"Well, well," Rev. Timothy said. "Here we tell the married men from the single by their beards."

Lydia smiled into the high neck of her blouse, fingertips

checking the buttons to make sure they were all done up. "Well, I guess," she said, "I would have caused some commotion, confusion, at your barn-painting party."

The doctor was the only person who didn't laugh with Lydia. He squared his massive shoulders, peered through the lace curtains as if watching for someone to rescue him from the Hutterites and the bearded missionary.

"It isn't ever going to let up," he said.

"If you can't wait for patients," Lydia said, "you can practise on me."

The doctor glared at her over his raccoon collar.

Somewhere, outside, a bell tolled.

"Milking time," Rev. Timothy said, "and the cows must not be kept waiting."

The four Hutterite men laughed into their short, cropped beards, downed the dregs of the rhubarb wine. They got up and left.

From the hallway, Ruth beckoned to me. "Come along," she said, and I followed her outside.

Wind had settled. Snow, heavy and moist, drifted on our heads and shoulders. It spun under the yard light like ghosts of a million fat sand flies who had returned from a forgotten summer night. I wasn't sure if the weather had let up or if it only seemed to be better due to the trees' protection.

The colony was laid out on a square, all buildings joined by a crossing network of cement sidewalks. I wondered who had shovelled them clear.

Ruth pointed out the dormitories. They looked like Legion halls. "I live there," she said. "See in the window, my plants? White-flowering prayer plants. They fold their leaves at night."

I smelled something toasty, and I thought it was snowing puffed wheat.

"That's the feeder," Ruth said.

I looked up, and through a filter of snow I saw a large tower that looked like a missing part of a refinery. Long pipes led away from the tank into the barns surrounding the feeder. A long stairway curved up to a loading platform. It looked like a fire escape.

Ruth was silenced and stilled by something she found at the base of the feeder tank. I bent my head into the slanting snow and moved closer to Ruth.

"It's a bear I think," Ruth said. Slowly, she backed away. "I get gooseman to bring his gun." She clutched her long skirts and ran, feet splayed out and head down, to the fenced section where hundreds of Canada geese were caged. She disappeared into a large shed, then returned with another Hutterite man bearing a shotgun.

There was a breathing hole at the top of the humped snow, and whatever it was sleeping there — hiccoughed.

"Bears don't do that," gooseman said. He poked the mound with the rifle butt.

The mound moved, it shuddered, it shook like an animal shaking off snow. A head appeared first, a large head with long shaggy fur — no — hair falling to shoulders as huge as a bear's. The dark face had smooth skin. Eyelids fluttered.

Gooseman poked the mound again, and snow slid away from the fattest person I had ever seen. He sat cross-legged, hands folded across thick knees. He hiccoughed again, and opened his eyes.

"He is just sleeping it off," gooseman said, laughing. "Come up to the dining hall where it is warm."

Lips pressed together, the mouth quivered, then lips shaped the word, "Godsum wine?"; and the man rose up.

"Sure," gooseman said. "Or you going to sleep all winter?"

It was still snowing. Wind played with it, sweeping in gusts across the sidewalk, spinning it on banked snow on each side of the walkway. I heard the sound of a shovel scraping cement coming from the direction of the dining hall.

A long line of huddling people moved into the hall. Rev. Timothy lifted his black hat and waved at us. The bearded missionary and impatient doctor were filing into yellow light that beamed warmly through the doorway.

Inside, the smell of hot bread. I hung my coat on a peg beside Ruth's black shawl. Gooseman went ahead with the man from the snow.

"Well, well," Rev. Timothy smiled, "Donna Brown meet Mister Francis!"

Mister Francis had been given a Hutterite sheepskin jacket. The ends of the sleeves were tight around his bulging upper arms, and it wouldn't close across his great stomach.

Rev. Timothy sat me beside himself at the center table. The doctor slouched on my other side. Mister Francis spread himself on the bench across the table, flashing smiles at Lydia, whose mixed-up hormones were making her forehead blush. There was another pale stooped man on the other side of Rev. Timothy. I looked around for Ruth, but she hadn't followed me into the dining hall. Was this table and this meal reserved for outsiders?

The long table was spread with wooden platters piled with hot sliced bread, bowls of chicken soup, trays of golden crisp potatoes. Before each person, a whole boiled duck. The cups and plates were enamel, cutlery plain.

23

A thudding of work boots on polished tile, and a long line of black-suited Hutterite men marched into the dining hall, stood silently at their places before a long table under the east windows. Rev. Timothy nodded, and the men sat down in one unified movement.

Then the children, aged seven to fifteen, were led in a tapering line, tallest to smallest, by their German teacher. Again, Rev. Timothy nodded, and the children took their places, the teacher remaining rigid and standing at the end of their table.

The Hutterite women, in another line, according to age, eldest first, entered the room silently, hands folded in their skirts. At the given nod of the elder's head, they took their places along the table behind the outsiders.

Rev. Timothy rose to give the blessing in German, then prayed in English, "We give thanks this special night of celebration for the safe return of our painting party, for granting safety to our new friends who found their way through the storm to this colony. We give thanks for the food we are about to receive."

Heads bowed, a collective "Amen!" from both the men's and women's sides of the room.

The hot bread was passed around the table first. I wanted to make a meal of the bread alone. Each time the platter was emptied Rev. Timothy ordered more from the woman serving our table. "My wife," he said. She was the dumpy woman wearing wire-rimmed glasses, the mother of Ruth.

Mister Francis plowed through food heaped on his plate and nodded at whatever Lydia was whispering to him. The doctor mumbled into his plate about not being kept waiting. Rev. Timothy had his back turned sideways to me, his right arm around the pale shrunken man on his other side.

No one was talking to me. I was the only one with no place of belonging, no real home. The Hutterites had a well-defined, orderly, safe world. It was a retreat from mine, but I was the outsider. I looked at Mister Francis in the sheepskin jacket, at Lydia's hairy face, at the doctor's separateness; and I suddenly saw where they came from, the choices they had made; and a feeling warmer than Hutterite bread surged through me. But I remained isolated, removed from them, and worse — alienated from all that I had once known as familiar.

Rev. Timothy, swivelling around, introduced me to the pale man.

"So I am happy that we have Frank here with us, who is just released from the jail and wants to work in our mechanic shop. Very good at fixing trucks he is!"

I ducked my head forward, "Hello!", not seeing Frank, the fixed image of caged men in the Prince Albert Jail barring all other thoughts.

His Lordship and I had toured the cell blocks. Five floors, walls iron bars, floors wire mesh, so the guards on the bottom floor could watch all the prisoners right up to the fifth floor. Cages stacked on top of each other, and notes floating like feathers through the bars, hands grasping at them, but the prisoners' messages fell at their guards' feet. And the clanging of cups against iron bars as His Lordship and I walked by the cells.

Now I couldn't think. My scalp tightened, skin on my forehead stretching, overhead lights hurting my eyes. I took a deep breath, but couldn't let it out. My rib cage expanded, and I felt as if I were trying to break through it.

Rev. Timothy rose, and silence fell over the room like a dark cloak. "Tonight we draw the lot," he said. "For our guests I must explain. Our new colony to the south is ready, and tonight we choose who is going to stay at the old and who will go on to the new. You all have decided whom you follow, Reverend Jacob or me. Place your paper in the box as you leave the dining hall. After prayers Reverend Jacob and I draw the lot to see which one of us goes and which one stays."

Listening, I poked the grey pimply skin of the duck in front of me. I felt cut off, a stranger among strangers; as if I were suspended between earth and sky, belonging to neither; floating now, not knowing whether to rise or fall.

Mister Francis pointed a hand thick with silver and jade rings on every finger, and I passed him my uneaten duck. He ripped a wing from the breast and gave it to Lydia. Her face burned, but she nibbled the tip, leaned towards Mister Francis.

Then I thought it for the first time: *why am I Donna Claire Brown? Why am I me and not Mister Francis? Why am I me and not Lydia wanting to work with children?*

"The children are so well behaved!" Lydia said to Rev. Timothy.

He waggled his beard at her, winked. "The German teacher, he is always making sure they are good!", waving a carpenter's thick hand at the teacher who paced between the table and east windows.

Why was I born in Saskatoon instead of a Hutterite colony? Why was I raised in Haultain House and the child of no one, and not a Hutterite child? I suddenly wanted Rev. Timothy to hold me. I thought of how easily Ruth had touched me; here, on my arm, there, her arm around my shoulder.

No dessert, the meal finished, and Hutterites marched out of the dining hall the same way they entered: men first, then women, but each head of family dropped a slip of paper into a wooden box atop the iron stove at the rear of the room.

"Ruth will show you where to sleep tonight," Rev. Timothy said to me.

Ruth led me to the dormitory. "I get things ready," she said, "a place for you to sleep."

"I'm dying for a cigarette. I'll come in," I said, "in a moment." I sat on the stoop, and Ruth went inside.

I needed to be alone. I stood up. My feet had a forward motion of their own; and, head bent beneath the still falling snow, I found myself pushed, or rather pulled, to the nearest barn.

Inside, hens, thousands of them, all stacked in tiers of wire mesh, four chickens to each cage. Claws hooked around wire. They were tightly packed as if for shipping, and I couldn't hear anything but the racket of squawking hens. They were all white with red combs, yellow beaks and feet. They were beating each other with wings, pecking at necks that were featherless, raw, and bleeding. Feathers littered the aisle, in piles deep as snow on the outside sidewalk. Feeder pipes sprinkled grain into a tin tray that looked like an eavestrough. Eggs dropped onto a leather conveyor belt that whirred under the cages and disappeared through a square hole in the south wall.

Along the top of the highest layer of cages, three white roosters strutted.

I fled.

Back at the dormitory, Ruth stood back from me. "Ohh," she said, "you are wet from snow."

She gave me her felt boots, warmed from the oil burner, and I kicked off my cold leather boots. She gave me a towel to dry my hair, but there was no mirror in the bed-sitting-room, and Ruth brushed my hair.

"You should let it grow long," she said. She had removed her skull cap, and now her burnished hair hung long and red down her back. I noticed her freckles, on hands and wrists, for the first time.

I ducked my head so she could brush the back. "Ruth?" I said. "Don't you, didn't you, want to go with the others to draw the lot? I mean, aren't you anxious to know whether you will go to the new colony or remain here?"

"I go with my family," she said. "It will be the same there as here. He has put all of his ideas, all of his energy, all of his strong hands into the building of the new, my father, so I think he wants to go there."

"What about the painting party?" I asked. "Did you meet someone?"

"Yes," Ruth said. "But I belong to the colony before my family, before my husband. When the new colony is ready, if we go there, then there will be time for my wedding, and I go to the colony in North Dakota to be with my husband. The people, the way of life is the same there as it is here." She folded the wire brush between her hands. "There is too much struggling in you," she said.

Why am I me and not Ruth with a hope chest filled? "If I wanted to stay here," I said, "would I have to marry a Hutterite?"

"No," she laughed, "but you might want to!" Then she said, "You would have to be baptized."

I wasn't given a chance to reply. We were both startled by coarse voices yelling in German, the thudding of work boots on cement. Dark shapes of men racing by the window. The fire's glare.

I dashed outside with Ruth.

The grain in the feeder tank was on fire, the pipes running into the barns a yellow glow in the black night. There was no way to stop it, the platform was burning, the stairway too hot to climb.

Ruth and I bent our heads into the rising wind. Snow blurred our vision. We ran towards the pig barn.

Under the burning feeder tank was a dark and moving hump. Mister Francis, Lydia on top of him, humping. She had her head thrown back, face lifted to the sky, and she was crying, "It's God's will!"

Ruth kicked her bare backside before she ran into the pig barn.

Inside, the cement floors and walls couldn't burn, only the grain; and fire burned its way through every tray. Bits of straw flaming. Fire running along feeder pipes. Grain burning in troughs. Outraged screaming of pigs. Smell of singed hide and roasting pork. Hutterite women and girls gathered piglets into their skirts and ran them to the safety of outside snow. Hutterite men led the mothers, by ropes, through the open north doors.

I dropped to my knees. Gathered squealing piglets into my coat. I tied a knot in the sleeves, made a handle of twisted woolen arms, and carried the litter outside.

It was suddenly important to save the colony. Anger drove me to the chicken barn, Ruth right behind me. Shrieking of chickens in my ears, smell of singed feathers searing my nose, smoke stinging my eyes. I soaked my coat in a water trough and dragged it across the floor of the chicken barn, smothering burning feathers with wet

27

wool. Water streamed out of my eyes and down the sides of my sooted face. My hands and arms were blackened, pain where skin was burned by bits of flaming straw. My feet were too hot, felt soles of Ruth's black boots smoking.

The roof was reinforced with steel rafters, but made of wood, and the shingles caught fire. The feeder pipes cracked, fell from the smoking roof. "Ruth!" I yelled. The roof fell: pipes and planks and flaming shingles. The downward force of the crash thrust me backwards, my feet slipped on feathers, and I fell through the doorway onto my back.

I scrambled to my feet. They were on fire, and I was screaming, running, my feet freezing, snow up to my legs burning; and I was running away from Canada geese flying up and battering their heads and wings against the wire holding pen. I leaped through snow, then crawled over a downed barbed wire fence to the tree-lined Hutterite lane. An RCMP cruiser, its red light whirling. I don't remember anything after that, except it was still storming.

What I don't understand is how the municipal council and court officials all managed to hang their thinking caps on the same wooden peg and hook onto the assumption that someone started the fire in the feeder tank. Of course, I can't speak for the others, His Lordship would say that evidence is inadmissable, although I believe it will be corroborated by their testimony.

It happened the same way a fire sometimes starts in grain elevators. It was an Act of God. The same as the sudden blizzard.

No, I don't believe any of the others had reason to start that fire. Rev. Timothy drew the short straw and had to stay in the colony, but he wanted to stay and rebuild. Frank was given work in the mechanic shop. Mister Francis only stumbled onto colony land. Lydia found out that she is a woman after all. And the doctor, not to be kept waiting, left the colony two hours before the fire started.

I don't know why I'm not a Hutterite girl, a man huge as a bear, a brooding doctor created in the image of God, a missionary with hormone problems, or an ex-prisoner from a provincial jail. I don't know why I survived the night, the storm, the fire; and not Ruth. I don't know why I am Donna Claire Brown.

But I will find the answer.

SWORN BEFORE ME at the city of   ,
in the Province of   , this   day
of   , A.D. 19

28

COMPOSITION IN BLACK AND WHITE

MICK BURRS

"How to make photographs more striking and unusual is one of the main quests of every photographer, amateur or professional."

Phillipe Halsman, **On the Creation of Photographic Ideas**

One. "The rule of the direct approach."

I am preparing my breakfast, but the ripping sounds coming from outside are interfering with my usual calm concentration on toast-buttering, coffee-brewing, and grapefruit-squeezing.

"What *is* that damned noise?" I yell at the window, then look out.

That grating noise, like having your teeth drilled in an echo chamber, is coming from the old wooden house down the alley from my apartment.

I remember. Its second floor was gutted by fire in the summer. The family living in that two-storey corpse had no choice but to move out. After they left the house, no one came to restore it.

Until now. But it's not being restored. It's being torn to shreds by that most vicious of scavengers — a wrecking company.

The instrument of destruction does, indeed, resemble a big

threatening bird. It has a long steel pipe for a neck, and a giant ripper-tooth for a beak. This ripper-tooth, held up by the pipe, would make any vulture envious. It tears away at the old house as if it were meat.

Through my window, I see the bird-shaped bulldozer pulling down part of the back roof. I watch, fascinated, as the innards of the house are exposed for the first time. Part of the upper wall has been peeled back like an orange. There's the bedroom with a scorched brass bed still resting in it. From this distance it looks like the cut-away section of a doll-house.

I'm always on the lookout for unique visual metaphors, fancying myself a better than average still photographer. (Some of my pictures have been exhibited — and sold — at local art galleries.) That vulture-like beak, as it tears away at the ribs of the two-storey corpse — well, I've never seen anything like it. I must capture it! I must cage that vicious bird in the frame of a black and white glossy print, and hope that it turns out be a classic graphic symbol of our destructive age!

With such a creative flood pouring through me, I have no time to eat breakfast. I turn off the coffee pot, leave the toast to grow cold and stale in the toaster, and let half a grapefruit shrivel on the sink. I pick up my light meter and my old dependable reflex camera and clank in my black shoes and denims down the iron fire escape two floors to the alley.

It's chilly outside, a mid-October morning. I head quickly and directly to the demolition site, the scene of my projected composition. I don't expect anything to hinder me from my simple, straight-forward objective: I will make a memorable portrait, in black and white, create a dramatic image of destruction.

Two. "The rule of the unusual technique."

The driver of the wrecking machine — it belongs to the FLATLAND EXCAVATION AND DEMOLITION COMPANY — seems too occupied with his duties to notice anyone watching him. But another spectator, wearing scuffed cowboy boots, faded jeans, and a thin blue parka, is also standing in the alley, and from a safe distance is observing the destruction. Of the two of us, I'm the only one with a camera. This makes me feel somewhat conspicuous.

The man is much older than me. Retired rancher, I'd say. When he glances sideways at me, his mouth tightens, as if he's thinking, What do you want to take a picture of this for? Are you morbid or something?

His disapproving silence makes me feel even more conspicuous.

I won't be able to get a good angle and make the picture I want, until I feel comfortable about this man being here.

"Something, isn't it?" I say, trying to be jovial. With his hands thrust in his thin blue parka, he turns slightly towards me, not looking me in the eye.

"It's to get it over with as soon as possible," he says.

Three. "The rule of the added unusual feature."

That remark of his sends a chill through me. I step away, determined not to get into any dialogue with him. If he weren't here, I'd be making progress toward that picture right now.

We both watch the vulture tear out more of the back wall, including the first floor's rear door and a window. The ground trembles. Dirty brown smoke blows out in spasmodic puffs from the vertical exhaust pipe as the bird-shaped bulldozer backs up, turns left, turns right, gets into position, moves forward for the next mauling of the two-storey corpse. Boards and planks crunch below its revolving steel tracks, reminding me of a relentless military tank gliding over rubble.

Then I see something crawling out of the pile of broken boards in front of me. It stops and licks its light brown fur.

"Hey, look at that! It's a mouse!"

As soon as I say it, something in me wishes I hadn't. The old man turns and gruffly asks, "Where? Where is it?"

Instantly, I sense he doesn't like mice — in fact, I can tell he detests them. But, quicker than I can think, I point with my camera hand in the direction of the mouse.

I could have left the mouse to myself. I could have watched it with silent curiosity, maybe even taken a picture of it.

Why . . . that's it! The last occupant. The lone survivor. A dazed mouse, leaving what used to be its home. I'll take it from a low angle, with the house looming up and being eaten away in the background. I'll make sure I catch the gnawing beak of the vulture as it hovers hungrily over the mouse.

Four. "The rule of the missing feature."

But the old man has another idea. He moves toward the mouse and reaches behind it for a two-by-four. He steps back, gripping the plank. It has a bent nail at the other end.

Had the remaining survivor been a *rat*, grey and fat and ugly, I might be feeling differently. But before me stands a creature smaller than a crumpled pack of cigarettes. Its small chest heaves in and out to a rapid rhythm. With the breath of life in it, I can identify with the mouse more than with the two-storey corpse.

Its eyes, though, are slits, temporarily blinded, not accustomed to the sunlight. And it can't crawl straight. It inches forward, sideways, then stops, then inches forward again.

But it has no visible injuries. I feel it's only trying to get its bearing, having abruptly lost its home, not knowing what to do next, where to go, where to find shelter.

So I speak up, my voice firm yet pleading. "It's only a mouse!"

The old man has the board upraised in his hands. Hands that are thick, gnarled, weather-worn, those of a man who has always worked outdoors. Yes, a rancher who has retired to the big city, and has had his share of experiences with rodents and other pests. Now he has appointed himself the executioner of a homeless mouse, and he's about to perform his simple duty with one sharp blow.

He doesn't look at me as he explains. "Might carry a disease. It's no good for nothin'."

I visualize the outcome. A few ounces of fur, its heart and lungs still pumping, will in one second become a bloody, lifeless pulp on the ground.

Five. "The rule of compounded features."

"No!" I shout, my determination surprising me. My voice mingles with the indifferent roar of the rest of the back wall as it crashes to the ground.

For the first time, the old man looks directly at me, faces me squarely, the board with its gleaming nail still raised above his head.

My eyes are asking him to be merciful, to spare at least one living thing from the surrounding destruction. His gaze communicates contempt — as much toward me as toward the mouse. But I also notice a definite flickering in his eyes. A flickering of guilt.

And that, apparently, is enough.

He lowers the board to his side, then pitches it onto the pile where it came from.

He looks down at the mouse. The creature has no awareness of the drama that has been flaring up around it. It is still dazed by the sunlight, its pink feet gripping the earth for support, its ringed tail a semi-circle on one side of its fragile body.

My basic response is relief. I helped save this lone, defenseless mouse. But as the old man just stands there staring down, I begin to feel another emotion compounding the situation. In some small way, I realize I've crushed something inside the old man. His self-respect, perhaps. His pride. His dignity. I don't know exactly what . . . but it makes me feel small. Smaller than the mouse. I can't look at the old man now, for a flickering of guilt is rising inside *me* and I don't know how to stop it, how to make amends.

What if the old man's right? What if the mouse *is* diseased? I begin haranguing myself. Or what if it's dying? Wouldn't it be an act of mercy to kill it? And what, in God's name, is more important anyway — the soul of a doomed mouse, or the soul of a living man?

I'm beginning to wish I hadn't come down to take that damned picture.

Six.   "The rule of the literal method."

It's the mouse who makes the next surprising move. I feel like I'm witnessing one of those instant miracle cures you see at a prairie tent revival meeting. The mouse has suddenly lost its awkwardness, its wobbling gait. Opening its eyes to the light, it darts into the middle of the alley and stops to rest. It doesn't look back, probably thinking of only one necessity: I've got to find a new home now.

What a smart mouse! I think. Even more than before, I'm glad the old man didn't kill it.

But the old man isn't finished. He walks up to the mouse while it rests. He nudges it with the pointed toe of his left boot. The mouse turns over, then rights itself. Its eyes are slits again.

Soon it is clear to me what the old man is doing. He has to prove something, as much to himself as to me. He nudges the mouse again. Once more the mouse turns over, then rights itself. The boot is used like a stick, and the mouse is prodded like a warm coal in a fire.

As it's poked for the fourth or fifth time, all I can do is stare. I can't interfere this time.

I tell myself that he's only nudging the mouse, not planning to raise his boot to crush it. Yet I can't be absolutely sure. With each poke it feels like he's gradually restoring that something he had momentarily lost.

All this takes place to the background accompaniment of pitiless destruction.

Who will be the first to grow tired of playing this little game in the middle of the alley?

After being poked once too often, the mouse opens its eyes while righting itself. The old man and I both watch it scurry away, in the direction of a trash bin across the alley, into the shadow cast by an old one-car garage that over the years has acquired a severe tilt in its posture.

But at least the old, tilted garage is still standing. In the next moment I turn back to see one of the side walls of the two-storey

33

corpse come floating to the ground. It bursts in an enormous explosion of planks and splinters, of glass and nails and dust.

The old man turns away from me in silence. He swings his arms, as I watch his back, his heavy cowboy boots marching him down the alley like some crusty war veteran.

He's left me alone, at last, to take that picture.

But not of the two-storey corpse. And not of the noisy vulture. And not of the mouse, who has already disappeared into the shadows. They each lack interest for me now.

So here it is.

That picture of him.

THE VOCATION

ANNE CAMPBELL

We were sifting along the highway to Saskatoon in Uncle Elmer's car. His cars always make you feel like you are floating like when you ride a balloon-tired bike. They're pretty good to us, Uncle Elmer and Aunt Ellen. Always taking some of us kids along to the city with them. My mother says it's because they don't have any kids of their own and they get lonesome. But they don't have to be that good to us. They're always buying us something or taking us somewhere and they don't have to do that. It's a funny thing but I don't even mind it when Aunt Ellen lectures. That's when she tells us something that is good for us to do or something that is good for us to know. When she does that her voice gets a sound to it that makes you feel ... well ... it's hard to say how it makes you feel. Something like somebody is holding you and rocking you and humming you to sleep. I like it when she does that. I get the feeling then that the important part of what she is saying is in the sound of her voice. One thing she does do that isn't right though is give spit washes with her hanky. I have never had one and I never will. She spits on her hanky and washes my sister Nomi's face or my cousin Jean's. I always make sure my face is clean. I would die if she touched me with her spit.

Anyway, here we were this day like I said, sifting into Saskatoon. This time only three of us kids were along: Nomi, Jean

35

and me. We didn't have any little kids along so we thought we might get to eat at the Elite Cafe. If little kids are along we have to go to Aunt Eve's. There are lots of people around Aunt Eve's apartment, in fruit stores and butcher shops and pool rooms and hotels, but they won't let us play on the street and something in the air doesn't make you feel good anyway. Aunt Eve isn't as interesting as the other aunts either. I don't know if it's because her kids are grown up or if it's because she doesn't have anything interesting to say. I know I wouldn't have anything interesting to say if I lived there. Even though sometimes her voice sounds a bit like Aunt Ellen's, it isn't the same.

But the Elite. There the food is wonderful. Crackers in cellophane wrappers, and bread in a basket. You can hardly keep from eating it all before your soup comes. And it's wonderful too. Tomato, not thick like Campbell's; it's runny and it has rice in it. We always have fish and chips and it's funny but I can't ever remember finishing mine. Even though I've eaten there a dozen times, every time I do everything seems new.

Saskatoon is like that. Every time I go there it's this same wonderful feeling like I've never been there before and everything is new. I know it's hard to believe a place can be like that, but every time we go there it's like it just finished raining and the sun is out and everything is clean. I partly have that feeling when I go to my cousin's on Sunday after church, or when we go to my Grandma's and all of my cousins are there. But that's different because there we have such a good time playing that I can't really notice the feeling of the place too much. But Saskatoon. The feeling you have on your skin when you drive into that place, even before, when you're just getting close. It's like gold. Gold light all over you, waking you up and pulling you into it. Getting close to Saskatoon you can hardly stand it. Not being there already. The feeling really is different: not like the ordinary good feeling a person gets playing alone in the deep grass by the old Anglican Church, or in a good game of covered wagon or cutouts with Jean. It is definitely a different feeling.

Speaking of playing. Jean is a good person to play with. She has good ideas of what to do. Some kids don't seem to have any notion of how to play. I wonder about that. I guess they don't have any ideas of what to do, but then I think they should get some from a book or a show. It is hard to get hold of a book in Earley, that's true, but there are good stories in the Star Weekly which you can get every Saturday at the Red and White. Sometimes people surprise you though. Like my sister Nomi. She studies a lot, and when we play she usually does what we tell her. But once in awhile she comes up with a real good idea of her own. I like Nomi, but I have never been able to figure her out. Most of the time that's what I think, that I can't figure her out. I do have one feeling about her. That she knows something that I would like to know.

When you are in Saskatoon you can hardly wait to get out of the car and get going, everything seems like it is practically dancing around and you want to get going into it. This day as usual we went to Eaton's and parked the car. Aunt Ellen lets us go around by ourselves if we stay in the block by Eaton's and if we are right where we are supposed to be when she wants us to be there. Sometimes we go with her, at first, anyway. Like this day we went with her to look at material in Mikado's Silk. There's lots of material in there, and the people who wait on you are Japanese. It usually takes Aunt Ellen a long time to get material. We looked at material with her for awhile, then we left to go back to Eaton's. To tell the truth, Mikado's is not the most interesting store in Saskatoon.

Going back to Eaton's from Mikado's you walk past the Ten Cents Store and that is an interesting store. That's the thing about Saskatoon, there are always different things to look at. Like the Ten Cents Store. The people in there are something to see. They look like they all come from different countries. Sometimes at the Lunch Counter you can see redheaded ladies with makeup that's painted on, and eyebrows that are special shapes. There are old men in there too, with white hair and wrinkled faces talking to each other and drinking coffee. I like the look of them. Like they know everything, and what they know is everywhere inside them, not just in some part. You see Retarded people with their mothers, and people talking to themselves, and people dressed in black clothes with long skirts like they've come from an old-fashioned country. You see men with beards and ladies dressed like you know they only live in the city. You see things like you never see in Earley. And the counters. They have every colour of everything you can imagine. Balloons, crayons, combs, knee-socks, panties, crepe paper, anything you can think of. Aunt Ellen says every person is different, but the people in the Ten Cents Store really are different. I can't imagine where they live, but I wonder about them and what they do when they go home.

Outside, on the street, part of the sidewalk is made with shiny black bricks that you can see through. I always wonder if you are supposed to walk on them. I don't really think a person could keep from walking on them unless they really tried not to. It makes me a little bit shaky, walking on them, but I do. One place I would not like to walk is on the high steel bridge that crosses over the railway tracks downtown to the other side of town. I would not like to walk on that bridge, and I don't think I ever could.

Two really interesting stores by Eaton's are Bricker's Shoe Store and Birks. Bricker's has the most beautiful shoes you have ever seen. They are leather and they smell so good and look so beautiful you'd want to save them just to look at. Maybe put them on once in awhile. Once I had a pair of red leather loafers something like the ones they have at Bricker's. I liked those shoes a lot. I can't remember what happened to them. I guess they must have worn out, or maybe got too small. I miss those shoes; sometimes I actually miss them like you'd miss a person.

In Birks it is like in church. Everything is blue and gold and velvet and quiet. I always like it in there, at first. I like looking at the gold bracelets and necklaces on the blue velvet in the dark cases. But after awhile, if we stay longer than I think we should and I look at the ladies, I feel like we shouldn't be in there. I feel like the ladies are only letting us stay for awhile and pretending they don't know we shouldn't be in there. Then I start pretending too, and when I get that feeling—that everybody is pretending—I get Jean or Nomi or whoever I am with to leave. Even though everything is nice in Birks, I do not like that kind of feeling of pretending.

This day we went back to Eaton's like we usually did, to wait for Aunt Ellen in the Shoe Department. They have this X-Ray machine there. You can put your feet right into it and look down and see right through your shoes to your bones. It looks like a weigh scale. It is interesting to look at your feet, but they say you aren't supposed to do it for too long because too much of the X-Ray isn't good for the bones in your feet. Usually some man comes along and tells us to stop doing it anyway, so we never really get a chance to have a really good look at our feet. Someday I'd like to get in that store when no one was around and just take my time looking in that machine at the bones in my feet, until I felt like I was finished looking.

While we wait for Aunt Ellen, like this day, I think. I think a lot about what's on the radio. I like listening to the radio. You can get a picture of what's going on so you just know what things are like from the words. I kind of get lost in some of the programs, but then it's like when Aunt Ellen lectures and I keep listening anyway because I like the sound of the words.

You never know when Aunt Ellen will show up, and sometimes you have a long time to think. When she does show up you never know what she might want to do. She might want to go home, or she might take us to eat. Or she might take us to a show at the Capitol Theatre.

And what do you know, this day that's what happened. She took us to a show at the Capitol Theatre. There was singing and dancing and the show was in Technicolor, and I can't remember anything more about it than that. What I do remember is that I thought the same thing about the Capitol Theatre that day as I always did. It is the most beautiful building in the world, and I love it. Before the show starts you can sit there and look around. There are stars on the ceiling that look like real stars. They sparkle, and the ceiling behind them is dark. Dark blue. It's always night. There are windows on the sides of the Theatre that you can look up to. And there are gold balconies that come out from the windows right into the Capitol Theatre.

I wondered about the people who lived in the houses those windows are attached to. Sometimes I thought they were lucky to live there. Sometimes I wondered how the houses got built so close to the Capitol Theatre. I wondered if it was an accident. I always thought of asking somebody about it but I never did. I wondered if it bothered the people to have the Theatre so close. I thought it must keep them from sleeping sometimes. I wondered what they were doing in those houses, and I thought of things they could be doing. Like at one window I always thought there was a boy, with his mom and dad behind him, and none of them talking. Sometimes I thought I saw him at the window, then I thought his mom pulled him back. I had lots of ideas about the people who lived in those houses. Sometimes I'd remember an idea about them exactly like the first time it came to me, and sometimes I'd change it. When it came to finishing an idea, I could tell I didn't want to. It didn't seem right, to me, to make the lives of those people come out a certain way, when I didn't really know them. I thought they might want their lives to come out different. I thought it wouldn't be fair for me to think of their lives coming out my way. Sitting there, I'd always think that when I was outside I'd look to see how those houses were built. Most of the time I forgot, and when I did look I could never tell where they were. The best thing anyway about the Capitol Theatre is just being there, in it, sitting there waiting for the show to start.

It was just past the middle of the afternoon when we got out of the show, and we started right home. It was early fall and the sun was out, warm and still. On the way home I usually look at magazines that Aunt Ellen has in the car. They are about the United States and how people live there. I like looking at them. The United States always reminds me of a show, the way everything is planned to come out a certain way. It seems like everybody knows what they are supposed to do, and they act it out. I don't know if they like doing it, but I wouldn't want to. This day though, the sun was so nice and warm, I just sat there and looked out the window. The way the sun was made the light and the air look different. It made everything look different, especially the colours. All the colours looked like you could feel them. Like if you touched anything its colour would stay on your hand, like coloured chalk.

The sky was light pastel blue, and the trees were the greenest green you have ever seen. A green so green you could *almost* see it moving. The crops were like that too. Different yellows. Some almost hurt my eyes, they were shining so bright. Some glowing dull, like gold necklaces in Birks. Everything was like that except for the straw. It looked like somebody had come along and tried to take the colour out of it. It looked like they almost had. All the colour that looks alive was gone, but what was left was a colour that looked like it would never go away. I don't know why, but I think I like that colour best.

We drove past some men working and Aunt Ellen said she thought one of them was Eugene. He is the son of the priest's housekeeper. Eugene went away to be a priest too, but at the Seminary they told him he should go out and work and have a good time and not think about being a priest. After that if he still had a calling to be a priest it would mean he had a true vocation and he could come back to the Seminary and be a priest. Eugene does have a nice face, but underneath the skin it looks sore. His face looks handsome and sore all together.

My Uncle Buddy has a different kind of face, and I like it. He laughs more than Eugene and he has a big moustache like my Grandpa's. When he isn't happy his face doesn't look sore or any different than usual. He just looks like he's getting bigger all over, if you can believe it. And he just keeps doing everything ordinary. Once when he came over to our house my mother asked him what he was doing. He said he wasn't doing anything, and my mother said he was just batting around. Batting around. I thought about that. Going where you land. I thought that's what Uncle Buddy does. He goes wherever he lands, like a bat. And he does whatever there is to do when he gets there. I thought about that. I thought how amazing it is that a word can tell exactly what is happening.

This day, sitting in the car in all that light, I was thinking of words again, and how they came to be in the first place. I was thinking that it is amazing that somebody could think up a word that nobody had ever said before. Then that other people start saying it too, a sound that makes people feel connected up to the thing it tells about. I think that is amazing. I was thinking about how it is too when you are the person who hears a word that tells exactly how something really is. How you feel like little things are popping open in your back and in your head, letting air in, and how you feel bigger. I was having a good time sitting in all that colour thinking about words. Then just like that, out of the blue, like it sometimes happens, it came to me. About the houses behind the balconies in the Capitol Theatre. I knew right then they weren't real. I just knew. For a second I felt like everything just stopped. Then I felt like everything in the whole world was moving and shifting around, and stretching, then like everything was dropping and settling down into the ground, bigger than it was before. While it was happening I felt like some great worry I didn't even know I had was rolling off my back. I just sat there after that for awhile, feeling it, a different kind of feeling than I have ever had before in my whole life. I felt rested and at the same time like my whole body was laughing, like everything in the world was wonderful. Everything. Then my mind kind of rolled over to the Capitol Theatre again. It seemed even more wonderful to me now than it had before. All by itself, without those imaginary houses hanging onto its outside. I thought how wonderful the person must be who made the Capitol Theatre. I wanted to go and find him and tell him that and hug him for making it. I thought and felt so many things bursting out of me in every direction at the same time. I felt like those people I'd thought of in the houses were bursting out too, just popping off the Capitol Theatre and floating up into the air on their own.

Now this is the amazing thing. Even though I knew they weren't real I still thought those people had lives of their own. Only now I felt like I could wonder about them and have ideas about them and not worry about making their lives come out wrong. I felt like that because—and this is funny—because I knew I would only get ideas about the people when they were really doing the things I thought about. How do you like that? I knew I couldn't make anything come out wrong because I wouldn't know what they were really doing, no matter how hard I thought, until they were really doing it. And then somehow I knew if I waited, somehow I'd know.

I KNOW WHAT I LIKE

ROBERT CURRIE

It was right after he hung the new picture that she asked him to go with her. He'd picked up a Blue Boy at Kresge's and put it above the television, taking down that other thing, the cockeyed face with the out-of-kilter mouth that seemed to laugh and frown all at once. Blue Boy wasn't exactly what he'd wanted either, though almost anything was better than the Pisasco —— whatever his name was.

Just as he was putting Nona's picture on the floor, she came into the room, not speaking at first, only watching him, her lips tight. When she did speak, she surprised him, asking if he'd join her on the visit, not once mentioning pictures.

He didn't much want to go, but Nona suggested that it would be good for him to get out of the house for a while after supper, to take a break before he settled in with a beer for the football game on television. He knew he couldn't argue with that, not really.

"Who's Mrs. Garland, anyway?" He heard Nona back in the kitchen, rattling cutlery on the drying rack, emphasizing that the dishes weren't done yet.

"The daughter of Samuel Bogue. The only child, in fact."

"And who's Samuel Bogue?" He flopped back on the fancy pillow he'd bought her in Hawaii.

"Come on, Frank. Samuel Bogue founded the church. That's his plaque just inside the door."

"Oh. Sure. The big metal one with the curlicues. I guess I've never really read it."

"No, you wouldn't. I phoned her and she said it would be all right to come at seven." The fridge door slammed shut, louder than necessary. The handle was loose, and he hadn't gotten around to repairing it.

"Mm, but I'm still not sure why we're going. Why *I'm* going with you."

Nona had perched on the end of the chesterfield, smiling that half-smile of hers. "You'd prefer to get into the beer even before the kick-off?" she asked.

"No, no." There she was, playing games with him again. "Put it this way," he said. "Why should Mrs. Garland want to see me?"

"Well, it's not exactly that she wants to see you." She paused, fingering the china figure of a woman, rolling it across her palm so that its tiny parasol spun above the woman's head. "She'll want you to see."

"Is that supposed to make sense?"

"No, I guess not. Just be patient, Frank."

"Say, she's not senile, is she?"

Nona's laughter tinkled like ice cubes in a cool, summer drink. "No, she's not senile. It was her father founded the church — not her."

"Well, I always thought your visiting committee was for sick people: the bed-ridden and the feeble-minded, the —"

"No, Frank, for anyone who needs it." She had risen once as if to leave, but she sat down again. "You're afraid to go."

"No, I'm not," he said. She could read him every time. Old people — hell. He'd be there soon enough without having to visit them. Still, he couldn't tell her. "Come on. It's almost seven."

As they drove down Oxford Street toward the older part of Moose Jaw, he noticed how the big homes stood shoulder to shoulder like rows of dowagers. He wanted to ask more about Mrs. Garland, to find out what kind of woman she was, but he thought it best not to ask. Besides, he knew that if he kept silent, Nona would eventually tell him. He paused longer than usual at the stop sign, giving her time.

Nona waited till they were through the intersection.

"She was widowed years ago. Taught school — art — and painted too. Had quite a reputation locally."

"Who?"

"You know. Some of her students actually went on to art school. That's quite a thing for this part of the country."

"Mm. Can you make a living that way?"

"Maybe. Someone good enough might. That's it. One eleven. The white one on the corner."

Pulling into the curb, he looked at the rambling three-storied house with its sprawling balconies and steep outside staircases which looked as if they might pull away from the building. "Huge," he said, trying another ploy. "The old family mansion, eh? Where she lives surrounded by the wealth of the past, tended by butlers and maids."

"No, Frank. She's got a small suite on the second floor."

The stairs were old and worn in the center of each step, creaking as they mounted them, but the climb was made colourful by the pots of geraniums at the top, the sudden red of their blossoms taking his breath away. He grinned. Nona would say it was the climb that did it.

Mrs. Garland must have heard them coming, for she was waiting at the landing with the door opened behind her.

"Hello, Nona," she said. "And this must be Mr. Stuart."

While Nona completed the introductions, he tried to study her without seeming to do so. She was a thin woman — no, he guessed slim would be more exact — slim and delicate, with features as fine as Nona's Dresden china figures. Her skin was loose at the throat and folded in deep wrinkles beneath the eyes, but her eyes were bright. There was something about her looks, something intensely alive in the way she smiled and motioned them inside that made him want to like her.

"It's especially nice," she was saying, "to have a visitor who hasn't been here before. And a gentleman caller at that." She laughed, a vivid, sprightly laugh that danced across the hall. Was she making some kind of reference, he wondered, to the annual little theatre play Nona had dragged him to again last winter? The one with the glass unicorn that broke so easily.

He smiled back at her, wondering what to say. There was a strange smell in the room, he noticed then, like perfume, but mixed with something else, odours from the kitchen perhaps, and he felt closed in, surrounded. He caught himself just as he started to sniff. It was lavender, he thought, lavender and boiled cabbage. He was wishing Nona would get on with the conversation when they stepped into the living room and he saw the pictures. The walls were covered with them: flowers tumbling from vases in great splashes of colour, vivid landscapes flowing into hazy distances, mountains rising to scrape at moody skies.

"Nona said you paint."

"Yes, I do." She paused. "Or, at least, I used to. It was the one thing that made me look forward to retirement. So many paintings to be done and all those hours to do them in. It was exactly like a dream come true."

"But, I thought you said . . ." He stopped, unsure of how to phrase it. It might be impolite to ask, probably would be. Why didn't Nona help him? He noticed her hands then, the way her fingers twisted over and bent back upon themselves. Blushing, he looked away, but she had already seen.

"The spirit is willing, but the hands are not," she said. "I'd hardly been retired a year before the arthritis came. For a while I could still manage, after a fashion. Now, well, I can no longer hold a brush. It's been a disappointment." Her tone seemed to suggest that it had not been so big a disappointment she could not accept it. "Do you like them?" she asked.

He found his eyes drawn again to her hands, but forced them away. Of course, she hadn't meant that. He hoped she hadn't noticed this time, but, glancing at her, he couldn't tell.

"Of course," he said, "I'm no judge of art." He paused, studying the many canvases.

"Frank's been heard to say, he may not know art," said Nona, "but he knows what he likes." The icy tone of her voice brought him around. Yes, she was doing it again. He glared at her, but her voice was fluid now. "Lately," she added, "I hardly know that myself." What did she mean? Was she apologizing?

"Well, what I like," he said, pointing to a cliff that rose darkly against a night sky, "is that." Sometimes he wasn't quite sure why he said the things he did. He added, "It looks real enough to climb."

"Yes, I had a realistic period, but I wanted to try other things. There wasn't enough time for everything . . . I guess there never is."

"No, I guess not." He felt embarrassed, without knowing why, and Nona was saying so very little.

"Realism just wasn't my style. I made that discovery twenty years ago in London."

"You went there to paint?" he asked.

"To study. It was a special summer course at the London School of Art, but Mr. Collier — he was chief instructor that July — preferred figure studies. Nudes."

"Oh," said Frank, "I see."

"No," replied Mrs. Garland. "I finished two, but they were big, blowzy women, rather cheap, I thought. Just doing it for the money. That's true of all models, I suppose, but they made it so obvious. The pictures are in the other room. I wouldn't have them in here. Besides, I grew tired of painting nudes." She nodded at the wall above Nona's head. "Mr. Collier let me do the flowers in his office. Big bouquets of chrysanthemums all over his desk. They were fresh every morning, the smell filling the room . . . Even Graham liked them."

He looked at Nona, but she was watching Mrs. Garland. "Graham?" he asked.

"My son. That was his last summer with me. He was the real artist in the family. Those are his." Her hand twisted towards the wall behind him. He turned and saw four paintings grouped together.

Strange ones. Of people who seemed torn from some perverse house of mirrors. Contorted men and women who had been wrenched by life, beaten down by it, and marked by shadow, touched by something dark. He was caught by one, a woman who seemed hardly more than a skeleton, yet almost alive, and somehow familiar, and now her eyes were like souls staring at him, telling him something, something he couldn't quite grasp. "Jesus," he said. "Jesus Christ."

"Frank!"

"What? Oh!" My God, and her a minister's daughter.

"Pardon me; I didn't think. They kinda caught me off guard. It's just that . . . well, they're so different." He realized immediately how silly he must sound. "They have a kind of . . . spectral quality to them. Haunting." He was a fool, must be. "They won't be easy to forget." He didn't suppose that helped either. "Nona understands these things better than I do."

He wished she would pick up the cue. Finally, she did. "Do you have more of Graham's work?" she asked.

"Yes. A scrapbook of his sketches. Some of them are very good — finished art, I think — though not all. He had great promise. I used to worry so about him."

She stopped, as if unsure about proceeding. Frank threw a look at Nona, who sat waiting for her to finish. Mrs. Garland seemed to have lost her place. He decided he'd better help her find it.

"There was something to worry about?"

"I thought there was. He started hanging around downtown, with the wrong kind of people. The ones who sit on the curb with their glazed eyes. But it turned out I needn't have worried. Not about that. When he came home at night, he was drawing them. Quick, flowing sketches that made John Groth look like a beginner. They're so good. I can't bear to look at them now. He was talented."

She moved uneasily in her wicker rocking chair. Nona was looking at Graham's paintings, studying first one, then another. Somewhere, at a distant window, he could hear a fly buzzing. He guessed he would have to ask himself.

"Graham. Is he dead?"

46

"No," Mrs. Garland said, and she looked at him for a long time, though he wasn't sure she really saw him. "He's a chartered accountant." She paused again, staring at him and through him, focusing just beyond him, on something else. "And married now," she added.

"Oh, I'm sorry. Not that he's married, I mean." He was stumbling badly. "For thinking he was ... You did use the past tense."

"I'm sorry too. He no longer paints. His wife isn't interested and ... well, neither is he. Wouldn't even pause for an art gallery now."

"Oh no," said Frank. "I can't believe that. Not after those pictures. Why it just doesn't make —"

"It's true though. Art galleries are the last things he wants to think about. He had a show once, you see, a small one, but in Toronto. It brought the critics out and they raved—oh, how they raved. And he didn't sell one painting—not one. Well, it doesn't take Graham long to learn. He's busy now, busy making money. Will you have some iced tea? I have it in the refrigerator."

They left shortly after tea, though not as soon as Frank would have wished. Mrs. Garland followed them to the top of the stairs, where they paused in awkward silence.

"They're beautiful pictures," Frank spoke suddenly. "And maybe he'll start to paint again some day."

"No, I don't think so," she said. "Once it's gone, it's gone. But I keep them for the grandchildren. Maybe they will like the pictures—if they ever come. She doesn't want them."

Frank waited for her to finish. "Pardon me?" he said.

"His wife. She doesn't want children." She took a deep breath, her right hand fluttering awkwardly at her breast. "Well, it was nice of you to come. Good-bye."

Frank felt her watching them all the way down the stairs and out to the car. He wondered suddenly if she were fair, if she were even objective about her son. When he drove around the corner, it was as if something cold and rigid had been washed away.

"You weren't much help in there," he said to Nona.

"No, I suppose I wasn't," she said. "I'm sorry. But it seemed somehow as if it were up to you. I can't quite explain it."

"Those paintings — Graham's — they were ... well, they did something. Got to me. Were they any good?"

"Yes, I think they were. You were right about them, Frank. Of course, I'm no expert either."

They made it home in time for the football game, but instead of switching on the television, he sat, motionless in a room full of

47

things, staring at the blank screen. Those eyes, those deep and hollow eyes, he could still see them, staring back at him, looking inside him, and through him.

"Shall I turn on the T.V.?" Nona asked.

"No, hon," he said, "not just now." He hadn't wanted to go in the first place; now, slumped in his easy chair, he wondered what had happened to him.

KOLLA, TICKS

KRISTJANA GUNNARS

July twenty one.

The ticks must be gone now. In the Wasagaming Museum they say the active time for ticks is between the middle of June and the middle of July. They had a bloated one in a plastic box. It was bigger than a lima bean. They said it came from a dog and was finished sucking up the lymph and blood. It must be the stupidest insect. It's got no head at all, just a large bloated torso. The disgusting thing about ticks it that they're parasites. Some insects spin webs or dig burrows or build honeycombs. But this one can't do anything except latch onto an animal and suck the life out of it.

June seventeen must be just the time for ticks. We never think of that. We always have to celebrate June seventeenth in the country by Pense. There have to be open fires in the dusk and races in burlap sacks in the afternoon and walks down a country road. It's dusty and crickets croak in the tall grass by the wayside. Far away a tractor pokes into a field in a dust cloud. Behind you someone laughs loudly. A joke about Gudbrandur Erlendsson whose cow sank into a quagmire in eighteen eighty. The air is dry. Straws crack, blackbirds fidget. Grasshoppers pounce across the road. For once the huldu-people are visible. People you've heard about and never seen. That day you see them. Next day they're gone. It's like that every year. They say things don't last in Canada. They're wrong.

Stories get told on June seventeen. Stories that never made it into English or into print. I know why. It's the odd people they show. You think your great grandparents must have been superstitious. I guess they were. That Johannes Bjarnason from Stykkisholmur, say. He stayed with Jonas Schaldemoes in a cabin by Lake Winnipegosis in nineteen sixteen. I heard that story five weeks ago in Pense when we got together for our yearly fest. They say Canada's too new for folktales and legends. That only natives have real legends here. They're wrong.

I'm sitting on the bank of the Lake Waskesiu panhandle in north Saskatchewan, here alone. I brought no provisions except for a tent and sleeping bag. There are patches of wild strawberry just below my tent site and saskatoons closer to the lake. My plan was to pick those and fish for the rest of my needs. I've got a licence and it's a good fishing lake. I just haven't made the gear yet. I've picked the branches and root fibres, but it's all still raw in the camp. This morning I put a sheet of birch bark into the lake to soften it up. I'm going to make a spoon and a bowl with it when it's smooth enough. I'm back to feel it, but it's not ready. I planned this trip a month ago. Now that I'm here I'm angry. Maybe I didn't sleep well enough. It was the first night. You have to expect to be nervous on the first night, but it's made me bad. I feel bad.

Maybe it's the ugly ticks. You come up here to think about beauty. To hear warblers in the morning and wind in the birch leaves overhead. But then you end up thinking about mites and ticks with lymph-sucking pipes that cut open your skin and dig inside. There they hang, getting big on your own blood. You don't think of purple hyssops or scarlet shootingstars or swallows swooping by. You think of white or yellow or brown ticks that don't have any shape or colour or character. It's mean. The whole thing is mean. Those pests don't have a right to lay eight thousand eggs all over the grass with nothing to do but climb onto a straw and wait for you to walk by.

Maybe you get that way when you're by yourself and everything is raw. That Johannes Bjarnason up in Lake Winnipegosis was like that. He got strange. Maybe it's in the family. He's supposed to be related on my mother's side. He stayed in this cabin with Schaldemoes' family, a wife and daughter, on a promontory into the lake. He was new in Manitoba, fresh from Iceland. The idea was that he'd help Jonas put the nets into the lake in the fall and gather firewood for winter. They were going to fish the nets out when the lake froze over. To do that, they hacked out bald spots in the ice and threaded a string underneath. Later they pulled the nets out of the holes, took the fish out, and put them back in. They had almost seventy nets and they lifted twenty of them every day.

If my folks knew about this they'd have a search party out for me. Maybe they've got one out anyway. It's a big argument with them, that I don't know enough to do something like this. It's dangerous for a girl who's only seventeen. But what about the first pioneers? What did they know about fishing in prairie lakes or camping in poplar stands? There isn't anything remotely like this in Iceland. You've got to be brave about life. You can't test yourself unless you step outside. It's true, I don't know what I'm doing, but I'll learn. I figure I'll be able to catch northern pike or yellow perch here. Pike are supposed to get so big that one catch might do me for a couple of days. They come where the water is shallow in the morning. You can probably just pick them up from the water-weeds. Otherwise you can put a worm on your hook and use a button for a lure. A shiny one, anyway. And perch are supposed to be around all the time. You can catch it from the banks, especially at noon or in the evening. It shouldn't be hard.

This Johannes, my great-uncle. In November the Schaldemoes family went to Winnipegosis town and he stayed in the cabin alone while they were gone. It was on Hunter's Island, twenty miles away and three miles from the nearest neighbour. Jonas Schaldemoes kept asking him if he felt all right about being alone, and told him not to work after dark and to stay overnight in the neighbour's cabin instead of sleeping alone. Friday morning the family left and Johannes went to work on the lake. It was slow work, lifting nets alone, but he didn't want to quit until he'd done enough to call it a day's work. So he didn't get back to the cabin till after dark. He was uncomfortable when he got there, but the discomfort vanished as soon as he started preparing supper for himself. He made the lunch-pack for the following day and went to sleep.

Next morning he went to work early and stayed on the lake till it was dark again. The hoarfrost was thick in the air and there was a dark heavy fog when he got back. He tried to open the door to the cabin, but it was as if someone pushed it against him from inside. He tried to get in twice, but both times the door slammed shut in his face. He thought about following Jonas' advice and going to the neighbour's cabin, but then he decided that would be cowardly. He'd slept all right in this one the night before. So he collected his energy, opened the door and walked in. As soon as he'd lit the lamp, he stood for a while and looked around. It occurred to him that he wasn't alone in the cabin. He couldn't see anybody else, but he felt sure he wasn't alone.

They say a tick goes through three stages. It's as if it's got three lives and in each one it has to latch onto an animal and gorge itself with blood. First it's the larva, then it's the nymph, then it's the adult. Each time it's bigger and takes more blood than before, and in the end it's so big that the shield on the outside of the body just about cracks. That's when it drops to the grass again. Then it's had enough. The lousy parasite. It isn't enough to have thousands of eggs from each one, but every one of those eggs gets you three times before it's dead. They're all over. There's no such thing as being alone in the wilds, is there? There's lots of company.

Johannes pulled himself out of his cowardice and started preparing supper. Stewing catfish, maybe. He knew he wouldn't get any sleep so he sat down to write a letter home. He didn't finish the letter till after midnight, but by that time he felt calm and tired. So he went to bed. There was a window over his bed and the stove stood on the other side of the room, a few feet away. He turned his face to the wall and lay still for a while. Then he looked over his shoulder onto the floor. There stood a man, halfway between the bed and the stove. Half a man, because the top half was missing. The legs, feet, and hips were there, but the rest was gone. He sat up in bed and stared at the apparition, but then it vanished.

You'd think he was getting bush fever already on his second night. Maybe it doesn't take longer than that. The trick is to stay organized and keep your mind on something specific. Like the birch bark. Even if a tree is dead, you can use the bark. The bark stays alive in a way. You just have to soak it in water and it'll work. Anything can be made with it: cups and bowls and plates. Pots too, with the dark side out so it won't catch fire. I'm going to fold this piece up into a rectangle and glue the ends up with sap. Then I'll roll up a small wad for a spoon and slide it into the slit of a twig. I'll tie it with roots. It's easy.

That man. He should have thought of something else when he lay down again after the figure was gone. Keeping your mind on something like that makes it come again. Sure enough, a little later he saw the same half-man on the floor. When he stood up, the vision was gone. He lay down for the third time, and soon he saw it again. Three times it came to him during the night. After that he couldn't stay in bed. He got up and paced the floor for the rest of the night. By six in the morning he was so tired that he lay down. Just as he was about to fall asleep, he heard a man call just outside his window: "Ho, ho, ho." He thought it was Hjalmar, Jonas' cousin from the next cabin. Hjalmar used to visit on Sunday mornings. But then he realized it was too early for a visitor. Johannes went outside and walked around the cabin, but he couldn't see anyone. The strange voice had sounded most like an Indian's call.

By noon the family was back home at the cabin. They asked

Johannes how he'd been and he said nothing about what he'd seen. Some days later, when they were at work on the lake, Jonas asked again if he hadn't seen anything while they were gone. Then Johannes told him everything. After all, they said he'd been strange when they got back. Jonas got more thoughtful after hearing the story of the split man in the cabin. Then he told his guest what it was he'd seen.

That's the way ticks are. You don't see them on the grass. You walk into them and they jump on you. You don't see them until they're burrowing into your skin and you have to get them out. The only way to do it is to stick a burning twig at the insect. That'll make it curl up and drop off. If you force it out or pull it, the mouthparts stay in your skin. But the whole thing doesn't sound as dangerous as they make it out to be. A few bloodsuckers can't do anything when they're that small. I guess they can give you diseases or sores or ulcers. That's what happens to cows and sheep. In the Rockies, the chipmunks and rabbits have spotted fever from ticks. People can get that too. But it sounds worse than it is. Just put some oil on the pest and it'll let go.

That birch bark still isn't ready. I didn't realize there were so many layers to a piece of bark when I cut it off the tree. Where do you stop with all those layers? They keep going. You don't know where the bark ends and the meat of the trunk begins. Maybe I didn't peel off enough layers. You peel one sheet, then another, some darker, some lighter. They alternate, but they always come back. Maybe I took too many and that's why it's so stiff. Maybe it's never ready.

Like that Indian on Lake Winnipegosis. He may never stop calling. Jonas said that a few years earlier, an Indian had been working on the lake during the winter. He moved fish bundles across the lake on a sled pulled by two horses. It was early in the winter and the ice was rotten. He disappeared on that trip and people said he'd fallen through. But no one knew what really happened. Next spring, when the ice loosened up, a man's corpse washed up just below Jonas' cabin. They decided it must have been the Indian who had vanished, but they couldn't be sure. The body wasn't recognizable any more. It was cut in half. All they found was the bottom half.

You'd think it was the top half calling for the bottom half. Looking for itself forever. But what harm can half a ghost do anybody? Without a head, without arms, it has to be harmless. But there's no real body there. Even if it were a real ghost, it'd be easy to shrug off. Just light a fire in the hearth and you won't see it any more. But what if it keeps coming back? Every spring it's there and you have to listen to the calls and the knocks clattering on your floor. By winter it's under the ice again. It only comes around when somebody's alone in a cabin and it wants to talk.

Maybe I've got my information wrong. Maybe you don't soak the bark in water at all. I guess I'll try a young tree next time, one with soft moist bark you can just rip off. Maybe I'm too mad to do anything right. It's only the second day. I'll come around. I didn't sleep after all. This sort of thing takes time. You have to move one step at a time. First you set up a tent, then you make a fire. Then you make the implements, one at a time. Soon you'll have them all. Bowls and spoons and plates and knives'll be dangling on the branches all around your tent. Like the sheep ticks. You don't see them, don't hear them, hardly feel them. But suddenly they're there. Right on you. They say in Europe the cows can have so many ticks hanging on them that they clatter and rattle when they walk. What a load. Think of having to take them off, one at a time. Burning them off with brands.

It's mean. The whole thing is mean. Like the name they gave me. Kolla. That's short for Kolbrun. I got it because I'm darker than the rest of them, as if I were the black sheep or something. Maybe they got the idea I'd be moody already when they had me in the crib. Kolbrun. That means brown as coal. Coal. That's a burnt forest, isn't it? It's mean.

Waskesiu, Wasagaming, Regina, 1978-79

A PROPER BURIAL

TERRENCE HEATH

The treed part of the cemetery filled up about ten years ago except for a few places reserved by older and more providential families of the town. Outside the caragana hedge, which was kept neatly trimmed by the town idiot, a piece of rough land bounded by the hedges and trees on one side and by a low, marshy area on the other had been divided into six large rectangles for the more recent dead. Saplings lined the intervening pathways and the idiot watered these two-foot high trees once in early June and again in August. One of the rectangles, the one closest to the town, was about two-thirds full of graves; the other five were only sparsely dotted with plots and these were located mostly at the west and nearest to the shade of the hedge and trees of the old cemetery. In keeping with the aesthetics of the landscape or, perhaps, in imitation of the fashion in urban centres for rolling lawns uncluttered by prominent tombstones, only flat headstones were allowed in the new part. As a result, the high, closely packed tombstones of the old cemetery seemed like a frightened giant people staring out apprehensively over their hedge walls at the growing, sprawling settlement of temporarily cowed serfs beyond their fortress.

Now, in the semi-night of summer, the trees, hedge and tombstones of the original cemetery were one crenelated shadow against the sky. Charles, bent over in the middle of the second rectangle from the edge of the town, was the only shadow in the new part, except for the very thin saplings in leaf along the paths. There were no lights in the cemetery but car lights passed about half-a-mile north on the highway down to the lake.

Charles had a seven-foot string, a collapsible shovel, a screwdriver, a book and penlight wrapped in a silk scarf and a wild rose in a jar of water. Except for the string, which he was using as a measure, the objects were piled next to the area he was marking off in the dirt with a stick. He first drew a line the length of the string and parallel to the pathway behind him and then he folded the string in half and drew a perpendicular line from each end of the seven-foot mark. He connected the ends of the short lines and noticed with satisfaction that they were exactly seven feet apart. The small rectangle was clearly outlined in the southwest corner of the large rectangle. Charles was a neat man.

He picked up the shovel and began to dig across the end of the rectangle furthest from the old cemetery. There were eight shovelfuls across the width of the rectangle and Charles piled four on one side and four on the other at about two feet out from the marks in the dirt. He worked his way toward the head of the rectangle, cleaning out the loose dirt from the six-inch-deep hole as he went. Halfway down, he stopped, took off his light jacket, folded it and put it at the head of the rectangle. Along the edges, he turned the shovel sideways and cut the sides even.

When he had almost reached the other end, he turned and dug carefully around the flat, marble headstone. After the dirt was cleared from the sides of the stone, he pried the stone up. It came up easily. He propped the slab up against his leg and moved it one corner at a time out of the rectangle. He let it fall flat again next to his coat. He returned to his digging. He finished the length of the rectangle and cleaned out the corners, before he walked back to the other end and began the second layer down.

Except for occasionally straightening up, Charles did not stop in his digging until he was about four feet down. By now it was quite dark. The stars shone brightly and the piles of dirt on either side of the four-foot-deep hole were higher than his head when he stood at the bottom of the trench. He was sweating heavily. At four feet, he hoisted himself out of the hole and stood next to the headstone, flexing his hands while the cool night wind blew his wet shirt against his stomach and chest. He drank some of the water from the rose jar, rolled it around in his mouth, walked over to one of the saplings and spewed it out around its roots. He listened to the wind in the leaves of the old cemetery. He raised his long middle finger and made an obscene gesture at the dark shadows of the graveyard battlements.

He walked back to the hole he was digging and lowered himself down into it again.

Now Charles no longer dug out six-inch-deep shovelfuls, but he pushed the shovel carefully in about three inches and removed much of the dirt by scraping off the surface. On the second time down the length of the rectangle, his shovel thudded hollowly on the wooden box. He cleared the dirt off the top of the box and began to work down the sides. He scooped the dirt out with his hands, piled it on the shovel and then threw it up onto the piles on either side of the grave. The cheap, pauper's box sat free on the surrounding earth.

Although the lid of the box was flat and not treated against water seepage, it seemed whole, almost new in its whiteness. Charles stood on it without any fear of falling through while he reached for his screwdriver and unwrapped the penlight from the scarf. With the aid of the light he was able to find the screws around the edges of the lid. He removed each screw and placed it in his pocket. He then stood on the lid again, replaced the penlight and took the wild rose from the jar. He held the rose in his teeth while he lifted the lid. The lid resisted his pull for a moment, then gave and he tipped it up and set it alongside the coffin. It was dark in the coffin and he had to get the penlight again before he could place the rose in what had been her hands. He climbed onto the side of the coffin and hoisted himself out of the hole.

The eastern sky had begun to pale slightly as Charles unwrapped the book from the scarf. He hung the scarf around his neck and adjusted the ends so that they hung evenly on either side of his chest. The wind stirred the silk tassels. He opened the book and with the penlight held very close to the print, he began to read the Latin side of the page in a low monotone. At the proper places, he made the sign of the cross and used the water in the jar as holy water to sprinkle into the grave. He climbed back down into the grave, replaced the lid on the box and screwed it down firmly. When he was up top again, he solemnly threw three handfuls of dirt onto the lid.

The sky was growing light quickly now but Charles read clearly and slowly to the end. Then he began the litany of the saints. After the fifth evocation, he was startled to hear the "ora pro nobis" response come from the old part of the cemetery. Charles did not raise his head but continued to read the evocations and waited each time for the response from the other side of the path. Their conversation drifted quietly back and forth on the early morning air. The birds had started to chirp and move about in the trees.

Charles wrapped the book and penlight in the scarf again, took up the shovel and started to throw the dirt from the piles into the hole. He heard a shed door bang in the old cemetery and looked up. The idiot was walking towards him with a shovel in his hands. The two of them shovelled the dirt into the hole, cleaned up as much as they could scratch out of the prairie grass and replaced the headstone on the fresh mound of earth. Charles put on his jacket, shivered slightly, picked up his tools and bundle and started off toward the highway. The idiot took the jar of water and poured it around the roots of one of the saplings.

THE RIVERS RUN TO THE SEA

JOHN V. HICKS

I was down by the river one morning in early June, watching the high water of the spring flood whisking along the side of the concrete retaining wall that runs east from the traffic bridge. It was one of those perverse June days that occasionally occur, making you think you've been tossed back into the first week of April, and I zipped up my windbreaker against the chill breeze from the north. Then, on a whim, I decided to drop in at Ahab Grundl's for a look around, and a warm up, before I went home.

As you enter Ahab Grundl's tiny curio shop on River Street, wedged in between a furniture dealer's and a small cafe, you cannot fail to notice a carefully lettered sign, suspended from the ceiling by an almost invisible thread, which reads: You Are Welcome To Browse. The faintly scented air stirs to the slight movement your entry has set up, causing the sign to revolve and let you read the other side, which in turn repeats the phrase: You Are Welcome To Browse.

It is as though an invisible hand, somewhere in the shadows overhead, were dangling the legend in front of you in quiet assurance that you are in no danger of being accosted by some enthusiastic salesman anxious to breach your defenses and send you on your way with something you may wish an hour later you hadn't bought.

Old Ahab sits hunched behind his counter looking less like a salesman than anything you might imagine. His swarthy features may crease into a smile as you enter, and on a particularly communicative day he may murmur a soft "How do you do, sir." But that is as far as his hanging sign will permit him to go, at least on early acquaintance. He stands by its unspoken guarantee that you will not be disturbed unnecessarily.

If you happen to be looking for something in particular, though, you have only to ask. Then he is at once at your service, with a courtly grace and a readily-tapped fund of information about every one of the fascinating articles that fill the shelves, the counters, and a large portion of the space available on the floor.

As I poked about among the welter of stuff on display, my attention was arrested by a meerschaum pipe set up on a shelf at about eye level. It was no ordinary pipe. The bowl had been delicately carved into the likeness of a man's face, with full beard. A sailor's face, I fancied. It was by no means the first meerschaum I'd seen with a face carved on the bowl, but this one had been executed with uncanny precision. And I couldn't help but be fascinated by the eyes, tiny as they were. They were fixed in the most intense expression, as though on the distance. The mouth, partly opened, seemed to be in the act of speaking.

Although I am not given to handling things displayed on shelves, I found myself on impulse picking the pipe up. It couldn't have been more than an ounce in weight, which was light for its size. Constant smoking had coloured the bowl to a mellow golden-brown hue, and it had a well-cared-for look. Even the carbon cake inside had been allowed to collect to just the right thickness and no more. Here, I thought, was a pipe that was rather out of place on the prairies. It should have been leaning against a marine-decorated humidor in the smoking room of some retired sea captain in Victoria.

It was when I turned the carved features toward me that I was momentarily startled to find those penetrating eyes looking directly into mine. In the silence, I could almost imagine a whisper issuing from the parted lips. How long I stood there I don't know. It must have been several minutes.

"The pipe fascinates you, sir," a soft voice said. I almost dropped it on the carpeted floor. Old Ahab was at my elbow, smiling. Only an extraordinary preoccupation on my part could have brought him from behind his counter to speak about the pipe.

"Yes," I acknowleged, coming back to myself with some confusion at being thus startled. "Those eyes. I mean, there's something about them —"

He nodded. "It is indeed remarkable," he agreed. "I am sorry if I interrupted your — meditation. I thought I had better come over. You were, as they say, as white as a sheet."

White as a sheet, was I? I certainly did feel a bit light-headed, for no reason that I could explain. Nothing wrong with my health, I was reasonably sure. But something had come over me — there was no doubt about that. I put the meerschaum carefully back in place on the shelf, and as I took my hand away I found the eyes once again fixed directly on mine. I blinked a couple of times and turned to Ahab.

"I certainly experienced a queer sensation," I said. "My imagination doesn't often run away with me."

He raised dark eyebrows in some surprise.

"Perhaps it was not altogether your imagination, sir," he suggested.

I guess my smile encouraged him to continue. I had encountered Ahab Grundl on one of his rare talkative days, apparently.

"You may be of a particularly receptive temperament," he said. "Who is to say? We know so little. The pipe is very old."

"You stir my curiosity," I told him. "You mean there's something out of the ordinary about this pipe?"

"Indeed there is, sir," he replied. He studied the floor for a few moments, collecting his thoughts. "It came to me from a man who had been a naval officer in World War Two. After he'd got his discharge he travelled out here and went into land surveying."

"That was a switch, for a sailor," I observed.

"Yes, quite," Ahab agreed, and it occurred to me that perhaps I shouldn't have interrupted him. He reached over and adjusted the pipe's position on the shelf.

"It belonged to his grandfather, apparently," he continued. "The grandfather was a mate on a merchant ship, sailing out of Halifax. He had attached some significance to the pipe which he would never divulge to anyone, and the story goes that he wished to be buried with it in his mouth. Insisted on it, in fact — even wrote it into his will."

"Good heavens," I muttered.

"A strange request," Ahab said, "but he was by all accounts a strange man. Something of a mystic. He had sailed in the far east for years."

"So somebody goofed?" I asked, glancing again at the pipe.

"Apparently the request could never be complied with," Ahab replied, "for he was himself lost at sea in a wild Atlantic storm. His few personal effects included the pipe, which seems to have been handed down from father to son to grandson. The grandson being a non-smoker, with little interest in strange pipes, he passed it on to me when he left the district last year. It was he who told me the pipe's history. He didn't set much store by the original owner's obsession, apparently. And an obsession it certainly was, not to bore you with any more details."

"So there you have something that ties in with the look in those delicately fashioned eyes," I offered whimsically. "I guess I do have an imagination after all, eh?"

"Even so, one should never distrust the imagination," Ahab declared, fixing me with a steady gaze. "I shall not soon forget your reaction of a few minutes ago. You seemed to be for the moment — under a spell, shall we say?"

"Possibly just a delayed heartbeat," I laughed. "Nothing to worry about, the medicos tell us. But I certainly was fascinated by the thing." I turned my glance back to the pipe, and there it was again — the same strange sensation. A wild thought occurred to me.

"If it weren't already so well smoked," I said, "perhaps I'd buy it and fire it up." Now, why had I said that? The last thing in the world I needed was somebody's second-hand pipe.

"You are a pipe smoker? Ah!" Ahab continued to fix me with that steady look, but now it was intensified. "I think you ought to have it," he said, "for a while at least. Perhaps you should become better acquainted with it. Would you like to take it with you when you leave? No hurry, of course."

He smiled briefly, and I thought he was reminding himself of the sign of hospitality inside his front door.

"That'll depend on how much you want for it," I countered, not feeling in the mood for haggling.

"Nothing, for now," he replied. "We can settle on a price afterwards, if you should decide to keep it. In the meantime, I'd very much like you to take it home for a day or two. Study it at your leisure. I have a feeling there may be some sort of affinity between it and you."

"What on earth do you mean?" I asked him.

"I — don't quite know," he replied.

On which rather indefinite note I walked out of the shop carrying the pipe, which he had carefully wrapped in tissue paper and put into a small cardboard box. A dead man's pipe, and a rumoured influence of some sort. What'll I get talked into next, I wondered.

It proved to be a morning for the nurturing of curious ideas. In the act of turning towards home with my non-purchase, it came to me that the logical place to light up a sailor's pipe, if indeed I really intended to, was on a wharf. A ship's wharf we couldn't boast, but we did have a tie-up spot for the Northern Airways planes that shuttled back and forth into the north.

Maybe I'm still under that spell of Ahab's, I thought, but just for laughs I'll do it. So I went off along River Street, took the road that led down the river bank to the Airways landing, and walked out on to the floating platform. I knew one or two of the boys casually, so if anybody was around I didn't expect I'd be labelled a trespasser. One tiny plane was made fast to a post, the current churning past its floats. I sat on a barrel and fished out my tobacco pouch.

I studied the carved bowl again for several moments before I began packing it. The eyes continued to draw me. If, as I could almost imagine, a flicker of excitement had been added to them, I attributed it to the outdoor light as compared with the lesser illumination of Ahab's shop. I gave the pipe a wipe and a good blow-through, packed it carefully, tamped the last bit of tobacco down firmly, and shielded the bowl against my windbreaker while I applied a match. Sailor, I thought, here's to your salt-cured bones, wherever they rest — if they do.

I found it surprisingly sweet. If I'd expected it to be fouled by the many years of disuse, I was mistaken. I puffed away for several minutes, watching the dark water racing endlessly east, listening to its small but insistent sounds, its faint hissings and lappings.

The sensation came over me without warning, some time later. Dizziness from a strong pipe I can understand. Fond as I am of my own briars, I never smoke one right down to the bitter end. But this was not dizziness. It was in fact an intensification of the feeling I'd experienced back in the shop. Apparently it was related to the trancelike concentration old Ahab had described, for I swear I do not clearly remember getting up and going to the edge of the wharf to knock out the ashes. I suppose I had sat for close to half an hour, since the pipe was out and appeared to have been smoked well down. Then indeed I did take a strange turn, a sudden light-headedness. Watching the fine grey ash spill down on to the swirling water, I lurched forward as though I'd been pushed.

A sharp blow to my right shoulder saved me from falling in. I staggered backward and sat down heavily. I had collided, I found, with a wing tip of the moored plane, for which I could thank my lucky stars. Had I plunged into the river in that state, and fully clothed as I was, I'd probably have drowned. There are undertows and cross currents that can carry you off without ceremony if you aren't careful.

I sat there feeling perfectly normal again, and a little foolish. My performance had not been seen, I judged, for nobody came running, nobody called out. I looked about for the pipe, half expecting to see it shattered at my feet. There wasn't a trace of it. But in my memory's ear I seemed to have retained the *plop* of a small object falling into water, and I knew then what had happened to it.

A fine thing, I thought. Now I'd have to square myself with Grundl — pay him for an art object I hadn't had for more than an hour and didn't particularly want anyway. I couldn't but imagine, though, that losing it had cleared my mind completely. I walked slowly back to Ahab's shop, my old down-to-earth self again.

"I guess I owe you for a pipe," I said, walking in with the empty box in my hand. "How much?"

His eyebrows rose. "So soon?" he asked. "You have hardly had time to get to know it, surely." He smiled. "You don't have to buy it unless you wish."

"I smoked it," I said, "and found it surprisingly good. Now I've lost it."

A wrinkled hand went quickly to his mouth. "Oh, surely not," he exclaimed. "You didn't have it when you got home?"

"It's in the river," I said. "I didn't go home."

He listened intently while I recounted my experience. When I came to the narrow escape I'd had, his face went grave. He waited, motionless, while I finished my story.

"I am sorry, sir," he said then.

"Thanks," I said, "but I guess there's no harm done. I'd like to pay you and forget the whole thing."

"You don't owe me anything," he said. "I should have told you. I am thankful nothing worse happened. It — frightens me, sir."

I must have looked puzzled. "Frightens you? Why? How could you know I'd be stupid enough to fall in the river — almost?"

"But I should have told you," he insisted quietly.

"Told me? What, for heaven's sake?"

He leaned forward across the counter, hands clasped. "The rest of the story. This sailor, now—" He closed his eyes.

"That sailor again?" I asked, becoming a trifle impatient.

"He was determined to be buried with his pipe, as you know," Ahab said. "And he vowed that if he was buried without it he'd get it back somehow, some time, no matter what, no matter where."

I smiled. "Well, he won't get it now," I said. "It's somewhere in the Saskatchewan River, travelling east at ten miles an hour or better."

He nodded. His voice dropped to a half whisper.

"The rivers," he said, "run to the sea."

PIECES

WILLIAM J. KLEBECK

wings lifted up the cultivator is in transport as they're getting ready
to move the seven miles to the South Half that is summerfallow this
year but before he heads out with the tractor Eddy helps his father
Milt load into the back of their half-ton truck a 100-gallon steel tank
they use for diesel since the tank at the South Half has a slow
leak

moving down the road in D4 the highest gear full throttle Eddy has
one wheel in the ditch because a blue-and-white Merc is passing
bang the car swerves as the driver jerks the steering wheel scared by
the sound of a tire blowing on the cultivator Eddy throttles down
pulls to a stop on a handy approach sighs he always wondered what
it would be like if a tire blew while he was in transport now he
knows there's enough clearance so the shovels don't dig into the
road even if the cultivator is riding on a rim only thing is he won't be
going very far on that tire Eddy turns in the seat to see the Merc
backing up stopping and Ollie Parkens in house-slippers getting out
Eddy climbs down to meet him Boy that sure scared me Ollie says
first thing I thought somebody was shooting at me Yeah says Eddy
can you give me a ride just a coupla miles my old man's down at the
field there and they get into the car Ollie shaking his head Didn't
know what it was until I got by you and looked in the mirror Yeah
says Eddy I always wondered what it would be like blowing a tire in

transport Well now you know eh Yeah Eddy points to his father's half-ton parked at the edge of the field Ollie stops his car on the shoulder of the road Thanks for the ride Eddy hops out How's your feet today Ollie Milt calls but Ollie is already easing the Merc back onto the road Eddy slams the door as he gets in with his father who has a wince of a smile on his face What happened Blew a tire on the cultivator Are you sunk in the road No there's enough clearance I'm in Ferguson's approach Oh that's not so bad then Need a new tire That's not so bad

they drive to town it being close to lunch time and Milt calls Norman who owns the tire shop tells him what happened Norm says he'll be out with a new tire shortly after dinner Milt tells Eddy while he's still eating dessert to fill up the tank in the half-ton and to go summerfallowing after Norman has fixed the tire What are you going to do Eddy asks I'm going hauling grain Milt wipes whipped cream off his whiskered chin with his sleeve and stands up Won't need you to shovel until tomorrow I'll be hauling from one of those big bins over at Dablanaca's Okay

Eddy stops by the Shell Bulk station on his way out of town and waits for the agent Ray Tamblyn to put one hundred gallons of diesel into the tank he and his father loaded in the back of the truck that morning

Eddy parks the truck within a hose-length of the tractor's fuel tank and since they use a little compressor hooked up to the truck's electrical system to pump air into the tank to pump fuel out Eddy attaches the air compressor to the valve on the tank sticks the nozzle into the tractor tank using the cap to hold the nozzle open and while the tank is filling he gets a socket and extension and in a few moments the blown tire is off leaning against the frame of the deep-tillage Eddy remembers about the fuel jumps up on the front wheel of the tractor to see there's no diesel coming out of the nozzle even though it's open and there's one hundred gallons in that tank Eddy glances over to see diesel spurting out where the weld has sprung around the pipe connected to the hose Christ he forgot to open the valve on the filter and the tank which had been lying flat in the back of the truck is raised four inches on the bottom bulged out by too much goddamn air Eddy tries to hop from the tractor tire to the truck but slips on the splattered diesel lands on the ground on his stomach umph but gets up opens that valve now he can hear the splash of diesel in the tractor tank but there's still too much pressure there's still diesel shooting out in thin streams so Eddy grabs the pipe-wrench cranks open the fill-plug that explodes so much air it blows his John Deere cap off but at least it relieves the pressure against the weld the stuff is not spurting any more just seeping that still means he's got to run the truck down to the South Half to pump the rest of the diesel into the tank there since that leak is a helluva lot slower than the one he just made

Eddy meets Norman on the road coming out from town but he's going so fast he doesn't have time to wave more pressing matters right now

long slow process pumping that sixty or so remaining gallons out of the leaking tank so Eddy's sitting on the tailgate spitting sunflower seeds swatting mosquitoes listening to the hum of the air compressor when all of a sudden the hum is gone probably the little compressor overheating and Eddy is walking to shut it off when the compressor shorts out sparks ignite the diesel splashed all over the truck whoosh into both tanks whooosh

THE BULLDOGS ALL HAVE
RUBBER TEETH

FREDA KORBER

It was good to kill.

At supper, after one of the long silences, the eldest child would raise cautious eyes and speak.

"We got fourteen gophers today."

And the father's ice-sharp gaze would impale the speaker, relent, and come close to approval.

"That's fourteen less," he would say.

For a good snare, you needed really old binder-twine, soft and limp as sugarbag dishtowels after they'd been blown on the line all summer. A soft snare would lie snug around the hole and stretch back smooth and straight. It wouldn't go springing up in crazy loops and coils the way new yellow binder-twine did. You'd never catch a gopher with a new binder-twine snare. Even the youngest knew this.

All three carried snares and short thick clubs. The eldest had two traps — small No. 4's, but even so, too strong for the other two to set. They would watch and hold their breath while the eldest stepped on the spring to open the rusty jaws, set the trigger under the pan, and ever so slowly let the spring up. There was a way to set the trigger just a little to one side, so that the smallest pebble would bring the empty jaws snapping viciously together and the whole trap would leap in the air, grabbing for prey.

A hot, dry wind blew from the west, as always. The empty sky was almost white, bleached by the sun's glare, as were the clothes and hair of the children. Heat flowed over their heads and down their backs like the boiling syrup their mother poured over fruit in glass jars. But their mother could not see them now. No one could. This was the far pasture, out of sight of any buildings, and the curve of unbroken horizon drew a magic circle around them. Here the children were free.

Only the shrillest sounds could pierce the rush of wind in their ears: the clear notes of a meadowlark, the high-pitched buzzing of grasshoppers, and the sound the children waited for — the squeak of a gopher.

"There's one. You get him."

The eldest pointed but the youngest was already running, bare feet scampering over the prickly grass and soft grey dust, toward what looked like a short stake driven into a mound. With a squeak of alarm, the stake doubled up, flicked its tail and disappeared. But its burrow had been marked.

The hole was small and round, and the noose of the snare easy to fit, even for the chubby fingers. One dusty foot on the twine held the noose in place while the child laid the rest out straight, squatted, wrapped the end twice around one hand, and began to wait.

The other two had separated; the eldest to set the traps, the other lying belly-down, picking idly at the scab on a fiery barbed-wire scratch across one thigh. The snare was set and there was time. Gophers seldom came out again right away.

But sooner or later — as now — curiosity brings the sleek head, the bright black eye, peeping up cautiously, an inch at a time. Not yet . . . the child sits still as a rock . . . not yet . . . wait until the head is through the noose . . . another inch . . . Now!

A savage yank and the child scrambles up, gopher dangling in mid-air, screeching, tiny claws scrabbling for purchase, eyes tight-shut in panic, jaws wide, gasping now for air. Lowered, it crouches, dazed and heaving, until its feet realize ground beneath them. Up in a flash, then, and dashing madly for the burrow. Is yanked back, runs again, is yanked off its feet. In short dashes, steered by the snare, the gopher is driven and dragged to perform for the other children.

But the last hard tug is too much for the soft binder-twine. Its worn fibers part, and the gopher, suddenly free, lunges for its life, zigzagging, dodging with swift leaps and turns; the children running alongside, swatting with their clubs, kicking, stumbling, laughing, sobbing for breath. "Kill it! Look out! Hit it! Kill it! Missed! Ouch! Watch what you're hitting!" A thrown club knocks the gopher off its feet. It rolls, somersaults twice, and flings itself down a burrow.

The children's cheeks are scarlet with heat and exertion. They turn away and the hot wind, which has erased their shouts, now glues strands of hair onto the damp, happy faces.

Gottlieb always sang to the cow when he milked. Head butted against the cow's flank, pail gripped between his knees, to the rhythm of milk chiming on galvanized metal, he would croon his way through "Red River Valley", "Springtime in the Rockies" and verse after verse of "Big Rock Candy Mountain." The children liked that one best. They stood, shy and silent now, in the shadowy barn, watching, breathing in the raw smells of new milk, oat-straw, sheaf-dust, ammonia. And listening.

"In the big rock candy mountain," sang Gottlieb,
"All the cops have wooden legs,
The bulldogs all have rubber teeth,
And the hens lay soft-boiled eggs . . ."
He squirted milk into the waiting mouths of the barn cats and they cleaned their whiskers with their paws.
"Oooh, the boxcars all are empty,
And the barns are full of hay.
I wanta go where there ain't no snow,
Where the rain don't fall and the wind don't blow,
In the big rock candy mountain."
The children waited for more.
"Oooh, the buzzin' of the bees
In the cigarette trees, by the soda-water fountain . . . "
Gottlieb glanced at the children.
"And the bluebird sings by the whiskey springs
In the big rock candy mountain."
He suddenly bent a teat and laid a stream of warm, sticky milk across the three sober faces.

Outraged, the children backed off a step, wiping at their cheeks with grimy fingers, while Gottlieb rocked gleefully on his stool, butting his head repeatedly into the cow's flank.

"Heeheehee! Heyheyhey!" he went, until the cow looked back, annoyed. With a powerful swing of her tail, she delivered a stinging lash to the back of Gottlieb's neck.

"God damn bitch!" screeched Gottlieb, punching the cow in the ribs and half-rising, the milk sloshing in the pail. This time, the cow didn't bother to look; she unerringly swung her tail again, then carefully moved one foot forward, shifting all her weight onto the pointed toe of Gottlieb's cowboy boot.

The children were helpless with giggling.

"You kids get the hell out of here!" yelped Gottlieb, tears in his eyes. "You know damn well your Dad don't like you hanging round the barn."

They got out fast.

The traps didn't make much noise when they were sprung but the gophers did. The squeals of rage and pain would bring the children running, ready with their clubs. Not that there was any hurry. There was no escape from a trap as from a snare, although the gopher would fight desperately, back arched, tiny pointed teeth clicking against the steel jaws, trying to bite and chew itself loose. The children took turns swinging, missing; the gopher ducking, rolling with the trap; the glancing blows falling anywhere, everywhere. A lucky hit might land squarely on the small skull and an eye pop out — a perfect white and glistening globe — to lie on the now-motionless tawny cheek, while two thin red threads crept slowly from the delicate nostrils.

The eldest, the only one strong enough to open the trap, would step on the spring and shake it free.

Only Gottlieb chattered at the table. He piled his plate with mashed potatoes and turnips and stewed chicken with dumplings, and described how bad the food had been in jail. He talked about how long you had to wait in line at the soup-kitchens down East, and about riding the rods and being chased and caught by the bulls, who would throw you in the calaboose or the hoosegow for being a bum; he told how many farms he'd seen deserted already, and how far he'd had to come to find a job.

"Talks to hear himself talk," muttered the father, who never did. The children enjoyed Gottlieb's stories even if they didn't understand the stories themselves, or why the father looked grim and the mother, out of politeness, smiled only a little.

After supper, the children would follow Gottlieb up the narrow stairs to his room and watch, wordlessly, while he spilled tobacco on paper, rolled, licked, twisted the ends and struck a match on his thumbnail.

"Yep," he would sigh through blue clouds of smoke, "I'm goin' West. Never meant to be no hired man on a farm. Gonna punch cattle on a big ranch. That's the life."

Gottlieb wanted to be a cowboy but the children knew he could not even ride a horse. "Spent a whole month's salary on that hat of his," the father would growl in disbelief. And, as always, after explaining his plans to the mute children, Gottlieb would reach for the tall box beside his bed, ceremoniously remove the lid, lift out wads of tissue-paper, and reverently hold aloft the snowy-white Stetson.

"Ain't she a beauty, now? This here's the best they make. Pure wool felt, this is. There ain't no better. Don't touch it, I gotta keep it clean. Ain't it something, eh?"

The children didn't say much. They secretly thought Gottlieb looked a little silly in the big hat, holding the white-framed mirror at arm's length, tilting his head this way and that.

The old sow lay on her side, grunting softly, while her litter squealed, fought and struggled for the best feeding position. The litter had been too large and one piglet was left out, too small and weak to win a place for himself in the free-for-all.

"Here's the runt," said the father, reaching into the pen.

The children froze. They knew about runts and cripples. They had seen the baby chicks, jostling and pushing; the sturdy healthy ones deliberately pecking and trampling the one with a blind eye or clubbed foot. Their clumsy fingers had felt, under the bright yellow fluff, little toothpick ribs and necks like tiny strung beads. They had also seen a matchstick, between their father's hard fingers, break in half as though of its own accord. And somehow, some morning, all the lame chicks would be gone.

Now, that hard hand was closing around the piglet. Frantic, one of the children begged, "Couldn't *we* feed it?"

"No use making pets," the father's word was final. "These are all for slaughter, eventually."

But with his other hand, he scooped up a greedily-sucking fat piglet. It came loose with a loud smack, its tongue still funnelled and full of milk, its pale eyelashes popping up in surprise. The father chuckled and the children's eyes flew to his face. He put the runt in the vacant spot, gently nudged it into position, waited to see it established, then turned and walked away. Amazed, the children watched him go.

Slaughter was something the children were not supposed to watch. They would only be in the way, their mother said. But no one had told Gottlieb.

"You kids wanta see something funny?"

The flapping hen he was holding upside down by its feet was to be killed for supper.

"Stand behind me," said Gottlieb, "and watch this."

With one swing of the axe, the hen's head was off, and Gottlieb quickly set the bird on its feet. Incredibly, blood spurting from the stump of its neck, the hen staggered in a brief, demented half-circle, wings spread and dragging in the dust.

"Eeeeeyah!" cheered Gottlieb, slapping his knees. "Lookit 'er go!" The children stared, wide-eyed.

"What's this?"

The words cracked out like rifle shots. The father's eyes were terrible to see, cold as ice — freezing Gottlieb — yet seeming to burn at the same time. The children stood paralysed. If those eyes should turn on them. . . Gottlieb's jaw was working soundlessly and his face was white. Without a glance at the children, the father bent and angrily snatched up the sprawled, lifeless hen.

"Any more of that, you won't be working for me," he growled, and strode off to the house.

At the supper table, Gottlieb ate in misery and silence, although the mother made occasional pleasant remarks to him, and even the father, who seemed to consider the afternoon's episode closed, said as much (or as little) as usual. After only one piece of pie, Gottlieb excused himself and went up the stairs to his room. Like shadows, the children slipped away and followed.

Gottlieb sat on the edge of his sagging bed, his head in his hands. He did not look up. It made the children uneasy and, after a moment, one said, "Can we see your hat, Gottlieb?" There was a muffled, "Naw."

"Please. We want to see it."

"Boy, was that dumb," mumbled Gottlieb to himself.

"What was? Spending all your wages on your hat?"

"Yeah, that too." He stood up restlessly and slumped back down again.

"No, it wasn't, Gottlieb. It's a beautiful hat."

Gottlieb looked up. "Yeah? You like it? You never said so before."

"Sure we like it."

"We like it, Gottlieb. Put it on."

"Please put it on, Gottlieb."

He looked thoughtfully at the earnest faces.

"Well. Whaddaya know. You really like it, huh?"

He reached for the box, lifted the lid, took out the wads of tissue. Leaving the Stetson exposed, shiny-white and brand new in its nest, he sat back a moment and rolled a cigarette. Then he stood and placed the hat carefully on his head.

"Boy, Gottlieb, that looks swell!"

"Yeah, Gottlieb, you look like a real cowboy in that hat."

"You sure do. Hey, a real cowboy!"

Gottlieb propped the square of mirror on the windowsill, backed off, tipped the Stetson a bit more to one side, and tilted his

head so that cigarette smoke drifted up through his eyelashes.
"Yeah," he breathed.

The grass in the pasture was brown and dead, although summer was not over. The hot west wind blew even stronger, snatching at the children's voices, blowing their words away.

"Kill it!"

"Hit it!"

"Wait," the eldest commanded sharply, and the other two halted in surprise. "Stand back. I'll do it."

The curled ball of fur, furiously intent on biting its leg free of the trap, was momentarily still, and the club descended cleanly and squarely. With a single, convulsive shudder, the tight body unwound, lay full-stretched and limp, the wind ruffling the almost-white fur of its belly.

Bending to open the trap, the eldest said something.

"What? What did you say?"

The wind was whipping hair into their eyes; little swirls of dirt were picking up, stinging their bare legs.

"That's better," repeated the first, voice raised above the wind. "I said, 'That's better.' "

The others heard and nodded.

PLAYBOY

PAT KRAUSE

Put 'er there, pal. I'm a Top Ten Man. That's what the TTM stands for on this business card, next door to my name. Been on the team five years — right since I made the shirt and tie brigade. You understand what that means?

Could be only another runt sired by a slippery Scot out of a thoroughbred Ukrainian would get the real glory of that. Mac, my old man, dropped by the Symetzki homestead seven times before he hopped the rails for good. Ma says I just squirted out onto her brother's sheepskin coat seven months and seven days after the CPR took Mac away. I'm lucky number seven in the MacSymetzki boys he left with her to raise. Always figured that's as good as being the seventh son of the seventh son, luck-wise. Muscled my way from Dysart to the Queen City at age fifteen. Worked for an outfit called Donald Duck Delivery when I first hit Regina. Pedalled an old CCM delivering meat to the South End's prime cuts for five cents a trip — winter and summer. Sent money home to Ma in Dysart, too. The big break was getting on with Zephyr Industrial Products. ZIP's cleaning and sanitary products Sweep the East and get you the Best Wipe in the West, like we say. Hustled myself up from errand boy, to stock, to repairs, to sales by age forty-seven. My TTM's earned. It matters. You know what I mean?

Anyways, the reason I look like this doesn't mean what you

think. I netted my TTM all right, all right. Did it by scoring a hat trick in this year's quota game. ZIP laid on a mid-winter calypso in the sun as number one prize to hype the old sales incentive. The Top Ten Men across Canada got a five day jaunt to Jamaica for the sort of re-lax-ation TTM's need — if you know what I mean.

ZIP always whips up a first class trip. We each got one of these Happy Face buttons, gold with black letters: HELLO! My name is Emil J. (Super Uke) MacSymetzki — Sales Rep. South Sask. Friendly touches like including our nicknames shows how it's no expense spared, you can see that, eh?

Well, old Bronco Berenson from Southern Alberta and a new TTM from Fog Coast somewheres, were on my flight out of home base. Bronco I know from away back but Peter R. Mathews-Moore from B.C. looked right off to be an exception to the old ZIP-zip. First off, there's no nickname on his Happy Face button. Then, he has a briefcase full of sales charts he hauls out with the company bonus catalogue and he pokes his thin nose into them like they were *Stag* magazine. St. Peter even turned down the free booze and got something called a Montclair cocktail, which Bronco tells me is just plain water jacked-up with minerals and a lemon twist. You know what I mean? St. Peter comes across as more than a bit aloof — like he's stern, if he isn't just plain stupid.

Anyways, the boys from the East turned out to be real shoulder-to-shoulder men. ZIP's always been kind of a family as much as a business to us guys. You know what I mean? I don't mean we wine and dine and hire the wife too, like I.B.M. — although our Human Resources Department wants to know their men got a little woman in the home to look after the care and feeding and assorted essentials. ZIP appreciates that. Wives of Top Ten Men get to pick a waffle iron, toaster, fry pan — any item they fall in love with, out of the "B" section of the Bonus Catalogue. (The "A" section's for us — golf clubs, suitcases, car and office stuff.) It keeps the little woman happy fixing her kitchen while her TTM re-laxes.

That four hour flight Toronto/Jamaica was lively as a regular ZIP Friday night get-together in the Empire pub. I led the sing-song, "Down by the seaside siftin' sand . . ." I pumped a little Al Jolson in with the Belafonte to ac-cen-tuate the matched set of Happy Face smiles I'm displaying, "I'd walk a million miles for one of your —"

"Hey, Super Uke," Tidy Ted Thompson from Bay Street in Metro-T.O. calls out, "The seat belt sign's on. Douse the cigar and sit down, pal."

"One more time," I said, getting up from my Jolson-pose for the finale, "Mary Anne — Mary Anne . . . and here goes." Old Bronco held out his arm in the aisle again for the Super Uke Limbo Special. I humped right under and on down past six or seven seats beneath the other arms that shot right out. I gotta thank my daily 5 BX, and the fact my centre of gravity's low, for making me flex-i-ble. I'm not stiff and solemn like St. Pete even if I am a dozen or so years older. It pays off to keep the old Super Uke muscles moving and a smile on my own face that matches right up with my Happy Face button. I practised the limbo under the wife's ZIP broom for two weekends and never got low as that once before. I turned and limboed on back to my seat.

"Mr. MacSymetzki. Sir. Please take your seat, we're landing. Sir?" The stacked Stew with the sour-o mouth, grabbed the collar of my new pink-striped shirt and tried to pull me up.

I give her my ZIP sales-pitch smile — all six hundred and eighty-five bucks worth of Doc McIvor's porcelain caps and pegs, for the big dazzle — plus, a pinch on her tight little ass.

"Re-lax, baby," I tell her as she grapples with me. "Enjoy! Guess we know what she needs, eh Bronco?" I give Bronco the TTM sign behind her back.

"Fly me," Bronco says to her. "Cowboys stay up longer."

The Stew's mouth goes into a capital O. She grabs Bronco's glass and snarls something about ZIP men being worse than a football club charter, then we're on the ground. Since I'm still standing, I'm just nat-ur-ally the first TTM to bongo-bongo down that ramp to the Kingston sun.

Turns out the ZIP hotel is the Half Moon, clear across the island in Ocho Rios. St. Peter lines up two cabs before we can knock back seconds of that rum punch Jamaica welcome. We chug-a-lug and pile in. I'm first, up front with the driver. I gotta admit that was a hair-ey ride. I'm used to doing my own steering, you know what I mean? And it's on Sask roads straight as a ZIP mop handle. I keep smiling but I've got this tidal wave of over-proof rum sloshing right to left in my gut as we career round those mountains. I can hear it, too, know what I mean?

St. Peter's sitting smack behind me calling out, "Tilt!", while we lean out over the edge of those cliffs, hanging to terra firma on two wheels, only. First off, I figure the mineral cocktails have sort of silted his guts to solid stone. Then I take a good look back and see he's close to spilling some gut-sludge over my shoulder. His face is white as a fresh roll of ZIP toilet paper and he's right up on the edge of the seat.

"You gotta garp, hang your head out the window," I yell at him, "I got on my new hundred percent virgin acrylic tropical suit." I reach back and roll down his window, in case. "You should of been drinking the joy-juice and moving around on the flight down, instead of reading," I say. "The ZIP travel list said bring one suit and that's what I've got — on me. I don't want it mucked-up with mineraled H2O and rubber chicken." I'm thinking, St. Pete's likely got the two pet bags he pulls behind him laid out with layers of silk suits. He's rolling up his window again and we lay into a curve that throws me onto the driver. Everybody yells, "Tilt," except me and St. Pete. I try a little ZIP buddy-to-buddy stuff on the driver, "You a *cum lawda* grad of the Indianapolis 500?" I ask.

He shows a keyboard of teeth pearlier than my caps and I swear he steps on the gas. I shut up. Everytime the ZIP men in the cab back of us get close enough to give us a back-slap, our man burns the rubber and tilts. By the time we get to the Half Moon, we're greener than ZIP liquid deodorizer and could've got lost in that jungle of plants around the entrance with no trace.

Anyways, we re-laxed right off. I got a bar set up in my room before some guys turned their keys. St. Peter sipped soda and kept trying to lecture us on some kind of new ZIP image. It took me until half-way through dinner to get the jokes rolling. We wound up to dawn playing poker on my patio. St. Peter took the pot — which was enough to send me off to bed sober — if you know what I mean.

ZIP had the works laid on for golf at 9 A.M. — clubs, caddy, carts, even free booze flowing at the ninth and the nineteenth. I set the pace. "You gotta move the old stick, men. Make it a TTM's game. Elbows up and make like it's a little white puck you're shooting," I yelled at the slow swingers. "Dysart Dynamites're still looking for a guy fast as old Super Uke here in a face-off." My score was lousy but I kept the boys en-ter-tained. St. Pete tried to damp things down with looks thick as B.C. fog. He didn't let a smile shine through until he collected the winning bucks at the end — and it was more smirk than smile.

I took a TTM poll back at the hotel, "Siesta or swim? Wanta zonk out or jump in?"

"In," old Bronco yelled, holding his nose. "It'll cool us down for the Playboy bunnies tonight."

St. Peter was at the pool when we got there. He was up and down, springing off the high diving board, flexing his puny muscles, like he was in some sort of ballet. You know what I mean? He bounced around on his toes, arms fluttering round his head, doing imitations of a swan when he dived into the pool. It looked like he was wearing some sort of G-string instead of real man's swim shorts, too. A blue jock-strap's what he had on.

The wife picked me up a pair of he-man, boxer-style swim shorts with a matching terry-lined shirt. Sure, I could've done without the sunflower blooms splashed all over, but trunks hid the family jewels from envious eyes — which was probably what the little woman had in mind. You know what I mean? Anyways, I doffed the shirt and dunked into the shallow end right away — so I wouldn't throw up watching St. Pete. I swam around with my feet on the bottom. The way I do it, splashing, flopping, and hanging a moon or two with my hands on the bottom, no one can ever tell I don't swim a stroke. Soon as my skin got wrinkled, I rose from the deep and grabbed me a middle-front lounge.

We lay around spreading some re-part-ee on the upcoming night at the Playboy Club. The boys pumped me for details about Bunny School training. Like I told them, I buy *Playboy* for the cartoons. But one month, the first article jumps right out at me like a bare bum. It's all about what they learn at Bunny School. Like I said to the boys, those chicks get lessons on how to do this bump and grind routine so they know how to waggle their bums in your face after they deliver a drink or something. I shook my field of sunflowers at them to demonstrate. Looked to me like a flicker of de-lights to come hopped through a few TTM minds, if you know what I mean. Gave us all something to con-cen-trate on when St. Pete took over to bore us with some lessons he'd learned in a *Financial Post* article.

Anyways, I showered, shaved and sprayed-up a storm in honour of Bunny bums to come. I must of splashed on half a bottle of Brut. That stuff hurts like hell on a sunburn, too, and my skin was red as my Scottish-side hair. Even my new tropical suit felt like barbed wire.

I hammered doors until I had all the TTM's rounded up. I led them down to the Half Moon bar to wait for our Bunny Wagon ZIP had charted for us. I showed the waiter how to deliver drinks Bunny-style. He was a real laugh and we were wound pretty tight by the time our Express to Bunny Heaven got there.

It was sure a slow express. "Wouldn't you know it?" I say to the boys. "This time, we get a driver who'd lag back in a funeral procession."

"Go man go," Bronco yelled, and the TTM's joined in, stamping their feet and snorting like bulls.

Then St. Pete butts into the fun with, "We're early. Our reservation is for nine o'clock." And next thing you know he's boring us stiff with Jamaican history, pointing out old buildings like this was some sort of ed-u-cation-al lecture tour. You know what I mean? Dates and everything. Boring facts. Bor-ing!

Anyways, I led the way into the Playboy Club. Took a few secs to focus the old eyeballs, you know what I mean? Plush? It made the

Hotel Sask look like Oscar's Greasy Spoon, no kidding.

"We're gonna need a seeing-eye dog to lead us through this carpet," Bronco said.

"No dogs in this hutch," I told him. My old ticker was going like a 400 cube V8 at fast idle.

Then this fluffy cottontail, all dimples and curves, nuzzles on up to us and whispers, "The gentlemen from Zephyr Industrial Products? I'm Bunny Penny. I'm your own Bunny for the evening. Will you please follow me to your reserved table?"

My V8 surged into overdrive, you know what I mean? I glommed the old headlights onto Bunny Penny and tailgated her right to the table. Like I told the boys earlier, I'm a bum man. Floppy, waffled, dimpled, or smooth, a waggling bum gets me where I live. I had a bumper-wide grin of Doc McIvor's gold, chrome and pure porcelain caps would've made an Edsel blow a gasket before it was launched. "Hey, Bronco," I said, without turning around, "Bugs Bunny she's not!"

"And th-that's not all f-f-folks," Bronco stuttered like a Looney Tune cartoon character, "I wah-wah-wasted six years with a cuh-cuh-company that suh-suh-sent whole families to D-Disney-le-land as a special suh-suh-sales in-cen-tive."

From what I see, Hugh Hefner's got a TTM's blueprint of in-cen-tive. We gotta go down three steps to a kidney-shaped couch covered with fur. Shaggy fur. Blonde. And there's this long table curved the same but covered with short fur. Curly. Blonde, too. I run my fingers through it as a guide, to the back, front row centre. And I sit — ginger-ly. It's like being in a fur-lined womb with a crotch-level view of that sweet little Bunny Penny. ZIP TTM's crowd in on either side of me. I grin ear to ear, stroke the short ones on the table, and wait for when she turns and waggles her plump little cheeks at me. I don't plan to grab. Just a gentleman's pat and stroke where it counts, is what I've got humping around in my mind.

"Something special from the bar, gentlemen?" Bunny Penny asks, like she was French-kissing each word of it.

"Spesh-ul!" I growl, adjusting the family jewels.

"Yeh, special-special," the other TTM's chorus.

Bunny Penny turns and bounces her cute little button tail off into the dark. "She forgot her bump and grind," I moaned.

"And to take our orders," St. Pete says, "I'll look after it, gentlemen." He's coiled into his place at the end of the table and looking right at me when he rattles this out.

"Hey, lookit this. Did she take an order or did she take an order," Bronco says, as Bunny Penny appears again in the pink spotlight in front of me. She's got a tray full of quart size glasses with more fruit on top than Carmen Miranda's turban.

"Ten Playboy Specials," she cooed. She steps down toward me, smiling. I'm flashing the porcelain and thinking ahead to that tan-tal-lizing flick of butt she's going to give me, dead centre, when I think I hear "tilt", loud and clear from the end of the table.

The tray's edge got bigger and bigger, spinning my way like an outsized puck that's left the ice. Before I can shut-out my gaping grin to protect my TTM bridgework, it hits. It felt like a full-fledged atomic grenade against my teeth. Four hundred and eighty-five bucks worth of ZIP Happy Face smile just cracked its moorings and exploded in a mushrooming cloud of shrapnel. Ten Playboy Specials hit my forehead, ears, shoulders, chin, chest, and shattered out over the edge of the fur table. Enough rum to float the fleet poured into my lap. Ice cold! Hunks of orange, pineapple, lemon, lime, shaved ice, and spikes of destructive glass crashed down on me like the Dunn River Falls. I'm numb as a banana with fear for the family jewels, you know what I mean? But what I feel is parts of Doc McIvor's built-for-ZIP smile biting down my gullet. I spit bits out onto the fur and the no-man's land on my lap.

ZIP TTM's peel off the couch on both sides. I stand up slow-ly and care-ful-ly while the glass, fruit and rum runs off.

Pink satin bunnies pop out of holes in the darkness. The manager appears under the spotlight, wringing a wine cloth, "Sir, our apologies, sir. We'll have your suit cleaned. I'll personally drive you to your hotel to change, and your drinks are on the house."

I tipped rum out of my shoes and ran my hand, gently, across my Happy Face-face. My ZIP sales smile's gum and two fangs, middle-front-upper fangs — the ones that Doc filed into points to hold the caps. I wantta give the old A-okay smile to Bunny Penny just to stop her bawling like a calf. But, I got a pretty good feel for the situation. I looked like a Super Uke Vampire and smiling wasn't going to help at all. I got no trouble hearing through the banana slices in my ears, though. I know Bunny Penny sobbed, "Your feet — I didn't see your feet, Sir," before St. Peter led her away saying he'd speak to the management so she wouldn't get fired.

Me, and the rest of the ZIP TTM's acted like the last of the great white hunters. We scare up a few bits of my smile out of the fur and carpet. It's not enough to match me up to my Happy Face button without accessories, though. Anyways, it turns out Jamaican dentists are scarce as palm trees in Wascana Park. Plus, I've got considerable concern about just how the dental works I swallowed are going to reappear — you know what I mean? Going down was bad enough. Coming out was going to be something else, what with my piles and all.

Anyways, I got this special death-case priority to grab this flight home. It's the hundred percent virgin acrylic tropical suit that smells bad, though. Sort of dead smelling. Festered fruit and dried rum smells rotten, all right. You know what I mean. Then all those virgin acrylics being defiled like that don't help, ha, ha. Thing is, takes weeks to get anything dry cleaned down there in Jamaica.

But, maybe I feel as bad as I smell, you know what I mean? The Stews on this flight might as well be bumless for all I'd care. I'm sombre and sober as St. Pete. It's him that comes to mind everytime I catch a broad's backside in the old headlamps. It's on account of what he did and what I figure he's going to try next. You see what it says right here in the *Globe's* B.S., "Peter R. Mathews-Moore named National Sales Manager of Zephyr Industrial Products." Goes on to say he's set to clean-up ZIP's marketing system and sanitize the sales force to attract real college grads into the family. And that's not all. His little woman's a niece of ZIP's President and she wants to get involved in the business. Gives me a sniff of a whole new as-pect in ZIP's old happy family.

Anyways, there's one thing for sure and you'd better believe it — I'm not called Super Uke or got this TTM next door to my name for nothing. You know what I mean?

LOOSE RUCK

KEN MITCHELL

Happy and me are playing Starship Destruction in the pool hall. After about twenty games we are still tied for top score, a hundred and eighty thousand kills with the Electronic Laserbeams. It's Happy's turn, and he's just about to score big, when all hell breaks loose at the front of the pool hall. Brennan comes running in like Intergalactic war has just been declared. "*Happy!* Where's Happy Hunchuck?"

This blows Happy's concentration. He not only misses a couple of Alien Starships, but one of their weapons blasts his fighter off the screen, and he's blown his chance at two hundred thousand points. "Ya fackin' dipstick!" he snarls at Brennan. "Look at that! The screen's gone dead! I was gonna beat Alex for the first time today!"

"Geeze, I'm sorry, Hap. But there's a game on in Regina this aft! Starts in half an hour."

"A rugby game?" Happy says.

Brennan is the manager of the Moose Jaw Gophers Rugby Club. He never has enough players, because they can never get organized. It's a big joke. In the winter, he manages the broomball team and that's even worse.

"Where's your cleats, man?" he moans. "We gotta get movin' right away! We're short at least three players."

"How come nobody told me about this game?" Happy says,

forgetting all about Starship Destruction. "You think I'm gettin' too slow or somethin'? Not good enough for you guys any more? Wut's goin' on?"

"No, Hap! No!" Brennan pulls off his CAT hat and starts twisting it round his hands. "If you'd only 'a come to practice on Thursday, you woulda known about it. What do you want me to do? None of you guys ever want to come to practice in the summer time. Everybody wants to play on Saturday, but nobody wants to come out on Thursdays. Everything gets left to me to organize. You think I enjoy it or something?"

"Aaaa, shut up," Happy says. "You know you enjoy it. Who we playing, the Condors?"

"Yeah, the Condors. And everybody's buggered off to the lake for the weekend. Same old story. Nobody's ever around in August."

"Yeah, it's really too hot to be running around a rugby field kicking the shit out of the Condors. How about a game of snooker, Brennan? I'll spot ya twenny points."

Brennan nearly swallows his CAT hat, though he really does get a charge out of organizing this sort of thing, especially when it's all going tits-up. He's the manager, right? But only because he's such a useless wing-three-quarters. Out on the wing he can't cause too much damage, and where would the club be without a manager? Somebody has to do the shitwork. Even so, he must be pretty hard-up if he's chasing round the pool halls trying to get a team together an hour before a game fifty miles away.

Brennan moans again, squeezing his hands against his head. "Hap — we're really stuck! Piston and Wombat both took off to the mountains for two weeks, and we got nobody at all to play in the second row. And if we don't have a second row, the Condors could *beat* us."

"Aaaa. That bunch a pansies? How about Alex?" Happy gives me the thumb. "He kin play second row."

Brennan looks me up and down, looking kind of glum, just like he does whenever I go to Thursday practice. "Yeah — maybe."

"I got nuthin' else to do today anyways," I say. "And I think I remember the off-side rule now."

"It isn't just the off-side rule," Brennan says to Happy. "He's always tryna rip some guy's head off."

"I been practisin', Brennan! I know the rules okay. It's only when I get excited."

"Yeah. And we get the penalties. If was your dumb penalties in Edmonton that lost us the game against the Barbarians."

"If Alex doesn't play," Happy says, "I don't play."

Brennan doesn't like this one bit, but without big Hap in the scrums and the loose rucks, the Gophers aren't going to get *any* ball for their running backs, and he knows it. "Okay," he says, "let's go."

Outside on the street, it's like walking into a furnace. I mean it's about one o'clock and *nothing* is moving on the sidewalks of old Moose Jaw. Brennan's car, a bright yellow fifty-seven Caddy, is waiting at the curb, and we climb in. This is the first time I ever got a ride in it, a real dynamite machine he's been working on for years.

"Man, this hot is too *extreme*," Happy says. "Let's grab a box of beer and head out to the lake!"

"The Condors got some booze laid on after the game."

"Yeah?" Happy says, looking interested again. "Maybe they're gonna start actin' human."

"Well, actually, they're callin' it a barbecue. It's gonna be on Willow Island. Wives and girl-friends. And they're supposeta be inviting a bunch a nurses."

"No shit!" Happy brightens right up. "Well, let's go! Stop by the Cecil on the way to my place and we'll pull a case of beer."

"Well — okay. After we get your boots and stuff. And no drinking in the car, okay? The cops are always pulling me over for a check."

"Aaaa — you should get rid of your pair a noya," Happy says. I look around inside the car for these noyas, but all I see is a pair of foam rubber dice hanging from the light. Maybe that's where Brennan keeps his dope stash or something. Inside of them.

Happy and me chip in together and buy a two-four of Labatt's plus a couple of bags of potato chips. Neither of us had any breakfast yet, never mind lunch. It's only a half-an-hour till game-time by the time we get out on the Trans-Canada Highway, and still Brennan won't break the speed limit. He's scared of cops ever since he got pinched one time for riding double on a bike across the Fourth Avenue Bridge. It's nuts, really, because the highway is four lanes all the way to Regina, straight as a donkey's cock and barely a car on it.

"Brennan," Happy says, reaching one hand into the back seat so I can put a bottle of Labatt's in it. "What's the point of *having* a machine like this if you don't burn highway? Aren't we supposeta be late or something?"

"It isn't for racing. It's a show car!"

"Come *on*, man! You're lettin' all these Volkswagens and Datsuns *pass* us! And there isn't a cop in sight! When are you gonna give these goobers the benefit of all that double-carb and high suspension you put into this pig?"

"Hey, you guys! I said *no drinking* in the car!"

"Aaaa, don't be a pill, nobody asked you to drink any of it. If I don't get some liquid into me, I'll never last five minutes in this heat. You want us to win, doncha?"

All the time we are guzzling away on the Labatt's, Brennan is checking all his mirrors and windows for the sight of a cop car suddenly appearing out of nowhere. With Happy egging him on, he finally starts passing the odd car. It isn't long before he pulls up alongside some kid in a Duster, moving about seventy. He revs the engine a couple of times to get him worked up, then takes off in a roar, leaving the kid with his mouth hanging open in the slow lane. That Caddy of Brennan's feels like a rocket taking off. He could make a fortune if he wasn't so chickenshit of racing.

Anyways, we polish off about half the beer before pulling up at the university field, where the Condors have their rugby games. The match is already started. All the Gophers are running around in their green-and-white uniforms and hollering at us to get onto the field. They're getting beat twelve to zip. Everybody is blaming Brennan for it like always. "Brennan, ya turkey!" they're yelling. "Didja stop for a wank or what? Cummon ya dumb bastard, get those guys out here! Didja bring the fackin' water jug?"

They're three players short, so they need me to play second row with Happy. By the time we get our cleats on and actually hit the field, the score is fifteen-nothing against, but the Condors are a bunch of cream-pouffs anyway, nobody figures we'll have any trouble straightening them out once we have a full side. Happy always make a big difference.

At the first lineout, he stretches way up and grabs the ball coming in, not even bothering to pull it down for a loose scrum. He just takes off, his bloodshot eyes glowing like bike reflectors, blasting through the Condors' pack and heading for their goal line. As soon as he busts through the forwards, he runs straight at their half-backs, levelling his head at them like a battering ram and picking up speed all the way, making this noise sort of like *hoooooom! hoooooom!* daring them to get in his way.

Naturally he scores a try right away, and all our boys start breathing a little easier. With Happy and me in the second row, we can shove the scrum all over the field if we want to. The only problem I'm having is in the loose rucking, when the ball bounces all over the place and everybody's trying to pick it up and getting their fingers smashed. As soon as somebody touches it you drill him, but there's offside rules too, which I can never get straight, so once in a while we get a penalty, but still the only way is just get in there and hammer away with elbows or heads or boots or whatever.

86

"Alex, you big dummy!" Brennan hollers from the wing. "Just the guys in *blue!* And only when they're carrying the *ball!*"

Sometimes in the excitement of the scrummage, I get carried away and try to break somebody's leg, so I got to try and remember what our team colour is. The whole game is heavy going on account of the sun, but Happy and the backs manage to keep on scoring. We finally beat them about forty to thirty. Everybody is just *shagged* by the end of the game, soaked in sweat and ready to fall over at the side of the field. They shouldn't allow rugby in August, really, it could kill people.

But both the teams soon get very buddy-buddy again, singing songs in the showers and making funny insults about each other, which Happy says is what rugby is all about. It's a neat game like that. There's one set of rules which make everybody hate each other on the field, so they can be friends off it. A guy who kicks your teeth out will buy you a beer fifteen minutes later.

The Condors' barbecue was a rip-off though. They brought about six boatloads of beer over to Willow Island, and no hamburgers. There was twenty cartons of buns and not a single chunk of meat to put in them. Somebody said we should cut up Brennan and barbecue *him* because he's such a jerk, but he gets let off if he agrees to sing ten verses of "The Hairs on Her Dicky-Die-Do."

It doesn't take long for the usual zoo to get going because there's three drunk rugby-players there for every spare woman, all chasing each other through the trees. Somebody from the Condors has brought good dope for once, and I manage to be standing in the right place at the edges of the crowd while a few joints of this Colombian is going around. Being stoned makes the entertainment funnier than it really is, which consists of guys whipping their jeans down and flashing their asses at the crowd. After a couple of times this can get kind of boring, unless you're one of them doing it.

Happy gets making out pretty good with one of the nurses, but when she won't go with him for a stroll into the bushes, he grabs Brennan by the arm and says, "Let's go and get us some Big Macs! I'm starved! Alex, you coming?"

I am still hanging out by the guys with the weed, and happy enough to stay there, but he comes over and pulls me over to the boat, which carries us back to Brennan's car. Considering there must be a hundred MacDonald's Hamburger Drive-ins in Regina, they're not easy to find. The city is all one-way streets heading in the opposite direction to where people want to go. What with Happy screaming directions from the back seat where he could be closer to the beer, and Brennan pretty stunned at the best of times, we are lucky we don't run over some poor bugger on the street, because by then it's about five-thirty in the afternoon and the rush hour is going full-blast. Downtown is crawling with pedestrians and some of them would have got a Cadillac "V" stamped on their asses if they hadn't jumped right smart.

Brennan is wheeling down this street near Victoria Park when Happy suddenly yells, "Look down there! Am I goin' blind, or is that a hot dog stand?" There is a shopper's mall in the next block, the kind of place where they put up barriers to keep cars out and fill the street with park benches and little barrels full of geraniums. Right in the centre of this mall is an old street-car which somebody fixed into a little snack stand. A sign on top of it says, "MARVIN'S DINER ON THE MALL."

"Haaaard *left!*" Happy yells. Brennan, like a dummy, does it.

You can imagine the look on old Marvin's face when this yellow Caddy comes blazing down the street and screeches to a stop right in front of the window where he hands out his Weenies-on-a-Stick. He stares at us, and back up the street where hordes of pedestrians are still scrambling for cover. Here and there a few tubs of pine trees are spilling their guts onto the pavement.

"Three weenies, pardner," Happy says to him. "And make it snappy, eh? We gotta be on our way in thirty seconds."

Brennan is revving the engine, suddenly feeling nervous about all the attention we are getting. There is a couple of sexy-looking bubblegummers giving us the eye from down the street and Happy brays at them in his best hog-calling style, "Hiya sweet-thighs! Wutcha want tonight?"

All of a sudden these four cops just *appear*, running up behind us and wailing away on the roof of Brennan's Caddy with these huge wooden nightsticks. Well, I dunno man, this is no way to come down out of a cloud of Colombian dreams, not knowing what they're after, or whether to run, fight, or just shit bricks.

Brennan flips out completely of course, flooring the old gas-pedal. We roar off in a cloud of burning rubber and flying cops, through a big squealing U-ie back the way we came in. It is *weird*, this mall full of cops jumping out of various doorways and pouring around every corner like a big riot was on. I figure they must have put on extra patrols because of the rugby game.

It doesn't do much for Brennan's nerves to see this horde of fuzz coming at us like some horror scene in a drive-in movie. He whips through a few fancy power turns among the litter-bins and park benches, past all the cops and heading fulltilt for the entrance at the far end of the mall. We are just about to hit the curb and fly over it back into the street when this big cop steps up right in front of us.

He has gold braid all over him, probably the chief, holding his arm up like some bigshot anyway, expecting us to stop. This is totally the wrong approach for Brennan. He goes spaz, tramping the gas through the floor and aiming straight at the cop along the hood ornament like an Electronic Laserbeam.

Somehow the chief flings himself off to one side as we fly over the curb and down the street. We'd have made a clean getaway, no problem at all, except that Brennan starts to *think* about all this. Just as we roar up to this red light a good block down the street, he jams on the brakes and brings the Caddy screeching to a stop.

"*What* the *fack* are you *doin'?*" Happy screams, frantically stashing all the beer under the back seat. "*Lay rubber,* ya turkey!"

"Fack you too!" Brennan yells back. "You want me to lose my licence for running a lousy red light? Doncha think they wrote down the licence number back there? I'm not stupid, ya know!"

The two of them start hollering at each other as the fuzz run up, about ten of their fastest sprinters I guess, and they don't make any mistakes this time. They haul us out of the car in about one second, throwing us face down on the hood and slamming our feet apart. They put us through a search that would have found the wrinkles on a grasshopper's ass, banging our heads on the hood a few times just for laughs.

"Okay," the chief says, hauling Happy to his feet, "what's your name, sunshine?"

"John Wayne!" Happy snarls back at him.

"Yeah? Smart guy, eh? Okay, hand me his wallet. Let's have a look at his I.D." He flips through the cards in Happy's wallet until he finds his driver's licence. "Says here your name is Harold Hunchuck. Is that your name or is this I.D. stolen?"

"You figure it out, Kojak!"

The chief turns to Brennan, white-faced and ready to piss his pants. "What's your name?"

Brennan looks around for help, trying to decide whether to make a break for it or to beg for mercy. "John Diefenbaker," he says. Probably the first thing that came into his head.

"Okay, I'm through playing games. Take these jokers down to the shop, while I find out what's going on here."

Then Brennan *does* fall onto his knees, blubbering, "I'm not with these guys, officer! I just gave them a lift in my car, see? I was on my way down here for this rugby game. I'm the manager of the Gophers, the Moose Jaw Gophers, and they needed a ride—"

"Moose Jaw?" the chief says, going very squinty-eyed. "Rugby game? Constable, check that car and see if there's any liquor in there."

89

One of the cops rips the back seat out and they find the remains of our two-four of beer. They start hauling it out with some very thirsty looks on their faces. You couldn't blame them, either, in that heat.

"Any of you even 19 yet?"

The other guys look at me, so I say, "I guess I am."

"And who are you?"

"Alex Dinwoodie. My dad's a lawyer."

"Well, you'll need him. We're going to lay charges against you punks till you can't count them. Take them and lock them up till they're ready to co-operate!"

Down at the cop shop they take away all our money and keys, then our T-shirts and the shoelaces out of our shoes in case we want to hang ourselves. Brennan looks like he wants to, too. We are in a row of cells where we can talk to each other, so we use the time trying to put together a story the cops might believe.

"I know!" Happy says. "We'll tell them we came down to enroll in university this fall. Cops love university students. They get away with everything."

"Are you nuts? You gonna try and tell them Alex is a university student? He never got out of grade six!"

"I can say psychology," I remind Brennan.

We decide to change the story to applying for a government job working in the parks. "Okay, nice and simple," Happy says. "As soon as we got to Regina we went to Wascana Park, and we're filling out the applications in the employment office when this dude in there, the head guy, asks us all down to the pub for a beer. *He* bought the beer, right?"

"That'll never work," says Brennan. "They don't ask guys like us out for a beer."

"How be if we asked *him*?"

"Shut up, Alex. Let's concentrate. Okay, we meet this dude in the street, an older guy, friend of Alex's—"

"I don't know a soul in Regina. I've only *been* here once before!"

"We're makin' it *up*, fer crissakes!"

Just then the cops figure we've sobered up enough and haul us down to the interrogation room. The chief is waiting there with a look on his face that would have cracked ice.

"Students, eh?" he says.

We all nod, not sure how far to go with this lie. Brennan takes evening classes at the Tech, and I'm still registered at the Adult Education Centre, but Happy's been out of school for a year, working on the wipe squad out at Valleyview Hospital.

"To hell, you're students!" he explodes. "You're all *bums!* Criminals! And I'll make sure you never hold a job in decent society again! We'll exterminate you!"

Brennan starts whimpering and crying. "Wha-wha-what're we charged with, your honour?"

"Shut up! I'm talking! We could charge you with a dozen things. Dangerous driving. Obstruction of police. Carrying open liquor in a car! Being a public nuisance! Buying liquor under age. And one that you don't even know about! The *worst* one!"

"What-what-what's that?"

"We got a tip a week ago that some gang of hoods was going to knock off the Woolworth Store at closing time today. We mounted a special operation, put the mall under total surveillance. I had twenty men waiting in that heat for *four hours.* We were all set for them. Then *you idiots* blundered along and scared them off!" He is getting redder by the minute, thinking about it.

"We're sorry, sir," I tell him. "We're very, very sorry."

He stares at me for a minute. "Get out!"

None of us can move, just stand there gaping at each other, hardly believing our own ears. He picks up a phone and roars into it, "Somebody come in and throw these punks out of here before I shoot them!"

Well these two enormous detectives come bashing in and chuck us straight into the street, throwing Brennan's car keys after. It is nearly sunset, the sun just going down, but you can still hardly breathe in the heat. That doesn't slow Happy down. He goes charging back to the door of the police station and gives it a huge kick that rattles the building.

"Hey, are you guys gonna give us back our beer?" he yells up at the window. "*How about our fackin' beer, huh?*"

Brennan and me grab him and hustle him down to the compound to get the car, which is sitting there with dents all over it where the cops did their number with the clubs. All the way out of the city, going the wrong way down these one-way streets again, Happy is badmouthing the cops. "Whaddaya expect from a bunch of pigs?" he says. "You could tell they had it in for the Moose Jaw Gophers! They hated us, man! We shoulda stuck to our university student story! Hey Brennan, we goin' down to Winnipeg to play at Labour Day?"

"I think I got the off-side rule figured out now," I tell him.

Brennan refuses to answer, just keeps doodling along at twenty miles an hour, muttering about his car getting all dented.

"Cummon Brennan," Happy says. "Don't be a *pill.* It's just a car, right? A pile of fackin' metal. It coulda bin worse — we mighta lost the *game!* And the game is life, right?"

"Right on!" I chime in, but I can see it will take a lot to cheer Brennan up tonight. I gotta try to remember the off-sides next Thursday.

RITES

BRENDA RICHES

I want to be an old woman so I can look back instead of forward. I want to stop wanting to walk outside when leaves rattle in a stiff wind or rain cracks on the roof; stop rubbing my mouth with my thumb when the phone alarms the late night silence of my house; stop wondering what the hell to do with myself because it wasn't you who called, and tramping long miles under clear stars that I can't look at because of you.

I'm sick of the urgency of sex.

I want to be old and arthritic, to sit in a chair that's worn smooth where my hands have pressed down to lever me to my feet, sit with a cushion at my back (a cushion that a neighbour's child embroidered, cross stitch) with my lap covered by a plaid blanket, tucked behind the knees for warmth, a faded plaid.

I want to sit and tell children how I used to love.

There was a pencil, ten inches long and candy striped royal blue and white. It had a blue eraser at the end, and I thought how superior it was since everyone else's was pink. I got it at a party given by Sara who always had better things than I did. She always had brand new shiny brown paper to cover her school books at the beginning of the year, when I had to make do with paper bags, some of them with lettering on. And she brought chocolate bars and blackcurrant cordial for her lunch. At her birthday party we were each given the end of a string and told to follow it and we would get a surprise. All the rest of us got pencils and suckers, and found them minutes before she got to the end of *her* string. So we stood around stupidly while she went on winding the string through room after room. A regular do-it-yourself Ariadne, she was, only her Minotaur was a brand new bicycle (no looking through the classifieds when it came to *her* birthday) all done out in red and blue ribbons.

That bicycle did it for me. I clutched my pencil in a passion and swore undying love, kept it in my desk at school, and only took it out to look at it.

Our schoolyard was a big grass field with a seesaw and a flagpole. I was only aware of the flag itself on three occasions. Once when the King died and it was brought to half-mast, and everyone spent the day crying. Once when there was a gale blowing and it flapped and battled up there, making such a noise that there was nothing for it but to lie flat on my back and gaze at it raging up there in a private tantrum, and forget about school friends who were better off than me and bells that marked the borders of time, till I felt a claw hooking into my shoulder and the math teacher was shaking me, asking me if I would be willing to give up my mystic inclinations long enough to attend her class. And the third time was when one of the boys from the private school across the road came and hoisted up a pair of red silk panties the night before parents' day.

But the seesaw was a different experience. For years I played on it, its peeling wood pressing thick lines along my bare thighs, my skirt swelling up like a sea anemone as I dropped to earth and flopping down again when I rose. On the days we had gym, which we hated on account of the gym teacher being a bitch, we played bumps. This meant you lifted your feet up so they didn't touch the ground when the seesaw did. As you bumped down, you yelled, "Sod *you* Mrs. *Pugh!*" The best bit was when you were on the high end because you were thrown into the air a little way, and the coming down was spongy, then hard. On other days, when I wanted to show *her* that money wasn't everything, that there were higher things to put the mind on, I stood, with my eyes shut mostly, right at the centre and balanced it perfectly level so it didn't move, till everyone but her was sitting round, stunned to a silent admiration.

Then she got hold of my pencil, I don't know how, and wedged it under the middle bit without me noticing, so when the bell rang and I jumped down and the board tilted, my pencil broke in half. I heard the crack, otherwise I wouldn't have known about it.

You slide through the cracks in my thoughts when I'm not ready for you. When I'm talking to Sara outside the drugstore, or to the woman at the library, you slide in like wet soap. I can feel you then pushing your hands under my sweater, telling me to glove your hands, and I want to stay with you, but Sara or the woman at the library makes some kind of sound and I have to say, I'm sorry, I didn't catch that. And I have to start all over again forgetting you and the things your hands did to me.

I was given two glove puppets one Christmas. One was a brown rabbit with a face as round and soft as a dung ball, and small eyes that gave him an unstartled look. He had a navy blue body for some reason. The other was a monkey with that look of constant hurt that monkeys have. His body was light grey like my winter skirt. I called them Rabbit and Monkey and wore them as gloves when I rode to school on the bicycle my sister outgrew.

They talked to each other across the handlebars about the quality of frost and how it could catch fire and not melt if the sun was in the right place, and how it looked pink but this was only how it looked and that really it was white. And then they would debate which they preferred, frost as it could seem or as it really was. They talked about frost on the days I had English, and referred to each other as 'my dear friend Rabbit' and 'most distinguished colleague Monkey'. On the days I had gym they referred to each other obliquely: 'That churlish sod Rabbit'. 'That thick-assed son of a one-titted bullfrog Monkey'. And talked independently to the air about the quality of bile and vomit and excretia. I like that word especially; I thought it ought to be the name of an Italian heroine. Or else I imagine myself daring to say after one of Mrs. Pugh's shitty sarcasms: My dear, how *excretiatingly* droll.

Rabbit and Monkey warmed my hands and threaded the air with the beads of their conversation for six weeks, till a boy from the private school moved house and had to take the same route as me. A girl who gets escorted to school by a boy doesn't wear puppets. For four days he rode behind me, close enough for me to notice, far enough away for no one to think he had any connection with me.

You are far away from me. A short time ago I watched your shadow moving behind the opaque glass of your office door. It had your name on it. A short time ago I could go in and see you at any time on any pretext because you hadn't touched me then.

The boy from the private school was painfully beautiful. He had smooth skin, sallow and translucent as if a light was on inside his face. His hair was thick and black and looked navy blue in certain lights. His name was Jon without the 'h' and he had a Malayan parent. "I have a Malayan parent," he told me on the second day he rode beside me, and didn't say if it was his mother or father or if he had a second parent at all. I imagined the two blended into one, wearing a bright sarong, a white flower in the hair, and lolling on a verandah, sipping punch under broad-leafed trees. Whichever it was lived in Malaya, and Jon lived with an aunt during school time and went to Malaya in the holidays. He never used the word 'home' when speaking of either place. It was 'my aunt's place', or 'my parent's place'. I was attracted to this unwanted quality of his. Ever since we had read *Jane Eyre* in English, I had fantasies of giving my all to a blind man or an outcast whose need for me was his only hope.

I'd like to say that Jon's first words to me were: 'Hya beautiful', or 'I have followed you for nigh on four days and must perforce yield to the pull of your beauty on my ravaged senses'. But what he said was, "What did my lady Jergens say when she saw those knickers?"

Aha. The hoister of the red silk panties.

So it was the raising of underwear that brought us together and the lowering of it that scattered us. It only happened once, but such is my luck that while others sin on a regular basis and never get found out, I was caught by the only teacher who stayed late that Friday to mark assignments and used a flashlight to get herself across the playground to the bus stop on Virginia Street. Jon got expelled and sent back to Malaya, and I would have got thrown out too, only there was no other school I could go to. The best my lady Jergens could do was moralise at me for half an hour and forbid me all contact with 'members of the opposing gender'. I liked her use of the word 'member', especially as I never did get to see his. From then on I stopped playing on the seesaw; I was envied and admired for other reasons.

It wouldn't be true to say I missed him. I missed what I came so close to having, and he left me wanting it more than I wanted my Saturday candy allowance (four ounces of liquorice which I ate in half an hour), more than I wanted Mrs. Pugh's death, and strangest of all, Sara melted like one of her chocolate bars into the boring ranks of all the other girls. No, I didn't miss him, but to this day I can't see frost without thinking of tropical flowers.

I sit here drinking tea and looking at the end of autumn outside. The tree nearest the window still has green leaves. They won't turn red, they'll just get dry and silver and drop off like cocoon casings. The top branches bow awkwardly in the wind, jerking down, then up, like a performer accepting applause. The tree nearest the gate is different. You have to go and look at it every day or you'll miss its changes, miss the pageant of its decay. I drink a second cup to warm me on the sidewalk of my longings, and watch the procession. Pencils and puppets and beautiful boys and more besides, and know that I'm not yet old, and reason that since there were many others there could be many more, and know that logic never was part of the syllabus of passion.

I must be all right really. I am drinking tea because it's too early for anything else. I still have my decorum, my fine sense of what and when. I shall wait and watch the leaves jostling each other and at the proper time I shall properly drink.

Children dear, I lost my maidenhead to my lady Jergens' godson. It was an occasion to put out bunting for. Flap flap, it would have got her nicely boisterous in that high-coloured way of hers if she'd got wind of it. Her tongue would have snapped and shredded in the gale of her outrage, her eyelids ballooned, her eyes come out on strings, if she'd known. It was a gala occasion. Grade eight graduation and me in my first long dress when a short skirt would have been so much more convenient. After the speeches and the pride and the remember-wherever-you-go-you-take-the-good-name-of-this- school and the fruit punch spiked with something else you didn't know about, lady J., till it was too public to comment on, after the ball was over your randy godson came up behind me two blocks from Virginia Street and laid the foundation of my high school career.

Oh but he was a good layer, now that I think back, though I couldn't have said so at the time, not having so much as a summer's day to compare him with. But I knew I was getting what my Malayan had left me wanting, and if that warm whirlpool was what it was all about it would do very nicely thank you. Looked at from the outside it wasn't exactly Hollywood material, that milestone in my life, that auspicious wanton occasion. It was a dominance of frantic yankings, his and mine, at my long dress, and too many thumbs in panty elastic, and my ankles rubbing together like dry sticks to get them off. (They were red silk, bought in a store in the neighbouring town. Me in dark glasses and Sara's wig, buying a memory of Jon). And finally I caught my toe in the right place to send them flying towards the moon. Only after the scrabbling and the engineering, his, and the unexpected porridgy spurting over my stomach (the Daddy plants his seeds, they'd told me; there'd been no reference to the Milky Way, to curds and cream — ah the *facts* of life were something else), only after the dabbing and wiping did it come to me that this was the origin of babies, and I told him so in case he didn't know, and was given the new and mysterious and secret knowledge: IT'S OKAY. I CAME OUTSIDE.

Dusk is here. A shredding and a crumbling if I wait long enough. And now the leaves on this tree and the leaves on that tree are the same colour; they are no colour. Yet they are vigorous and distinct, hard and dark and something to pull at, like liquor.

Lady J's godson, whose sins had been washed away with tremulous holy water as he lay in her arms, for whom she had fervently renounced the devil and all his works as he snuggled in her lacy clutch, Randolf (yes, that really was his name), ravisher of children (he was sixteen; he was full grown), celebrated my gala opening and his uprising with the contents of his father's secret supply, and his father couldn't raise hell about it because his mother would get wind of it. Randolf didn't care. Randolf had no loyalty to anything but the ceremonies of his emancipation and his dissolution. So we polished off half a bottle of whisky on the twenty-four-hour anniversary of our adhesive encounter. Two blocks from Virginia Street, on the very spot, we swigged, taking fair turns, and we were oiling ourselves nicely for an improvement on the night before when I spontaneously unravelled the contents of my stomach (pea soup laced with whisky) and spread them generously at his feet. I can see it all now, luminous and swirled in the moonlight.

It's getting dark and I can barely see the leaves. They are cut out and shivering against a blood orange sky. If I pull the curtains now I will be wrapping up the silence in my house. When the sky is drained and dried and the trees have gone far into the dark, I shall cover my windows and pour my wine.

My first true love gave me oranges to suck. I took him from Sara at the high school wiener roast. That's what they all said, and Sara said nothing to me for two years, until she pushed through her paper-wrapped silence the day after he finished with me, giving Sara and me something in common, something we could finally share. The desolation of a dead branch, bleached and smooth. Bearing nothing.

That's what it is. A swelling, a wetness, a draining, a falling away. Withered wood.

We made a bonfire of the shore's debris, twisted carcasses of trees, bone grey branches pale like clay. And logs in their ravelled skin, cut through and ringed like moons. I watched him with Sara, saw how she spiked his meat, how her face trapped the hot and crackling light and how her body made a shadow for him to lie on so he could touch her and no one could see. And it pleased me. That furtive drama set against the oilskin lake, against slippery water that hunched and dipped like seals, gave me some satisfaction, something to look at while Randolf went into the trees to hide our beer some place. But Sara's shadow paled, it must have, because he stopped lying there and got up brushing little stones from the back of his pants. He pushed his hands into the lake and brought them up again filled with oranges, touched one against his face, then reached it over to me. Sara held her face still and puckered towards the fire while he and I bit holes in the fruit and sucked. The juice leaked from my mouth and traced my chin, and he pushed me back into the shadows beyond the fire's reach and licked the juice off, licked my chin with his warm tongue.

PIES

W. L. RILEY

"The dirty cow, the dirty cow." Elena Meuser daintily drew aside the lace curtains and scowled at her neighbour. Across the road, Mary Cherwak was leading her milk cow home through the glowing late afternoon. She looked around at her spotless house. Nobody was allowed to wear their shoes indoors. Husband and children and herself removed their outdoor footwear on a special mat and put on clean slippers. Only the priest and the doctor were allowed to enter with outdoor shoes. When they came to the house, Elena kept her eyes carefully averted so they would not give away her disapproval of their dirty shoes. She wondered if they crossed the field. To bring in cow dung was unspeakable.

Just today she had taken the short cut to the store, across the field, thinking it would be safe in the daytime when she might carefully pick her way across on the clean dry prairie grass. She had avoided all the droppings deposited there by Bossie, but on the way home, as she was carrying her groceries, the cow put her horns down and ran towards her, terrifying her so much that she had run through two or three cow droppings, fouling her shoes. She thought of how she had carefully washed and changed her stockings and yet still smelled a faint odour of cow dung. But then it seemed to her that she could *always* smell a faint odour of cow dung.

"Ah no," she thought emphatically, "it's not fair." After all, they weren't farmers. They lived in a working man's village where the refineries and railyards were within walking and cycling distance and the end of the city street car line was only a half mile away. Some people took advantage of the closeness to the country-side and the many natural open areas to keep horses and chickens, but these animals didn't present the irritation to Elena that Mary's cow did, being directly across the street. Her suppressed temper boiled up in her as she watched Mary leading her cow. Mary was smiling, obviously talking to the beast, praising her no doubt, quite oblivious to the rights of her neighbours who had to take the long way to church and the village hall at night for fear of stepping into a soft round of cow dung.

She had asked her husband, Peter, over and over again, to speak to Mary's husband about it. After all, Peter and Stepan both worked at the refinery. Peter was a skilled workman while Stepan was only a labourer. Peter should therefore have some influence. Mary should at least tether the cow through the day as well as at night.

She spoke to Peter about it again after supper. She told him eloquently, in flowing German, of the filth and fright she'd endured that day.

"You must speak to Mary. She'll listen to you. Tell her plain that you'll get the village constable. She has no right to let her cow run loose all over the village. The next thing you know," she took her hands out of the hot dishwater and pointed a soapy finger at him, "that cow will be in our own yard, chasing the children, even . . ." Their two daughters, hearing themselves mentioned, became even more engrossed in their homework. "The dirty cow. That pig-woman. Why doesn't she get a farm?"

Peter took his pipe from his mouth. He fidgeted. He wanted to take his wife's part, but . . . Stepan was a work-mate. There was an unwritten rule among the workers that home problems must not be brought into the workplace. It could cause great trouble for everyone. On the other hand, he did not want to speak to Mary about it. First, she was a woman. It was not right somehow, and his position at work would still loom in the background. Then, although he wouldn't admit it, he was a little afraid of Mary Cherwak, as were many of his neighbours, for she was reputed to be a woman of quick temper. It was said that when Mary's daughter, Ina, who had married comfortably and lived in the city, had visited her mother and put on superior airs, Mary had given her such a shaking she dislocated Ina's shoulder. It would be difficult to speak to Stepan. It would be awkward. He wasn't Stepan's boss, but it might be seen as a pushy act, like he was trying to put himself above him. He sighed. Women had their own ideas of protocol. Elena couldn't or wouldn't understand. He tried to placate her.

"Well ..." he said vaguely, "I'll talk to Stepan tomorrow, maybe, Stepan is always very ..."

"No!" Elena wiped her hands on the special towel she kept for that purpose. "You must tell Mary, today. It happened today. Look!" She strode over to the window facing the road, and pulled the curtain aside. "There she is. She's taking her pails back to the shed. She'll be taking the dirty beast out to the field again. She tethers it behind her place at night. Now, you can speak to her."

Peter's instincts told him it would be disastrous to mix in this women's business. He took up his pipe and got up from his chair. Apologetically but firmly he said, "I'll talk to Stepan tomorrow. Calm yourself, Mama, calm yourself."

"Ai, yi!" she screamed. "It would be nice to be married to a *man* again!" It was useless to argue with him, she thought. She was now angry enough to speak to Mary herself. She put on her shoes which stood outside the door and marched resolutely across the road to Mary's place. She stood behind the shed and waited for Mary to bring out her cow.

When Mary came around the corner of the shed, leading Bossie, Elena disdainfully looked her over. Her shoes were filthy from the cowshed and the dirt. Her stockings were spattered. Her apron bore darkened spots. Her dusty kerchief was askew. But it was her features that disgusted Elena, above all. Her face was so Mongol, she thought ... wide, prominent cheek bones; slanting, deceitful blue eyes and a sallow skin. Elena didn't understand Polish and Mary didn't understand German, so they spoke in the new language neither had as yet mastered, due to their relative isolation in their homes.

"Mrs. Cherwak," Elena began briskly, "I vant speak viz you."

"Ah Meeses Meuser, how you today? Iss nice day, yes?"

"Mrs. Cherwak," Elena was not going to lose her edge through niceties, "I vant talk about your cow."

"Ah yes?" Mary's face became a little guarded. Elena's tone was stiff and strained. She looked so hard. Her little mouth was pursed, and the cords in her neck stood out. Her eyes were dark and cold.

"You vill have to keep her tied hup. Dis field ..." Elena swept out her hand, "belong to everybody, but nobody can valk for cow."

"Ah? Vy you can't valk? Is big field. Is plenty room."

"Today I valk to store." Elena's voice rose. "I come back, all parcels. The cow she run after me, to push me with horns!" Elena finished in a shout.

"No! Cow is alvays good. She see new grass. Come take." Mary's cheeks were reddening.

"No! She chase me. Look!" Elena pointed to her shoes, soiled with cow dung. "Who can valk? Is everyvhere shit! Shit! Shit!" Elena shook her head vigorously, her fists on her hips now.

"So vy you vant valk field? Is sidevalk not good?" Mary was also getting excited and came towards Elena. Elena backed up a little.

"So is filthy! Is dirty cow. You dirty voman for keep cow in city."

"Is city here?" Mary stretched her hand out around her. "Vy you not live city? Is nutting never good for . . . big shot lady?"

"Vy you not live on farm? You like cow shit, you go live in! You dirty like cow!"

Mary remembered the gifts of cream and butter she had given Elena, gifts which had been haughtily taken.

"You . . . suka . . . *lady!*" Mary shouted. "All time you tink you only good!" And she gave Elena a push. Elena leapt backward but her heel went into a fresh pile of dung and she fell, her hand skidding through the dung as she tried to save herself.

"Aiihh!" She scrambled to her feet and tried to shake the thick mess off her hands.

"Ho, ho! Who dirty now?" Mary jeered. "Dat's good, dat's good!"

"You pig-woman, you dirty Polish pig!" Elena screamed. She scooped up a handful of dung and threw it at Mary. It hit the front of her dress. Mary's lips curled back in rage.

"Ah! Is pig?! Hey! I show you is pig!" With both hands she scooped into a round of dung and threw it. Elena ducked, but not before some caught her on the side of her head.

"Ahhhh!" It was too horrible. Elena turned for home, trying to pull the muck out of her hair as she ran. Crossing the road, she could see her husband and daughters' shocked faces staring at her from the window. She screamed from the doorway for them to bring her a basin of water and in her backyard she proceeded with a hasty cleanup. Across the road, she could see Mary shaking her fist at her as she headed for her own house.

Elena's family said nothing to her when she went into the house. There was something about her bearing as she prepared to take a real bath that kept everybody very subdued about the whole thing. Her daughters' faces were particularly immobile, and as she washed herself in the tin tub in the little room she had set aside for a bathroom, she overheard a snickering reference to "cow-pies". Then she realised with shame and anger that they were probably laughing at her.

Elena lay awake all night. Her rigid position signalled to Peter that she was only feigning sleep so he put his hand across her stomach in a gesture of affection and sympathy. She gently but firmly took his hand away, rolled over on her side and lay in that curled-up position all the rest of the night.

The next morning she barely looked at her husband and daughters as she performed her morning tasks. Through the day she did not once look out the window towards her neighbour's house. She washed her soiled clothes separately and hung them to dry in the basement. Although she sorely wished to give them the sun and air for purification, she would not give Mary Cherwak the satisfaction of seeing her hang them outside. She worked automatically, with a deadly calm and slowness.

As the days went on, Elena's mood sank lower. She sat in her living room for hours, crocheting doilies and nursing her anger and shame. She was sure that everybody in the village now knew what had happened when she went over to Mary Cherwak's. She thought she could see the gleam of laughter in their eyes when she went to the store. One of her neighbours was sure to have been looking out the window and witnessed it. Even now, she, Elena, could not stay away from the window. She would look through the lace curtains across to Mary's house and sometimes she saw her tending her cow. Once in awhile Mary would glance over to where Elena stood, shadowing the lace, and it seemed that in her glance was an evil look of malice.

Elena missed church that Sunday, feigning illness. She could not bear to face people or see Mary's look of triumphant scorn.

She neglected her house. Cleanliness was maintained but she carelessly left things lying around. She kept her daughters and Peter at a cool distance. For his part, Peter treated her a bit like a convalescent. But for the first time in their marriage, Elena refused his lovemaking. She neglected her nails and even put no rinse on her hair to hide the few white hairs that were appearing in the lustrous darkness.

With the loss of her firm grip on household affairs, her daughters were becoming defiant. They giggled and dawdled about their chores. One evening, they did not come home immediately when she called them, and as she glanced toward Mary's house, she saw her neighbour look up from her gardening and it seemed that a look of spiteful pleasure, like a gleaming arrow, sprang out of Mary's face.

Elena would sigh heavily as she went about her work, and sometimes when she was alone she would weep from rage and frustration. She felt she had taken a deep hurt. There was a part of her which would not heal, she felt, until she had vengeance for her defilement and utter loss of face. She imagined, over and over again, Mary relating the incident to Stepan and perhaps others too. She could hear her coarse laughter and see the rude gestures she would no doubt make as she told of throwing the dung at her face. As she pictured these things, Elena's hands would tremble and her head would grow light. She wondered if she might lose her mind through this torment.

At last, as she was sitting all alone one afternoon, crocheting furiously, the solution came into her mind. It seemed so just, so fitting, such a perfect revenge, she wondered why she had not thought of it at once. Suddenly, she became a whirlwind of action. She got out her file of recipes, and leafed through them madly until she found the one she wanted, from a little-used section hardly specked with grease. She flew around the kitchen, opening cupboards and rummaging to the back. Then she made out a list and walked briskly to the store, taking the long way around. In the store, she felt a surge of the old pride and hauteur and did not look at anyone's expression. In a businesslike voice, her head held high, she ordered raisins and currants and spices from her list.

On her arrival home again, she engaged in a frenzy of polishing and tidying and when Peter and the girls returned home for a delicious supper of *suppenfleisch*, there was a new air about her and the house that put them all in a happy mood. After supper, Elena sat with Peter in silence for a time and he waited for her to speak what was on her mind. She sat crocheting in silence for several minutes. Finally she spoke.

"Peter, I have been thinking a great deal about what happened with me and Mary Cherwak." Elena spoke very formally. "And I have decided I was wrong to get mad about her cow and to act as I did, throwing. . . . Well, I just want you tell Stepan this, and . . . tell him I want Mary to come and have coffee with me, so I can tell her myself and show her I want to be friends. Tell Stepan tomorrow and say Mary should come day after tomorrow in the afternoon."

Peter was overjoyed that his wife had found the courage to face her feelings and he eagerly agreed to break the news to Stepan the next day and to urge Mary to accept the invitation.

They retired early that evening and Peter was rather surprised that Elena was still quite unresponsive when finally they made love again. He put it down to her nervousness about the invitation she was giving.

Actually, Elena felt sick with anxiety that Mary would snub her, and refuse to come to her house. She could just see Mary gloating about it and then grandly refusing. Elena fretted about it for awhile that day but finally she decided that whether Mary came over or not, the invitation was a stroke of genius. After all, if Mary refused, she would seem merely spiteful and carping, while she, Elena, would have a saintly aspect in the eyes of both husbands and the report of her spirit of *noblesse oblige* would spread around the village. Still, she felt nervous as she prepared the evening meal. However, when Peter came home for supper he was hearty and happy. Stepan had told him he was sure Mary would be glad to come because she had been feeling badly about losing her temper and she wanted to make amends. Elena was surprised to hear this, but she discounted it immediately, deciding that it must indicate a deviousness that even she did not attribute to Mary. She would require more evidence of real remorse before she, Elena, would change her stand.

Peter was delighted to bring her his news. It seemed to him a wonderful turn of events. His home life would return to normal. He did not notice that Elena's face bore not a trace of joy, but only grim satisfaction.

That night, Elena once more lay feigning sleep until the small hours of the morning. When all noises were absolutely silenced, she rose and put on her old shoes and coat. Getting out her scrub pail and a small flashlight, she crept steathily across the road. She found a fresh pile of cow-dung and put a generous amount into her pail. She went swiftly home again, covered the pail carefully and set it in a dark corner of the basement. Then, very quietly, she returned to bed.

That morning, after Peter and the girls were gone, Elena went quickly to work. She got out her recipe, her pie pans and utensils, the spices and the dried fruit. She fetched the cow-dung from the basement. Substituting the cow-dung for the applesauce in the recipe, she proceeded to make the pie. She added in extra amounts of spices, sugar and cognac, determinedly overcoming her own revulsion as she worked. She put a small amount of the mixture into a saucepan and cooked it thoroughly on top of the stove. Taking a little on a teaspoon, she tasted it gingerly. It was quite good. She spat it into a tissue and rinsed her mouth several times. The pie smelled sweet and spicy as it cooked. She put some crumbs and cooked mixture into the other pie pan, to make it look like a pie had been already consumed. Then the kitchen was cleaned and scrubbed to the ultimate degree.

After lunch, she dressed herself nicely, combed her hair carefully and prepared the table for her guest. She thought once about Peter's words regarding Mary. It couldn't be true, she told herself, that Mary really regretted what happened. She forced herself to stay away from the window, and then, just when she thought that Mary had played a trick on her, a knock came at the door.

Elena opened it. Mary Cherwak stood on the step. She had a clean kerchief on her head and her shoes were shiny, her rough brown stockings spotless. She held a little stone crock covered with a snowy cloth. She proffered it to Elena as she crossed the threshold.

"Here, I brink you. You like fresh butter?"

Elena took it from her. "Ah tank you, tank you," she murmured, peeking under the cloth at the rich yellow paste. "Is so nice, so nice." She went to the kitchen table and transferred the butter deftly to a deep bowl of her own, covering it with a plate. She hoped Mary would notice the empty pie pan with the crumbs in it that was beside her as she worked. "Is not too warm, no?" she asked lightly. Mary was taking her shoes off on the little mat.

"No. Is cold. All month July is cold."

"So come. Come into front room, yah?" Elena led the way into the pristine living room. The round parlour table was spread with an immaculate cloth. There was a coffee pot on a stand over a lighted candle. China cups and plates. The pie and server and a small plate of dainty cookies. The women sat across from each other on straight-backed arm chairs smothered in crocheted doilies. They both sat in shy silence for a moment. Mary picked gently at a doily on the arm of her chair.

"You do?" she asked softly.

"Yah," Elena replied.

"Is nice. Very nice."

"Tank you. You do dat?"

"Not so much. My eyes is not good for such vork. I knit covers, coats."

"Yah? Knitting is nice. I like too." Elena poured coffee into their cups. Now the moment had come. She must be just right. The same voice.

"You like pie? Is new receet. I get from my Angleesh neighbour."

"Oh yes? Vat is called?"

"Meencemeat. Is a special for Christmas. I bake special chust for you." She placed the pie on the plate and handed it to Mary, whose eyes, Elena noted, brightened with interest. "I eat already almost whole pie," Elena said casually. "Is very rich."

"Oh yes? Vat it's got? Meat?"

"Oh no. That chust name. You take him apples and chop very good and fat from beef the same, and much butter, vine, sugar,

107

spices, raisins, orange skin, lemon juice, flour for thicken. Like dat."

Mary's almond eyes crinkled in delight. She took the first forkful and ate it with interest. She put her head to one side.

"Ho, la, la. Is very much spice, much sugar. Is nice, very nice."

"Tank you." But this moment, which should have been so rich, so full, was somehow flat. It was like feeding poison to a trusting child. Mary showed not the slightest hesitation about eating the pie. Above her broad cheeks, her slanted eyes were open, remorseful. Elena wondered how she could have thought them evil.

"You like new statue of Holy Mother in church?" Mary asked suddenly.

"Yah. Is very . . . fine," Elena replied, trying not to follow the downward movement of Mary's fork with her eyes.

"I always pray to Holy Mother," Mary continued with a little sly smile at the corners of her mouth. "I always say Holy Mother is little bit like me. She is poor voman, vork hard, and she know vat it is to have troubling child." Elena stared at her in surprise. The sly smile had reached the corners of Mary's eyes and Elena saw that she was having a little joke. Suddenly, Elena found herself giggling hysterically. Mary laughed heartily. "Is true, yah? Everybody got trouble with their kids now, yah?"

"Ah yeh. Ah yeh," Elena agreed when she could catch her breath.

"I very sorry my cow give you much trouble," Mary said sincerely, stopping her forkful of pie in mid-air. "I don't know vat I should do. Cow must eat grass, must valk. All must come oudt. . . ."

"I know dat," Elena said miserably, watching the last forkful of pie disappear. "I should not feel so mad. I valk around, now."

"I can not help for dat," Mary said slowly, searching for words. "But I make good. Every day I brink you cream, yes?"

"Oh no! Is too much. Is not needed." Elena saw that Mary's eyes had strayed to the pie. She handed her the plate of cookies and refilled her cup.

"No tanks," Mary said to the cookies. Her eyes went to the pie again. "I vant brink you something for trouble. Ve be friends now. I vant be friends for much time." Elena saw that little beads of sweat stood out on her neighbour's cheeks. Her eyes were moist. Elena dropped her eyes in shame to Mary's hands on the table and noted for the first time the calluses on the fingers and the clean nails.

"Vill you have again, pie?" she asked in a high thin voice.

"Yes, tanks," Mary said shyly, holding out her plate. Elena

knew what she had to do. There was only one way, really, to redeem herself for this shameful act. She put another piece of pie on Mary's plate and then cut a generous slice for herself.

"Ah, so? You hongry again? Is good pie!" Mary pronounced.

"I can't let my friend eat . . . alone," Elena said haltingly. "Vould not be right. I share vid you." Resolutely she put a forkful in her mouth. The dung taste was completely disguised, but she felt a little thrill go through her as sometimes happened when she thought about the Mysteries or when the priest spoke of miracles. She swallowed mechanically and took another forkful. Mary was looking at her with that same kind, trusting expression.

"Ve not fight anymore, I tink. Is so good pie. Angleesh, you say? I not tink Angleesh cook so good. I get receet from you."

"Holy Mother," Elena prayed silently as she raised her fork again. "Holy Mother, forgive me that I hated my poor neighbour and help me swallow this pie." She had instinctively lowered her eyes as she prayed. When she raised them again she saw that Mary was looking at her with a quizzical smile. Whether from the tension or relief, Elena did not know, but she felt that she was as transparent and light as a butterfly. She smiled back at Mary, widely and sweetly.

"I get receet, yes?" Mary grinned broadly. "But I never make it good as you."

"Maybe better," Elena replied, finishing the last few bites. "Everybody got their own ways to cook. Their own secrets."

SUN

BARBARA SAPERGIA

Eleanor stirred her coffee in slow circles, pushed unwashed dishes from lunch to the corner of the table. The kitchen needed cleaning again. Jocelyn was always spilling things, always managing to spill things. It was bad enough when she spilled them on the faded grey tiles, but on the walls? the ceiling?

They had agreed to put off fixing up the kitchen until Jocelyn was older. It was only sensible, Jim said. But Jim didn't have to work here, day in, day out. It was depressing. The scratches and bubbles in the gold arborite counter. Chipped tan paint on the walls and woodwork. How had they ever picked the ugly indeterminate shade of dun that seemed to absorb whatever light made its way into the room? Neutral, the salesman had said. Goes with anything.

A plastic washbasket sat on the chair, reproaching her with its unfolded towels as she sipped coffee. The towels were getting old, stripes and checks fading, little frayed holes showing up here and there. That was one thing they would have to replace soon.

There wasn't enough light in here. They were going to put in a bigger window when they fixed up the kitchen. The one they had was a miserly little square over the sink that gave her a view of the neighbours' garbage pails while she did dishes. Most days she just left the curtains closed. "It's only for a while," Jim always said, "you know we're going to fix it the way we like." Today she was tired of putting up with it.

110

Eleanor tried to be happy. She knew that half the trick is to have the right attitude. She had heard this all her life, but had only recently come to believe it. It was astonishing how many of the old sayings were becoming simple reality. *Time heals all wounds. Money can't buy happiness.* Why couldn't they tell you these things when you were young in a way you'd understand? She was sure she could have understood, if only they'd explained things more clearly. *Handsome is, as handsome does,* her Mother had told her. Eleanor had complained about the long nose and craggy brows she'd inherited from her father.

"Nonsense," Mother had insisted firmly. "I don't know where you get these ideas, Eleanor, certainly not from *me.*"

Mother always said you should "just be thankful that you're healthy and normal and have everything in the right place." And Mother had been right. Eleanor understood now. In her body, not just her head. The trouble she'd known raising Jocelyn, the trouble some of her friends had known with their children, had been enough to make her understand. She hadn't known then what a gamble life was, how hard it was to go through it without major disasters. How impossible.

How could she have known then? Then it was humiliating to know that no one would ever consider you to be freshie queen or whatever kind of queen, even though your skin was clear, your eyes hopeful. Then she had plucked the heavy eyebrows into a thin line, slept on rollers, curled her eyelashes and brushed them with black goo, outlined her eyes in black. Always discreetly, though; none of the heavy eyeliner and beady mascara some girls used. Eleanor had always tried to make it look as though she didn't wear any make-up.

Remembering, she suddenly understood why. Then you would look good and people would think you *didn't need to wear it.* They would think you were better looking than you were. It was mortifying to express such motives in words, to realize how hard she had worked to keep anyone from seeing her real face. My God, she thought, I never had a decent night's sleep all through high school. Big round rollers, with little brushes like bottle brushes in the middle, pricking and gouging your scalp all night no matter how you turned. She sipped the cooling coffee.

Eleanor knew better now, of course, but the knowledge seemed to come too late. Age was beginning to show in her face, you could read the troubles, the downward pull of gravity and years. How could you ask that face to go out into the world on its own now, no defences? She wished she could, just once, without changing anything. (Jim said he liked her best that way, although she noticed that his eye was often caught by pretty women who used plenty of make-up.) She had stopped using make-up except for occasional parties, but she couldn't give up the plucking, the curling of eyelashes. They weren't like make-up. No one would *know*. For a moment she wondered if people would even notice the difference if she stopped. Would Jim? She couldn't quite remember what her eyebrows had looked like, but probably someone would notice if she let them grow out.

She looked through the kitchen door at Jocelyn, for once mercifully asleep, curled up on the living-room couch. She had begged to stay home from school today, and Eleanor could see it was one of those days she might as well give in, Jocelyn wouldn't shut up till she agreed. Oh well, she thought, it'll be a rest for the teacher.

Jocelyn looked very different sleeping, her face relaxed and peaceful, as it seldom was when she was awake. The shaggy brows, in a lighter shade of brown, looked better on Jocelyn; she didn't have Eleanor's long slightly bumpy nose, but something between it and Jim's short turned-up one. Eleanor had been relieved when she saw that Jocelyn would be pretty.

She felt ashamed, remembering the relief. She could almost hear Mother's voice protesting this latest example of moral sleaziness: "Eleanor, you make me *ashamed*." Lately, she could hear the voice as clearly as she ever had when Mother was alive. And had she actually thought that way? Had she fallen in love with Jim because she had unconsciously seen how his nose would balance hers in their children, his light hair soften the heavy brows? Unconsciously nothing, she told herself. You thought it out loud; out loud in your head. Never out loud to Mother, though.

Eleanor liked doing the washing. It gave you time to think, drinking coffee, waiting for the next load to be done. She'd even been able to get Jocelyn to help fold things for a while. (Jocelyn liked work all right if it was active enough, no nit-picking little tasks, and if it didn't last too long. You just had to watch for the exact moment when she'd had enough.) Eleanor had actually been touched by Jocelyn's willingness to help today, as if in thanks for being allowed to stay home. Although Jocelyn was eleven and had the beginnings of tiny breasts, she was still a little girl in most ways. She hadn't even asked for a brassiere yet the way Eleanor had when she'd first begun to develop.

Then they'd stopped for coffee, and after that Jocelyn had stretched out on the couch watching soap operas on T.V. When Eleanor came up from the basement with another load, Jocelyn was asleep, relaxed and graceful as a kitten. She quietly closed the drapes.

112

Now Eleanor sat with her coffee, enjoying the quieting of tension in the house as Jocelyn slept. The child seemed to use tension like a weapon. Eleanor had left the T.V. on, the sounds seemed to comfort Jocelyn, and muted fragments of earnest conversations came to her in the kitchen.

She looked at the cramped kitchen. The counters were too low. The sink was an old white porcelain one, stained beyond the curative power of bleaches and scouring agents. If she'd known this was the only house they'd ever have, she'd never have agreed. "We'll move to a bigger one when our family gets larger," that's what Jim had said. But after Jocelyn, who was going to risk more children? So she was stuck, in a small bungalow in an older part of the city.

She'd liked it at first, the small neat rooms freshly painted; two bedrooms, one for them and one for the child. It was only when you lived in it for a while that you saw the rooms were just a little too small, not really cute at all. A doll's house, the real estate woman had called it. The bitch. How many women had she betrayed in this way?

They'd been pleased with the brick fireplace too, at least in the beginning. Until Jocelyn got big enough to grab flaming newspapers and kindling and run all over the house with them when you weren't looking. They hadn't used it for a long time. Over the years, the house had come to leave a sour taste in her mouth. Jim still thought they'd fix it up when Jocelyn was older. Eleanor had her own plan. Sell the goddamn thing. But she'd have to wait.

Soon the school would be able to handle Jocelyn better. She was growing out of it a little already. Just two more years and she'd be in high school. Then maybe Eleanor could get a job at the neighbourhood day care centre. It didn't pay much, but it would be a job, a start. After that . . . But maybe they wouldn't want her? Who wants a woman looking after their kids when she's not doing such a hot job on her own? No! That was different, with Jocelyn, it was nothing we did or didn't do. The doctor said.

"Now, you must understand, it's very difficult to make a positive diagnosis, but we think Jocelyn is probably a hyperkinetic child." He'd waited, looking embarrassed, while she took this in. "We don't really understand what causes hyperkinesis, but we do know it's affecting an increasing number of children these days." Oh, terrific! It was affecting other children. Did they think that made it any easier? Maybe it did.

"At least," he had said, "you'll be relieved to know it's not due to anything you did or neglected to do." He'd smiled reassuringly, but she could feel the look of guilt spread across her face. "And it doesn't mean that she's a bad child or that she enjoys destructive behaviour," was he sure?, "she just can't help it." Well, that made her feel so much better about the scorched drapes, the smouldering hole in the couch. (Thank *Christ* she'd gotten out of her fire-setting phase.) Or the way she'd carved up the nice new coffee table and matching end tables. The excrement smeared on the sheets of their bed, invisible till they opened it and started climbing in. Of *course*, she hadn't enjoyed that. "And there are a number of therapies we can try." He was really trying to be kind. She ought to be grateful there were things they could try. Grateful!

It seemed so ironic. Jocelyn had managed to be born pretty. She was quite intelligent too, although she hated to be taught things. But she certainly wasn't popular.

Eleanor got up and found a light blanket in the hall cupboard and put it over Jocelyn. The days were getting warmer, but she didn't want Jocelyn catching a spring cold. The child looked totally at peace, her brows smoothed out, her small mouth soft and tranquil, moving slightly as she breathed. Jocelyn always breathed through her mouth when she slept, they'd never been able to change that. She looked so pretty, her light brown hair curling around her face. But mother had said not to judge people by their looks.

— I saw how you treated Martha Wright, she said, and I *sure* don't think it was nice. You treated her like dirt, Eleanor, and I know why. Just because she isn't good looking according to you and your smart-aleck friends.

but Mom, i've tried being nice to people like martha it doesn't work you remember judy clay? mousy judy? she asked me to her house one day after school i went because i felt sorry for her her parents weren't home from work yet judy was acting funny something was going to happen and i wanted to stop it i was embarrased but i was trying to be nice Mother i was *trying* i thought if i was nice and normal that would stop it then i could go home

she asked me to help with her homework something in the math book i was looking at the book Mother are you listening? and then she put her arm around me she put her arm around my shoulder and and she kissed me i slapped her face hard i pushed her away she just looked at me and then she started to cry i said i had to go home i never talked to her after that

i was *afraid* Mother afraid i was weird like her afraid no one would want me people would point at me and judy and say we were weird everyone would laugh no one would ever want me

oh that's funny isn't it? judy wanted me but you don't know she was fat and plain her face was wide and bland like a baby's no one wanted her i didn't want *her* to want me i didn't want her to touch

— Well, Eleanor, you certainly never mentioned this to me at the time.

how could i mention it Mother? we didn't talk about things like that i wasn't supposed to know but you didn't see her face Mommy you didn't see i hit her and she was crying i couldn't look at her she was just so lonely

—Because if you had, I would certainly have spoken to her mother.

spoken to her *mother* is that all you can think of? as if her mother *owned* her? do you think you can fix everything speaking to the kid's mother? speak to her mother speak to the teacher speak to the principal speak to THEM i remember when you spoke to carolann arnold's mother because she wouldn't walk to school with me and she told everybody and they all laughed at me

They'd tried a number of the therapies with Jocelyn. Tranquillizers had not helped. Then there was the theory that hyperkinesis was caused by the chemical additives in food, and could be controlled by a diet free of them. Eleanor had tried this, reading labels on everything, rooting out anything with artificial colour, artificial flavour, preservatives, stabilizers, anti-oxidants, extenders. It hadn't left much. Then she'd had to make everything from scratch. Even that hadn't helped, although Eleanor was sure it was a healthier diet. But she'd felt a keen pleasure, quickly suppressed, telling Jocelyn she couldn't have ice cream because it wasn't *good* for her.

They had achieved encouraging results, however, when they started her on regular doses of strong coffee and Ritalin, an amphetamine compound. Funny, Eleanor thought, these things stimulate normal people, but Jocelyn they calm. "They usually start to grow out of it when they approach their teens," the doctor had said, and this seemed to be happening with Jocelyn. She was able to go to school pretty regularly now. The doctor had congratulated them on their management of Jocelyn's condition.

Eleanor sighed. She got to her feet and picked up a pile of folded clothes, tiptoed through the living-room past the sleeping child, and into Jocelyn's bedroom.

She put the neatly folded clothes away in the drawers of Jocelyn's dresser, the brightly coloured T-shirts, ruffled perma-press blouses, printed nylon panties. She didn't think it was an extravagance to buy pretty things for Jocelyn. Poor child, she needed any advantages they could give her.

115

The white framed mirror above the dresser reflected back Jocelyn's room: pale pink walls, white wooden furniture, frilly white spread. The light coming in through pink Priscilla curtains cast a rosy glow in the room. They'd thought maybe if she had a pretty room, she'd take pride in it. Eleanor still had to keep it tidy, but Jocelyn had stopped trying to destroy it. She'd had the same spread for over a year now.

Eleanor caught her reflection in the mirror. There was more grey in her hair lately, she noticed, especially around the temples. She told Jim she liked it, it was what happened in life. Mark at the beauty parlour had tried to persuade her to have a red rinse that would put "highlights" in her hair and "cover the grey." Or, he could "sun-drench" it, bleaching in delicate steaks of gold, like the sun-tanned beauties on his wall posters. She was tempted. It would be a real change, a different way of facing the world.

"Why don't you dye your hair blonde?" Cal, a long-ago lover, had said, just as he was getting ready to leave her. "It'd be a real change for you." He said this as though compelled to offer a little cheap therapy before decamping, as though resistance to change might have been her real problem. As though the information might help with the next one.

She'd been confused answering him. Men never seemed to realize that you don't *dye* brown hair blonde. You bleach it, strip it of colour, *then* you dye it, in the sunkist shade of your choice. He wasn't interested in the mechanics of it, he said, it was the idea.

"Because I'm not particularly *interested* in being blonde," she had said resentfully, not taken in by the pseudo-kindly manner, as if now that they wouldn't be sleeping together any more he could finally be objective. But she'd considered it for a moment, as a possible diversion from the unhappiness of being left. She had rejected the idea though, for once too proud to fall into his humiliating traps.

She had Mother to thank for *that* anyway. They had never been able to make her feel that blonde hair was better than brown. Guided by her mother's triumphant contempt (was she trying to protect me, Eleanor finally thought to wonder), she had never quite got over the idea that blonde hair was rather a misfortune, that even the natural kind looked cheap and sleazy. Nonetheless, at the beauty parlour she'd considered sun-drenching.

On balance, though, she didn't think so. Soon the pale streaks issuing from her temples would have expanded into two silvery wings around her face, and that might look quite interesting.

She examined her eyebrows. Not as thin a line now as when she was a teenager — she'd been slowly letting them grow into a fuller shape. Nothing like their full shagginess, of course, but still, she was pleased to have achieved a more natural look.

Her nose she didn't mind so much now — at least she no longer fantasized about nose jobs, couldn't really imagine any other nose shape connected to her face. She saw now that the turned-up creation of her teenage dreams would actually look ludicrous.

Most faces are more or less asymmetrical, Eleanor's a little more so than most. She held her hand out at right angles in front of her face, neatly splitting the image in the mirror. As always, she saw that her nose wasn't straight, but came down at a slight angle. It had been that way since she was ten and her brother Alan punched her in the nose.

Eleanor smiled experimentally at the reflection. The smile was tentative, a bit crooked like all her smiles. The left eyebrow was rounder than the more pointed right one. In the mirror the left side of her face was smiling, but when she looked at the right side, it looked more as if she were about to break into tears. This effect of her face always puzzled her. She had first noticed it in a studio portrait of herself where the smile just didn't seem right. She lowered her hand, which was growing tired, relaxed her face, which was also growing tired, from smiling.

In the living-room, Jocelyn still slept peacefully, her breathing deep and regular. Eleanor turned the T.V. down, watching to make sure the child never stirred, and walked quietly back to the kitchen. Her coffee was cold now, the cream separated into a curdly scum on top, like an oil slick. She gathered up the coffee cups, plates and spoons, and stacked them by the sink, then got out stewing beef for supper. It looked like good meat, she had had the butcher cut it in fine little pieces. She decided not to brown it, the sizzling might wake Jocelyn. You never woke Jocelyn if you could help it. Instead she put the meat in a large saucepan, covered it with water, and set it to simmer gently. Jim said he liked it just as well that way. She only browned the meat because it was in all the cookbooks. From now on she wasn't going to bother.

Mother was certainly right. You could be thankful to have your health and everything in its right place. Eleanor was glad Mother had never known about Jocelyn. She felt ashamed, as if she'd failed somehow. Mother only had babies that were healthy and had everything in the right place. Of course, Mother had only had two babies, but she, Eleanor, had had only one, and even that one hadn't turned out right.

Very quietly, Eleanor got a big Spanish onion from the cupboard and began slicing it for the stew. It was very strong, and soon water was streaming from her irritated eyes and nose. Damn!

117

Spanish onions were supposed to be mild, that was what you paid extra for. She concentrated on breathing only through her nose, that was supposed to help. If only she didn't always chop onions so fine. She began to feel very tired. She needed to get out. There was a good movie on at the theatre in the shopping centre. She would ask Jim when he got home from the refinery. It was nice having him work days, they could go out. They could get that nice sitter, Mrs. Comstock, who seemed to be able to handle Jocelyn so well.

Yes, that was what they'd do. The theatre was just five miles away on the freeway. Jim was usually too tired but tonight was important. It was just for the evening, but she had to get out. Your troubles didn't go away, but you were allowed to forget them once in a while.

She brushed the onions from the slicing board into the steaming stew, caught again by the onion fumes mingling with the steam. She grabbed kleenexes and began to blow her nose, just for a moment crying a little in self-pity. She sat down.

There was a rustling sound. Eleanor tried not to stiffen her body. Jocelyn was awake now, had come to the kichen door, and stood watching her with steady serious eyes. She hadn't even heard her get up. The child looked so quiet, just like any child, and suddenly Eleanor found she was really crying at the thought of a normal average sort of daughter. Jocelyn just looked; then she stepped forward and put out her hand, gently touching Eleanor's shoulder. Eleanor looked at her, surprised and hopeful; she held out her arms to Jocelyn.

Jocelyn shrank instantly from her touch, jumped back to the door. She stared at Eleanor, the drying tears on her cheeks. She made a choked sound as if she were going to cry. Then she started to laugh, boisterously, heartlessly. She pointed her slim fingers at Eleanor, and laughed and laughed.

Eleanor felt savage anger boiling up in her. She wanted to hit Jocelyn, hit her hard. She jumped up, and Jocelyn ran into the living room, laughing, just ahead of Eleanor's aching hands. Eleanor caught hold of the edge of the kitchen door, and flung it shut as hard as she could, horrified as she heard a terrible squealing sound that must be coming from her own throat. She stood trembling a moment, fighting the desire to chase after Jocelyn, to hurt her.

There was a sliding, grating sound. The living-room drapes being flung open. Then ripping cloth, splintering wood. Eleanor opened the door. Jocelyn was standing on the couch, pulling at the drapes. One tore apart at the fraying seam. She wrenched at the steel rods, trying to rip them from the wall. Plaster sprayed from the wall to the couch, the worn carpet.

118

"Jocelyn!" Eleanor screamed. "Stop it!"

The child didn't look at her. The rods still clung to the wall on one side, but she finally managed to pull the drapes free, to fall in a sighing heap around her. She stood tearing at them with all her strength, making little grunting sounds. The tough fiberglass wouldn't give. Still she tore, eyes staring, sweat popping out on her forehead. Eleanor watched her, but didn't move. Jocelyn sobbed with frustration. Then she looked at Eleanor, and her eyes were pleading as she wrenched at the unyielding fabric.

Eleanor looked at her. This is my daughter, she thought. This is what I've worked for. Sunlight streamed into the room, the television people faint as ghosts in the bright room. Behind her, there was a sudden hissing, sizzling sound; the stew was boiling over. Eleanor turned and walked back to the kitchen.

FISH-HOOKS

REG SILVESTER

Out they flew — *skreeeeeee-splopsh, sk-sk-skreeeeeee-splopsh* — the fish-hooks into Jackfish Creek, just above the dam the engineers call a control structure. Walley Dyer watched the lures twist and glint in the morning sun as they arched and plunged.

Walley didn't fish. He had no tackle box. He sat by the creek, watching. Sometimes, not often, fish would be dragged flopping from the water. Walley imagined the panic of the fish as they struggled, wondered what it would be like if he bit into a sandwich some day and found it dragging him into outer space. Death, conceived in his own hunger and delivered by the sharp blow of a club in an alien atmosphere.

Walley's favourite sight was a rod bending and tugging, then suddenly yielding. A hook snagged and a line broken. Fishermen curse snags and reels that drag in limp ends of fishing line. But not Walley Dyer. He owned the snagged hooks. Let the casters swear.

Mondays in the mid-afternoon, when the creek was quiet, when no one would be fishing, Walley slipped into the water in face mask and flippers, to snorkle down to the log. His log, lined with hooks. A dozen Len Thompson spoons. The plain brass of Len Thompson Number Zero. Black and orange Len Thompsons like deadly ladybugs; yellow ones with five red diamonds on their backs; a white one with a winding red stripe down the middle. He found spinners, Deadly Dicks and one-eye wigglers, with their fatal ruby eyes staring nowhere.

He dove with his lungs full, unsnagging hooks, and when he felt about to burst, he broke to the surface. He resnagged each handful of lures for safekeeping on a floating anchored log. Down and up, down and up again. He was careful not to get a barbed hook in his finger.

Once in a while, quite rarely, he would find a Lucky Strike hooked down there. A large white-bodied plug with simulated scales, a red head and a lethal hook hanging from its underbelly. Walley never saw anyone using a Lucky Strike. No one would cast a Lucky Strike with somebody watching. Too embarrassing. It's not a casting lure.

He would take his hooks away when the log was bare, and later return to watch fishermen filling it up again. Fishermen casting. Unwinding sidearms. Spinning out overhands. Cursing backlashes. Self-consciously comparing styles. Comparing catches. Cursing snags.

Walley hasn't always gathered fish-hooks. He spent much of his life reeling in lines with the rest of them. In his place in line along the creek. *Skreeeeeee-splopsssh*, winding in words. Minding words. Listening to his mother: "When you grow up and get married, you won't be able to fool around all the time. You'll have to be responsible for your wife and children and provide them with a good living. If you concentrate on your school work and get ahead, it won't be so hard."

He swallowed those words, never questioning the certainty of marriage and children, never wondering what "get ahead" meant.

Skreeeeeee-splopsssssh. He wound in the words of the high school teacher who wrote numbers on the green blackboard: "Many of you probably think you should go straight to work after high school. You might think that going on with your schooling will cost you the money you could make in those three or four years. Well, I'd like to demonstrate how wrong you are. The figures are these. The average yearly income of a man with a high school education is $7,000. If he works 48 years, his lifetime income will be $336,000. But a university graduate earns an average of $10,000 a year, making his lifetime income over only 44 years come out to be $440,000. So you see, going to university does not cost you money. It will gain you $104,000 during your lifetime."

While at university, Walley wound in the wordless dialogue of love: the flash of an eye, the warmth of a smile, the gentle yielding of selves. He was married two weeks after graduation. He became a civil servant the following week and a father a year later. *Skreeeeee-splopssssh.*

It was his job to analyze tourism statistics. If surveys showed that all Iowans visiting Canada chose Ontario destinations, he would recommend that advertising in Iowa should stress the beauty in beautiful British Columbia. If the number of British Columbians holidaying in the prairies showed a downward trend through the years, it was up to Walley to figure out how to change the trend.

Job, wife, child, Walley wound them all in. He kept casting but he was catching less and less. The love he once compared to a soft sweet candy was exposed for the jaw-breaker it really was. His kid became a pain in the ass. The weight of his responsibilities seemed leaden; the demands of his job seemed twisted and barbed.

Skreeeeeee-splopssssssh. He wound in the words of his boss: "Walley, I've been wondering what's bothering you. I'm finding mistakes in your figures. Your maritimes survey is two weeks late. What's the matter, Walley? Let's get this straightened out."

Walley walked home muttering. "Straightened out. Straighten out the fish-hook. Uh-uh, I'm not casting any more." He jabbed a pin in a tourist book. It took him to Jackfish Lake, to an old house not far from Jackfish Creek.

It is midnight. Walley Dyer churns up the still lake, skimming through dark in a stolen outboard motor-boat. Walley turns on the running lights, red and green on the bow, white light aft. He is gobbling up the silver highway laid out by the moon. The motor's roar is part of the silence. There is no other boat on the lake.

There is a log, once part of a child's raft, now broken free and floating just below the surface. It is to be Walley's launching pad.

Suddenly there is no boat, just Walley flying in a moonlit arc, flying in a shower of spoons and wigglers, Deadly Dicks and spinners. There is the dim red and white of a Lucky Strike.

In the lake, a jackfish slides along, bending among weeds. The stars in the sky beyond are twisted by the gentle motion of the lake surface; the moon is an elastic oval. In the pea-sized brain of the jackfish there is a spark. Where there is no possibility of thought, there is an intuition. The jackfish begins to swim faster, angling down, faster and faster, skimming the bottom. Its eye fastens upon the shining oval. With a jerk it turns up, takes off, fins and tail beating, pushing. It breaks the surface like a bullet, fins flailing the thinness of air. It drives for the moon. There is another flicker in the small brain — this is too far, too hard; air is not water, fins are not wings, I'm just a fish — its effort and desperation combine to burst its heart.

The jackfish drops to the surface, flat. It lies there still, floating on the silver highway.

EMILY

LOIS SIMMIE

Every year we rented the same cottage at the west end of the lake. All through the dry, cold winters, when snow lay thick on the town, I dreamed about the lake; and in the summer, too, when parched prairie grass crackled under my feet and the caragana hedges were covered with dust. And still I was surprised, every year, by the shimmering immensity of it; you could barely make out the hills on the far side, and cottages were mere specks on the horizon.

On the first of July we were always up by six-thirty to get an early start. That year my sister, who was fourteen, complained about getting up, but I didn't mind. In a corner of the back seat, made fort-like by a stack of pillows and blankets, I hugged my bathing suit and imagined how it would be. The imagining was always the same, made familiar by months of practise: I would run along the warm wooden pier, dive into the cold water and swim — just like that I would know how, my body as easy and casual in the water as a fish's. Sometimes I saved someone from drowning, most often my mother, though how she was in danger of drowning when she never went near the water I had never worked out satisfactorily. She was always wearing a jersey print dress and a straw hat, so I supposed she had fallen in.

But when we arrived and I raced into the water, I sank like a stone. It didn't matter, it never mattered, the lake itself was enough, the luxurious wetness of the water, as clear as a crystal glass — no matter how deep you walked in, you could always see the hard ribs of sand on the bottom. I splashed in it, wallowed in it, soaked it up through my pores, longing to pull off my tanksuit but afraid my father or Val would catch me. I dog-paddled furiously, arms and legs churning foam, breath held hurting in my chest, but when I stood up and looked back, the stirred-up water extended only a few feet behind me.

I was building a sand castle when Emily floated into my life. A movement made me look up. She was floating in the water about fifteen feet from shore, enormous mounds of breasts and belly above the water, the back of her head completely submerged, long hair drifting out around her face like strings of brown weed. Just floating there, without a sound, in that clear still water. She passed silently by, parallel to the beach, and I shaded my eyes to see her better.

She must be dead, drowned bodies rose to the top, I knew that, and was just going to run for my father when I saw her white foot move, just a flicker but still a movement, and farther on another, stronger flicker, like a fish's tail, and she began to move faster. I watched her for a long time, and then she rolled over and began to swim. Until I saw her white arms gleaming rhythmically in the sun, I still half-believed she was dead. I watched for her all that day but she still hadn't appeared by bedtime.

Ours was a plain two-bedroom cottage with a screened verandah, its board siding weathered to a pale silver grey, soft and fuzzy to the touch, like suede. It was set back in the trees, close enough to the lake to hear the waves on a windy night, and fat spiders hung outside the screens. The trees gave us the illusion of privacy, though in fact we were close enough to our neighbours to hear them talking at night, their screen door and toilet door slapping open and shut, bursts of laughter. And sometimes other sounds in the night. My father always reserved the cottage, on the day we left, for the first of July the following year. It gave us a proprietary feeling and made it easier to leave.

Mr. Jacobson, the man who owned the cabins, called renters "summer people", which made us sound faintly glamorous. In fact we were quite ordinary, and this didn't bother me yet, but bothered my sister considerably. She had met some kids from the city last year, and was afraid that we were going to shame her in some way, do something horribly gauche or gross that she could never live down. I swore I would never be a dumb snot like her, but of course I was, a few years later.

It was almost dark when my father came in from fishing that

first night and told us he'd had the scare of his life. He was fishing in the rowboat, a long way from shore, when a fat girl came floating by. He'd almost snagged her with his fish hook. It was downright spooky, he said, seeing someone that far out in the lake, just floating along as if she was ten feet from shore. He asked her if she wanted a ride but she didn't answer, didn't even lift her ears out of the water when she saw him speaking to her. She smiled and swam off, he said, and he followed her in to shallow water to make sure she didn't drown. She floated in and out of my dreams that night, a strange little smile on her lips.

"That's Dummy Morrow's daughter," Mr. Jacobson said the next morning in answer to my father's question. "Your wife would know the family." Mother had grown up only a few miles from the lake. "Floats like a cork," he said, aiming a stream of tobacco juice into the long grass beside our cottage; a sturdy dandelion swayed, straightened, and dripped brown. "Emily, her name is, you'll get used to her. Swims like a fish and floats like a cork — swim clean across the lake if she takes the notion. And that ain't all." He didn't explain what he meant.

My mother had finished the dishes and was rolling cigarettes on the oilcloth-covered table when I went in. She was expecting company later and her hair was twisted onto hard metal curlers with rubber knobs. Because she had grown up near there she had a lot of company.

"Dummy Morrow," she said thoughtfully, lighting a clumsy, hand-rolled cigarette, "I haven't thought of him for years." She blew smoke toward the ceiling while charred bits of paper and tobacco drifted onto her wine chenille robe. "In fact I thought they'd moved away." She absently scooped the loose tobacco into a pile on the table. Not many women smoked in those days, and Val had asked Mother not to smoke in front of her new friends, but she just laughed and went on lighting up whenever she felt like it.

"Did you know Emily?" I asked.

"No, I wouldn't know her. But I remember her father. He used to come around to the farm, sharpening knives and scissors and mower blades. He knew everything you said by watching your lips. And when he wanted to tell you something, he wrote a note."

"Was he deaf and dumb?"

"Of course," said my mother, "that's why he was called Dummy Morrow."

I accepted this without question or surprise — that was the way people talked then; Chinny Sawyer had a huge chin, Gimp Brown had one leg shorter than the other, Fat Faber weighed three hundred pounds. No one seemed to think anything of it, not even the

Chinnys and Gimps and Fats who waved and grinned when they were hailed by name.

"Do you think Emily is deaf and dumb?" Mother was putting things away in the bright blue cupboards on which someone had painted fat yellow fish with bubbles rising from their open mouths.

"She probably is," she said. "It's hereditary."

Emily was sitting on what I thought of as my stretch of beach when I got there. Even sitting, there was something of the same stillness about her, but she looked up and smiled as I went past her into the water. She was wearing a faded blue bathing suit and her wavy brown hair hung past her shoulders. Because of her size, I found it difficult to guess her age, she could have been thirteen or twenty. I attacked the water headlong, willing it to hold me up, but I could not keep my feet from touching bottom for more than a few seconds. Each time I glanced ashore, Emily was watching me intently.

And then she was in the water, gesturing for me to lie down, supporting me with her hand on the small of my back. I was stiff and awkward and she set me on my feet, shook her head and arms and legs and let them go limp, then she flopped back in the water and lay there. She put her hand on her chest so I would notice that she was breathing naturally. She was able to tell me with gestures what she wanted me to do, and I did it. There was authority in her manner, firmness in her hands, and before that first lesson was over, I trusted her completely. She smiled broadly when I managed to stay up for awhile without support, and then she signalled the end of the lesson.

While we were building an elaborate sand castle, my father walked down the dock with his green tackle box and fishing pole. I waved. "My Dad," I said, making sure Emily could see my lips. She smiled and nodded.

"Do you want to go fishing, Bethie?" he called, his voice sounding different across the water — distant, remote.

"No," I called back, "we're going swimming again." I pointed to Emily and myself and made swimming motions with my arms.

He nodded and lifted his arm. "Be careful," he said, and stepped down into the rowboat, almost losing his balance before he sat down. As he rowed away, I promised myself I would go with him the next time he asked.

I don't know why, but we were not a family who did many things together. I've heard it said that the Depression made families close, but it was not that way with us. For one thing, there were four years between my sister and me. There had been a baby who died two years before I was born; a girl, too. She was beautiful, I'd heard my mother say, with thick black hair and a perfect little face. Her name was Elizabeth and they named me for her; you'd think my mother would be afraid to do that, afraid it would bring bad luck.

No, we didn't do that many things together. For that matter, my parents didn't do many things together that I remember. Certainly not at the lake, where my father fished and my mother visited friends or read on the screened verandah, drinking iced tea and fanning herself with a cardboard fan with DRINK COCA COLA printed on it in red and white. She liked the stories in *Liberty* magazine and saved them all up to bring to the lake. She enjoyed all the company she had there, too. She was a woman who liked to talk, and my father was a quiet man, maybe it was years of poring over figures in the small office in the back of the Co-op Store, maybe he just got out of practice.

I discovered that first day that Emily was a fine person to build sand castles with. When we needed a flag for the turret, she raked the sand with her fingers and unearthed a small piece of silver paper, which she folded into a triangle. A quick raking on her other side produced a small twig which she split part way down with her strong fingernail, and, sliding the paper into place, she poked it into the wet sand. She laughed when the wind caught it and turned it around. The sun was hot on my neck and arms, between my shoulder-blades, and the warm wind fluttered and dried the wet sand on my legs.

Val came down to swim, walking in carefully, riffling the water with her fingers. In her white two-piece bathing suit, her blonde hair in a green net snood with small green bows on it, even I could see that she was pretty. "My sister," I told Emily, and she smiled and rolled her eyes in a complimentary way.

"Can I come with you?" I called. It was always better to ask, with Val.

"Sure. But don't splash me," she said, as I ran in. And I kept my distance, fearful she'd change her mind. I cavorted around her, telling her about the swimming lesson, telling her who Emily was, scarcely able to contain the huge bubble of joy in my stomach — I had to expand my chest to the limit to hold it. The sun, the lake, the absence of school, the swimming lesson, Emily, my sister ... sometimes things were so good you could hardly stand it. I fell in the water face down and slowly sank to the bottom, my arms flung wide to take in the whole lake, the whole world.

Emily and I went in a half dozen more times that day, and while she sat on the beach, I went on practising. By the end of the day I could float on my back easily, though I had to move my arms and legs more than Emily did.

Once, while I was in the water, two boys came down to the beach and seemed to be asking Emily to go somewhere. She jumped up and ran off with them, her long hair flying, joy in the pumping of her fat legs. They disappeared into a clump of dense bush down the beach. They were gone about twenty minutes and then Emily was running back, looking over her shoulder and waving to the boys who didn't wave back, but who were giggling hysterically as they staggered off up the beach the other way, shoving each other into the water every so often, and they weren't even in bathing suits, they were wearing pants and shirts and shoes.

I wonder if anyone else ever learned to swim as quickly and easily as I did, for there could be no other teachers like Emily. We were together every day, and almost as easily as she had taught me to float, she taught me how to breathe, how to move my arms and legs. I never wondered who had taught Emily, it seemed as if she must have been born knowing how, as if her mother had birthed her in the lake and she had swum easily from one fluid to another. Sometimes, with motions for me to stay in the shallow water and practise, she would strike straight out toward the centre of the lake until I couldn't see her for the reflection of the sun on the water. She always came back. And every day we floated, side by side, wrapped in water, the sun warm on our faces, open-beaked gulls hanging in the blue air above us.

Val got a boyfriend, a boy from the city. I didn't like him, though I couldn't have said why. He was polite and good-looking but there was something about him I didn't trust. They wound up the old Victrola gramophone on the cottage verandah and danced to Bing Crosby singing "Moonlight Bay" and "Sioux City Sue." My mother grumbled about being relegated to the back yard with her books and her visitors, but you could tell she was pleased.

More boys came for Emily, they beckoned to her from down the beach almost every day, and I soon accepted these interruptions as part of our routine. I put in the time while she was gone perfecting moats, straightening flags — we had one on every turret, all different colours — and squinting at the bushes now and then to see if she was coming. If there were more boys, Emily was gone longer. She always came back smiling, and sometimes there were leaves in her hair.

Once her father came to the beach just as Emily and two boys emerged from the trees. He was a thin, bald man with thick glasses; his hands moved so fast they were almost a blur at times, and I knew he was shouting at her in his way. Emily's hands, which were slim

129

and graceful compared to the rest of her, moved more slowly and there was no anger in her face. When he started pulling on her arm, she just shook him off, walked into the water and swam away.

Emily was not there when we went back the next year. She had been sent away to a special school for the deaf, we were told.

I could make a collage of that summer with Emily if I had to, and I know exactly how I would do it. There would be the immense shimmering blue of the lake and on the far shore, my father in the rowboat, fishing. My mother and another woman are in deck chairs, words falling out of their mouths into their laps; they are wearing dark glasses. Off to the left, my sister in her white two-piece bathing suit is dancing with her boyfriend and there are notes rising from the gramophone. From a clump of bushes on the edge of the shore, boys' faces are grinning.

And right in the centre of that blue water, Emily and I are floating, floating in the silence like a strange pair of sea creatures. Emily's eyes, the colour of the lake, are open, and her long hair is drifting out around her face.

IT BODDER ME

GLEN A. SORESTAD

The young attractive physiotherapist came to a stop before Ward 218. She inhaled deeply, set her lips firmly and strode determinedly into the ward and directly across the room to the corner bed.

"Good morning, Mr. Desrochers. It's time for your exercises again. How are you feeling today?"

"Worse," was the reply.

"Well, Mr. Desrochers, I'm trying to help you so you'll feel better. Now would you sit up on the edge of the bed and we'll try some deep breaths." She leaned over the bed to offer her arm to the man who lay motionless on his back on the hospital bed, clad in hospital pyjamas and gown.

Desrochers brushed her arm away abruptly and struggled slowly to a sitting position with his feet dangling over the side of the bed.

If the young physiotherapist regarded this independence on the part of her patient an affront, she did not show it. Rather, she seemed to take it for granted. Her facial expression still retained its determined character, as if she had decided that from this point things were going to be done her way, or not at all.

"Have you been coughing up phlegm, Mr. Desrochers?"

Desrochers ignored her.

"Have you coughed up anything?"

"Yeah, I cough."

"Good. Now let's see you breathe in deeply through your nose and breathe out through your mouth."

Desrochers breathed in and out.

"Breathe *deeply*, Mr. Desrochers."

Desrochers breathed again.

"Oh, come on, Mr. Desrochers. You can do much better than that."

"It bodder me," said Desrochers without bothering to look up at the physiotherapist.

"I know it bothers you, Mr. Desrochers. But you have to clear the congestion from your lungs. Even if it hurts a little."

Desrochers gave no indication that he either agreed or disagreed, or even understood.

"Now try it again, Mr. Desrochers, and this time breathe *deeply*."

Desrochers breathed more deeply this time. The physiotherapist placed her hands lightly on each side of Desrochers' chest along the sides of the rib cage.

"Don't touch me there. It bodder me."

She removed her hands.

"I can hear the phlegm rattling in your chest, Mr. Desrochers. You have to cough that up now." She reached to the small table beside the bed and extracted several facial tissues from a box. "Now *cough*, Mr. Desrochers."

Desrochers made an imperceptible sound.

"*Cough*, Mr. Desrochers."

The sound this time was barely more audible.

"Come on, Mr. Desrochers. You've *got* to cough it up, you know. I know it hurts, but you'll have to try harder. Now cough it up from down here." She indicated by laying her hand on the upper part of her stomach.

Desrochers coughed again. The sound was there, but it was all in the throat.

"*You're not trying*, Mr. Desrochers. Now try harder."

Desrochers coughed. The same as the last one. "No good," he said resignedly. "Nothing there."

"Yes, *there is*, Mr. Desrochers. You're just not trying hard enough."

"You go now. I cough later," Desrochers offered hopefully.

"No, Mr. Desrochers. I want you to cough up some of that phlegm before I go. Now *try again*."

"It bodder me. Hurt like hell down here." Desrochers indicated his right side below his armpit where a week previously the surgeons had removed the upper half of his lung in an attempt to check the cancerous growth that threatened to choke the whole lung.

"I know it hurts, Mr. Desrochers. But you won't get better until you clear out your lungs. You *have* to cough that phlegm out."

"I cough after you go. Nothing there now."

The physiotherapist shrugged her shoulders in resignation. It seemed that each session with Mr. Desrochers ended the same way, with her in a state of complete frustration and Desrochers as unperturbed as she was agitated. She stared in silence at the aging Cree as if reluctant to let it end as it had on both previous sessions. Yet she felt certain that nothing she could say would have any great impression on him. It was almost, she thought, as if Desrochers was unaware of the seriousness of his condition. She had tried to explain to him the danger of pneumonia from the congestion in his lungs. She was not sure whether he failed to understand, or whether it just didn't matter to him. She was not even certain whether Desrochers was aware of the nature of the operation which had been performed on him. Several times in the past two sessions he had referred to the hurt in his side, both back and front, and she had acknowledged that the operation had caused it.

"Mr. Desrochers, have you been drinking lots of fluids? Water, milk, tea, coffee, juice?"

"I just like tea. Not coffee. Coffee bodder me."

"Well, I want you to drink plenty of fluids, Mr. Desrochers. It'll help you. Drink all you can, especially in the evening before you go to bed."

"Tea is good. I drink tea. Don't need nothing else. On trapline I make tea. Tea save me once." Desrochers looked at the young blonde-haired woman, as if almost embarrassed by his own sudden volubility.

The physiotherapist appeared to lose some of her composure in the firm hold with which the deep hazel eyes of the sixty-five-year-old Indian had fixed her. It was really the first thing she could recall Desrochers saying about his life. She felt an inner urge to follow up this revelation with the natural question, but instead she glanced at her watch and realized that she should be moving on to her next therapy patient.

"Well, Mr. Desrochers, drink as much tea as you like. And any other liquids you can. And lots at night before bedtime. I'll see you again this afternoon and we'll got for a walk and try to cough some more. You can lie down again now." She offered her arm again but once again he ignored it and stretched out carefully without her assistance.

As she turned and walked away she heard Desrochers say to no one in particular, "Tea is good."

The early spring weather was unseasonably mild when Desrochers reached the trap sets along Blackstone River. It was nearly noon as he reached the river's edge and he stopped to heat a tin pail of tea. Firewood was plentiful in the heavy coniferous forest land of northern Saskatchewan. Forest and waters, furs and fish, the only environment with which Louis Desrochers was really familiar and of which he was a completely integral part. He had set his first traps and snares as a small boy, taught patiently by his own father. And Louis Desrochers had been trapping each winter since that time. And he had passed on his knowledge of the wild to his two sons who also ran traplines now. But Desrochers' trapline was the same one he had always had, a legacy to him from his father by the right of family. For fifty years now he had wintered in the same cabin, his father's before him, on the small lake, and had made his livelihood from the winter's catch of furs. At the end of the season Desrochers hauled his furs out to the town of Lac La Ronge where he spent the summer, occasionally acting as a fishing guide for one of the fishing lodges centered there.

Desrochers sat back on the log beside the little fire and rolled a cigarette. He smoked leisurely and watched the flames dwindle as the fire burned down. The hot tea had revived him, warmed him, and now he glanced at the sky and decided that it was time to move. Time to cross the Blackstone and check all the trap sets on the other side, following the usual loop which would bring him back to recross the river at this same spot in about three hours. He left the tea pail beside the fire. One gnarled piece of firewood was left by his tea pail. He tossed it on the coals and left.

Midway across the Blackstone, Desrochers noted the ominous crackling of the river ice. It was too early for the ice to be breaking up, he reflected without alarm. The early spring thaw must have weakened it somewhat, he realized, but the ice never broke up until much later in the spring, at least a month yet, he knew. Nevertheless, he knew the ice sounds very well and he didn't like the sounds he heard as he finally gained the far bank of the Blackstone. Safe on the Blackstone's opposite bank, he dismissed the ice warnings from his mind completely and strode off on the familiar trail along the river's twisting course toward the first trap set.

When Desrochers had completed the trap loop and was approaching the same crossing again it was late afternoon. He was in good spirits and carrying a better than usual catch of fur with him. As he stepped out on the river ice, he had completely forgotten the noon crossing and was thinking only of making a quick cup of tea on the opposite side at the site of the morning fire where he had left the tea pail.

The ice complained even more vociferously now than it had the few hours previously. For the first time Desrochers had a definite feeling of alarm. This was not good, he thought. Never before had he ever heard the ice speak its warnings like this so early in the year. In a month, Desrochers knew, a man would be a fool not to listen to the voices from the river ice. But now? It was too early. And anyway, he must cross. He walked gingerly toward the opposite side, trying to shut his ears to the river voices that were telling him of his danger. Three-quarters of the way across the Blackstone, the ice gave way abruptly and Desrochers plunged through.

The unexpectedness of his breaking through the ice shocked him, but it was the coldness of the water that was the greatest shock. He knew the water would be cold, but now as he clung to the ice's edge he realized that a man could not survive long in such bone-chilling wetness. The Blackstone, he knew, was no more than five feet in depth, except for occasional holes where the depth might reach six or eight feet. Here at this crossing he knew the river was four or five feet deep and he had no fear of drowning. It was the coldness that was quickly sapping his strength. Desrochers knew the fire of pure fear racing through his mind. Could he pull himself out of the numbing, paralysing coldness before his body was completely immobilized? And what then? This thought exploded on him as he broke and rebroke the ice in his frantic attempts to gain the bank. He blotted out the consequences of his deadly exposure and concentrated his whole being on getting out of the frigid water. Already he was aware that he was losing the feeling in his legs and feet.

A partly submerged tree projected a branch through the river's crust and Desrochers plunged steadily toward it, finally lunging desperately at it and gasping with relief as it held. He pulled himself out and crawled the remaining few yards to the bank. He clambered up the bank and got to his feet. He took two steps forward and pitched face down in the snow. His legs had no feeling. He had no control over them. Now Desrochers knew his worst fears. He must get to his feet and walk. He must get the blood circulating through his body. Freezing to death was imminent if he failed. He slowly gained his feet again, but it was as if his legs and feet were not there at all. Much as he willed them to move he could not seem to transmit his desperate urging to those benumbed limbs. He stumbled forward and fell full-length again.

135

Fire. He must make a fire. He must warm himself, restore feeling to his numbed limbs. He knew now the ageless instinct that coursed through every living being. Survival. He mustn't die. And he must make a fire to survive. The little container of wooden matches in his pants pocket would be soaked, he knew. No help there. He got to his knees and began to crawl on all fours toward the noon campfire site. It was his only hope.

When he plunged his hands into the ashes he was rewarded by the warmth of several smouldering coals. His hands were burned slightly, but he didn't really notice this. All he knew was that he now had a chance. Why had he thrown the gnarled old branch on the fire when he left to cross the river? What inner force or power had caused him to do this, to perform this casual and unnatural act, one which he would seldom do in winter and never in summer? Whatever had prompted the act had provided him with his last hope, his last chance to live. He blew across the coals and was rewarded with wisps of smoke and the slightest glow. He plunged his hands deep into the snow to the ground below to gather moss to feed the fire. Suddenly Desrochers knew he would live. His movements became calm and deliberate and even though his hands were also numbing he had no doubts at all that he had cheated death.

Later, when the fire was blazing fiercely and the combined heat from the blaze as well as the rubbing and kneading of his legs had brought some circulation back to his legs, Desrochers had time to reflect on the experience. It was clear to him that someone or something that he couldn't quite understand had controlled the whole incident. Perhaps the whole of his life. Maybe all men's lives as well. The priest had said such things to him before. And he had read the prayer book in Cree where these things were said. Now he believed them. It was a good thing he had decided to have tea this morning, he thought. He thought that making tea was something a man did to warm his body and quench his thirst. Now he knew that God meant him to drink tea this morning for another reason as well. Desrochers was amazed at this insight into the workings of divine power. He wouldn't ever forget this day, he knew. Tea was a good thing.

"Good morning, Mr. Desrochers," said the physiotherapist. "Are you feeling better today?"

Desrochers was sitting up in bed when she walked into the ward. He was reading a battered black-covered book intently, his lips moving steadily and his right index finger tracing its way across the page.

"Not so good," Desrochers replied without looking up. He continued to read.

The young woman stood beside the bed and peered closely at the book. The characters on the yellowing pages were strange to her.

"What language is that, Mr. Desrochers?"

"Cree." Again he answered without taking his eyes from his reading.

"That looks hard to read."

"Not so hard." Desrochers now looked up at the physiotherapist. "I could teach you — easy."

"Maybe. I have enough trouble reading English, Mr. Desrochers."

Desrochers looked at her skeptically, then resumed his reading.

"Mr. Desrochers, you haven't been smoking, have you?" She had noticed several butts in the ashtray on the bed-side table.

"Sure."

"But Mr. Desrochers, don't you know you're *not supposed to smoke?* It's not good for you."

"It don't bodder me."

"But it does, Mr. Desrochers. How can we clear up the congestion in your chest if you keep smoking?" She felt the frustration building once more. How was she to explain to this stubborn old man that smoking had been the cause of his problems, the reason for his being here, the danger that threatened to kill him. "You won't get better if you keep smoking, Mr. Desrochers. How can we let you go back home until you're better? You better not smoke any more, Mr. Desrochers."

Desrochers looked up at the young woman. What could she know of the things that were good for a man like him? God knew. But this woman only knew how to make his chest hurt doing things there was no reason to do. He always smoked. God didn't object. Even the priest smoked.

"I smoke since I was five. It don't bodder me."

The physiotherapist shrugged. What was the use? Desrochers was unflappable. He was stubborn. He was independent. Nothing she could say seemed to have the slightest effect on him. She could get him to do some of the exercises she wanted him to do, but she always felt that when he did co-operate with her it was on his terms and not hers. It was as if he were simply trying to keep her reasonably satisfied, or maybe it was humouring her. She couldn't say that he was defying her, but she realized that in every way Desrochers was asserting his own particular individuality, his complete self-reliance. She couldn't help but be impressed at how this old trapper, three hundred miles from home, completely away from his natural surroundings in a totally alien environment, could still maintain such an imperturbable independence. He amazed her, frustrated her and thwarted her efforts to help him. Yet she somehow felt that he had to do this, that this was absolutely essential to him, what he must do to maintain his identity. Desrochers was sixty-five, according to her file on him, and he was not about to change his ideas or habits to please her, or anyone, she realized.

"Have you been coughing much since yesterday?"

"I cough. Look, I show you." He indicated the small paper bag attached to the side of his bed near the pillow. It was half-filled with soiled facial tissues.

"Good, Mr. Desrochers. Now let's try coughing some more, shall we?" There wasn't much conviction in her voice today.

Desrochers shrugged lightly. He swung his legs carefully over the side of the bed and began the pretended deep breathing in preparation for whatever coughs he might be able to produce for her. He wondered if his sons had left Lac La Ronge for their trap lines yet.

HOW THE WEST WAS WON

EUGENE STICKLAND

Hip-Hip-HURRAY!
Happy Days!
Salad Days!
Boyohboyohboyohboy
Goin' a be a lot a winners tonight.
Some lucky person somewhere
A lot of dreams hanging tonight
In the balance of a
Drop.
THE MACHINES HAVE BEEN ACTIVATED!
What's it goin'a what's it goin'a
Be?
And it's a "5"
    girl holds up a "five"
One more
What's it goin'a be?
And it's an "8"
    girl holds up an "eight"
Some happy winner somewhere
    Priestly watches on
    sans slippers
    sans ticket

And we haven't even started the big ones yet
Heading this time for
ONE MILLION DOLLARS!
Now we're looking at a
What is it?
I can't make it out.
Another "8"?
No no
It's a "3"
    girl holds up a "three"
And the crowd cheers
      Priestly knew, of course, all along that it was indeed a "three"
      and not an "eight", sitting there vacuously
      sans slippers
      sans ticket
      can't really be blamed for his terrible fate, sitting there as he
      does in his threadbare bathrobe gazing blankly across the
      expanse of worn carpet at the gaping shadows on the not
      quite antique black and white, set not religiously upon an
      inverted green plastic container for two litre sized milk
      cartons which he had not two weeks previous scavenged in a
      darkening alley behind the local co-op store
Ah the dream tonight of becoming a MILLIONAIRE!
And the crowd is whipped to a fever pitch longing sweating
drooling over their tickets
Just takes one to win
But you can't win without a ticket
    Priestly
You need a ticket
You need a ticket
Buy a ticket
Just one ticket
One little ticket
    Priestly
      tugs at his three or four days growth of pepper-coloured
      stubble that for three or four days has aggravated the tender
      skin of his cheeks and chin and looks at his wrist watch and
      stretches yawns thinks out loud perhaps for the benefit of the
      cat "morning comes *so* early" and the cat it would have to be
      said is appreciative of this small effort at communication and
      seems to answer by stretching out an arm at an impossible
      angle from the entanglement of legs arms head and tail and
      matted fur
Mr. Eddy Savilto of Brandon, Manitoba.

Hi!

I'm going to put it to you bluntly, Mr. Savilto:

Did you ever in your wildest dreams ever ever think that you'd be a winner? A . . . MILLIONAIRE?

Well . . . I look at it this way . . . If you don't buy a tigget . . . how the hell you goin' ta win anyway?

Good thinking, Mr. Savilto! It's thinking like that that changed your life.

It sure is, you know? I was sitting at home one day and not knowing what to do with my last five dollars. Do I buy beer? Or do I buy a tigget? Well . . . you can't win without a tigget . . . so I bought the tigget . . . And now I got all the beer I can drink.

Crowd laughs.

Smart thinking, Mr. Ed Savilto of Brandon, Manitoba.

You can buy a lot of beer with a million buggs.

Thank you, Mr. . .

I mean, you might as well pick your ass and hope to find a million buggs up there . . . that's how good your chances are without a tigget . . . Shit . . . you don't stand a hope in hell if you're too fuggin' cheap to go out and drop five lousy buggs to get a shot at a million . . .

Thank . . .

I mean a million buggs is a million buggs . . . am I right?

Crowd cheers.

    slowly the picture fades and is replaced with the row of shining spitting electronic grasshoppers and Priestly wonders out loud as if for the benefit of the cat "I wonder if there is something to this lottery business after all" but the cat merely casts a cold eye back at Priestly and arches the mass of fur and bone and sinew for an ecstatic moment and shrugs leaving Priestly alone with his thoughts and the worn out black and white again

A lot of dreams hanging

In the balance of a

Drop.

One more

What will it be?

And it's another "2"

Amazing isn't it, the number of "2"s we've had tonight

Some happy winner somewhere

    girl smiles holding up a "two" which she has delicately plucked from the snout of the grasshopper whose red light begins to pulse again *even though* the numbered ball has already dropped

A SECOND BALL DROPS OUT!!
And it's a "0"
And a hush falls over the studio audience as it sits stunned at the
failure of grasshopper number "four" which has erringly dropped
two balls
The host points an accusing finger at the innocent from the studio
audience
Did you push the red button twice?
No! No! cries the innocent cowering from the formidable wrath of
the not smiling now host who with his back to the rank of
grasshoppers is unaware of the goings-on on stage all of which is
captured on live t.v. for the benefit of the home viewing audience
P.S. We're you ever in the Services?

 starts at the strange scene on the black and white the
grasshoppers beneath their halos of flashing red begin to spin
their drums with more than reckless abandon good god! the
numbers in the drums the drums themselves the grasshoppers
themselves will surely be destroyed and the hostess not
smiling now runs back and forth in a desperate but futile
effort to fight excess of energy with excess of energy the
grasshoppers begin to shake and tilt dangerously as if at any
minute the momentum of their spinning drums might cause
them to fall from their moorings but she stops at number
"four" who seems to be the ring-leader of this little uprising
and for some unknown reason perhaps in an attempt to get at
the heart of the matter she shoves her arm into its snout and
is sucked into the opening by the vacuum pressure which has
been created by the velocity of the spinning drum and some
of her can be seen coast-to-coast spinning at maytag speed
while some of her most of her an arm a leg the better part of
the head slides down the metal torso and falls to the floor
before the vicious number "four" like scraps on the butcher's
floor while the host in the by and by frantically runs to save
the hostess and stupidly suffers roughly the same fate at the
snout of the canivorous number "four" and slowly the picture
fades
Priestly sits
sans slippers
sans ticket
last cigarette burning all too quickly down towards his elegant
yet nicotine stained black in some places even "my my my I
must do something about those terrible stains!" fingers and all
that can be seen in the darkness of the room is the fiery glow
of Priestly's last cigarette and the glimmer of two saucer-like

cat's eyes coming ever closer to Priestly through the darkness of the room perhaps she is preparing an attack perhaps she has bared her claws and is now preparing to rip out Priestly's eyes with those sharp little knives of hers but no and once again Priestly thinks out loud from the abyss of his shabby living room perhaps for the benefit of the cat who has curled up in the warmth of Priestly's crotch "maybe there *is* something to this lottery business after all"

DAS ENGELEIN KOMMT

GERTRUDE STORY

When my sister Elsa was a baby she was an angel and my father called her das Engelein. At our house people never spoke in German. My mother would not allow it. Only my father ever did, and we children could hardly understand him. I should not say me. I will tell you later. It was the fury of his life having non-German children. One of the furies. He had several. The Brotherhood of Man was another. My father loved the Brotherhood of Man with an ardent, vocal passion.

He loved his daughters, too, I suppose, but they never knew it. He loved his son, and his daughters knew it. He loved him like Isaac loved his Jacob or like Abraham his Isaac. My father never sacrificed his Floydie on any altar; never even tried to. But he killed his daughters a thousand times over, and this is the story of the last time he killed my sister Elsa in her snow-white Engelein gown, her wings spread and ready to soar at the church Christmas concert one year in the sandy, dry, hard farming district where we used to live.

It had to be in German. That whole church concert had to be in German. Some of the kids did O.K.; they had mothers who hardly spoke English. In that community the fathers went out into the world and did the business and learned to speak the language of business. The mothers stayed home and plucked geese, and made quilts and perogies and babies, and crooned them to sleep with Komm' Herr

144

Jesu, and sent them there with a few slaps to the ear if the child went unwilling.

So it was at our house, too. Except for the German and the Jesu. My mother didn't believe in either one. She had had it different at home. Her father was just as German as anybody else in that settlement but his mind had a different order. His daughter was to go to Normal School and be a teacher but she chose Papa instead. No wonder, I suppose. Papa was tall and black and imposing and he courted every woman in the district atop his large white stallion, taking them for rides into the hills to show them the wood violets.

I think the violets stopped when my mother agreed to come into his kitchen, but his passions did not. At least I know we had violin and lots of talk and booming laughter when the neighbors came, and cold lips and steel-blue eyes when they left again.

It was a hard life in a lot of ways, but this is not that story. I tell it to you this way, though, because it is very hard, at fifty, to keep it going well. To keep the order. I've had too many other voices inside my head for so long and Papa bellering from his bed, after Mama died and the third white stallion threw him, for tea and beef broth and a pen to write his newest orders.

Papa was a difficult man. He lived for too many years. I looked after him for twenty-three of them. Mama, I think now sometimes, almost had it easy. She spoke back, you see, and the hate did not gather, black and hard and festering, around her heart as it did mine.

But I want to tell you about Elsa. I think that is what she means me to do when she comes now and stands by my side when I am writing away the blackness and drinking the coffee Papa forbade in this house because it repelled him. She has been dead thirty-eight years now, I counted it out today, and I suppose she has forgotten how to speak. On account of not knowing the sacred language, ha ha, I never believed it. Papa used to say it was all in German up there, a German preacher once told him.

For all these years I was careful not to care, but now I see that Elsa did not even go there. She couldn't have. The church says not, and they should be right on some things; it is too terrible otherwise to try to live.

But all these years I thought it was an accident and I'm sure Papa did, too. But I think now Mama knew. I do not want to do the thinking sometimes, there is a danger in it, but I think now she knew because it raised a real uproar the way she went to bed and stayed there the day it happened and wouldn't get up for the funeral.

But that's ahead of it again. I need the order. It is harder than to have it in your head and know it, this setting of it down. Once I wanted to be a writer and read King Arthur over and over until I knew the order of telling things but now I cannot keep it straight.

It goes like this though. We always went to church. All but our mother. Papa said we had to go to church and learn the glory; it was not safe to live in this world otherwise. And the glory was only good if it came in German. It was holy that way. It was important because it had to do with Christus and the angels and your holy German soul. The words you spoke in the old tongue, he said, helped to get you the glory.

That pastor, I knew him, said so, and Papa believed him, but our mother didn't. She said it was a peasant's attitude and it was either all true in any language or it was not all true and maybe none of it true and so what, it didn't put bread on the table; but you sure couldn't break it up into German and English and French, it wasn't logical. And Papa said what was logical was if she allowed his daughters to speak German at the supper table, but the Schroeders seemed to be such English boot-lickers it seemed to be more than a man could expect to have the old tongue spoken around his own fireside. And our mother said it seemed to be Schroeder money brought the coal to keep the fire going in it. And Papa said, Yes, yes, rub it in; and he took his box full of blue socialist tracts and saddled his white stallion with the red wild eyes and rode to Elmyra Bitner's to discuss the Brotherhood of Man.

And Mama would scrub hard at the fading red apples on the oilcloth on the kitchen table and make mouths at the way the corners were wearing through and she'd say, Come on, girls, we'll make brown sugar fudge tonight.

And our mother made brown sugar fudge with butter and walnuts most nights he did that. And sometimes when my sister Elsa peered too long into the night from the kitchen window straining to see his white stallion coming back out of the dark night my mother would say, Don't be silly, girl, do you think a bear will get him or something, he's only gone to get educated, come on and we'll make ourselves some popcorn.

But Elsa wouldn't. She just turned her back on our mother and went and rearranged Papa's pipes neatly beside the family picture taken when there was only Papa and our mother and Elsa and me because our sister Laura already lived just at Grampa Schroeder's, she had to, Papa said she was not his child. I hope that is the order. It seems to fit here. Laura is important; she got lost in a different way. And while Elsa looked at herself being an Engelein in the family picture on the sideboard our mother and I would pop popcorn, shelling it first, plink-plank into a pan off the cob first, and heating the heavy iron frying pan on the back of the stove while we did.

Not Floydie, though. Floydie was a boy and anyway he was young and fast asleep by that time of night. But Elsa would only pick away at her bowlful now and again and when Mama said, Come on, eat up, it's just the way you like it, Elsa would get that tight look around her eyes and say, No, I'm saving it for Floydie. And Mama would say, He's spoiled enough, and Elsa would say, You don't like anybody, do you? And she'd go back to the window and look some more for Papa and his stallion and she only left her place when Floydie cried and then she always ran to him before Mama could go.

And yet Floydie was the reason, I don't care, why Elsa had to look out into the dark night for Papa with her pink barn-goose eyes that got teary from too much watching. And Floydie was the reason Grampa Schroeder got so mad he kept giving our mother money to buy us girls new dresses for the school picnic and the church concert. Floydie was Papa's Sunny Boy Cereal and Elsa used to be his Engelein, but now she was just a girl who had grown a long Schroeder neck and couldn't do arithmetic.

She couldn't learn her German piece, either. For the church Christmas concert you had to learn to speak a piece in German, no matter what. You had to or your folks were shamed for ever. Even my mother went to the church Christmas concert. It was called the Tannenbaum and nobody missed going. It was holy, and not even the littlest ones expected to see Santa.

It was as if to say the white light of Jesus shone those nights. The church was lit with candles. Not even the coal oil lamps were lit and certainly not the gas mantel lanterns with their piercing twin eyes. Only candles were holy.

And that year, that last year, Elsa said she wanted to be an angel. An angel in German yet, and with twenty-eight lines to speak. When Pastor asked who would take the part Elsa's hand shot up and it surprised me. Elsa was not that way. She would rather not speak, even in English, and to do anything in German killed her.

Especially speak to Papa. When you have been an Engelein and aren't any longer, to stand before Papa and say Ihr Kinderlein kommet, zur Bethlehem Stall into his pale slough-ice eyes doesn't help to make your wings grow, and if you're one to have had the wings clipped you know this is the right order to say it.

Kinderlein, not Kidderlein, Papa told her. Baytlah-hem, not Bethlehem; what do you want to put a thuh in it for? The people will think you're not raised right. Now start the first verse again from the beginning and stand straight and speak it right. Twenty-eight lines only, a big girl like you, and you can't even learn it.

Hellslänzendem was the word that did it. Hellzadem, Elsa said.

147

Who wouldn't? It's hard in German to get all the zeds and enns and urrs in, and lots of times the Germans don't even care when they talk it. But when it comes to their kids, watch out, they're supposed to all speak like preachers.

I talked German in my head all the time. Nobody knew it. One of the voices in my head was a German man and he told jokes sometimes in German on the pastor when church went on too long. Hier ist mir ein alter Fart, he'd say sometimes, and I would try not to smile; to smile was dangerous. And the voice would tell me to go look up Fart in Papa's German dictionary when we got home. But we never touched Papa's books, that was dangerous, too, and I would have if I'd wanted, but I didn't want to care about it.

Elsa cared too much. It was dangerous. Day by day she sewed on her Engelein costume, looking quite often at the picture on the sideboard. She sewed in the parlour where you weren't supposed to use thread because it worked itself into the carpet. Mama told her she could sit there when she caught her sewing at four o'clock in the morning once by the kitchen lamp. Its flame flickered pale and yellow.

Silly goose, Mama told her, it's too hard on the eyes and I could do it on the machine in a minute. But Elsa only turned her back on Mama, pretending she was looking for the scissors, and said, I want to do it. And she'd show Papa after supper how it was coming and he'd say, Yes, yes, yes, but you're not gonna spend your life in a dress factory, how's the piece coming? And Elsa would stand there and speak, one angel wing drooping. Bei des Lichtleins hellzadem she'd get to and Papa would look up quick and say, Hellslänz—, hellslänz—, put the zed in it; how come you can't remember; people will think you aren't raised right.

And then he'd call Floydie to him for a game of clap-handies and Mama would say from the parlour door, Come work in the kitchen, the light's better. But Elsa would take her piece out of her apron pocket where she kept it to learn even in the toilet, I saw her once, and her mouth made the words but she did not say them out loud and she watched Papa and Floydie whenever they laughed until Papa said, You could likely learn better in the kitchen. And then she folded her piece up and put it in her pocket and went.

And on the Tannenbaum night she spoke it pretty well, so I don't know why Papa had to do it. The candles were lit in the church and you could almost smell the glory and people shook hands with everybody they could reach even after they got sitting down in the pews, the fat ones straining hard over their chests to shake with ones sitting behind them.

Grown-ups even shook with two-year-olds, and graced each

other fröhliche Weihnachts whether they were mad at each other or not. And you could smell the Jap oranges from the brown paper bags, each one packed two man's hands full of peanuts and almonds and striped Christmas candy made into curlicues almost the size and shape of Floydie's new bow tie, and each one with two Jap oranges at the bottom so that you had to dig through all the other good stuff if you wanted to eat them first. Germans never were stingy when it was nuts and candy and they had the money.

Only we never were allowed to open our bags until we got home. But that night we girls were wearing our new dresses Grampa Schroeder had given the money for and Floydie looked like a prince, true enough, like Papa said, in his royal blue breeches and snow white shirt with the ruffles. And Mama looked nice and came along to the concert and people graced her, too, and only a few made remarks like, Well at least we see you Christmas. So it was all good, very good, for once, and Elsa spoke up, spoke right up Ihr Kinderlein kommet only with not enoughs zeds and enns in it. But she spoke it clear and good, her eyes shining and her hands folded and looking up into the candelabra so that her eyes became two candles, too. But the trouble was, her one wing drooped because she would not let Mama help her sew.

And Mrs. Bitner said afterwards to Papa, Now Floydie, you tell that wife of yours I got time on my hands I could help her next Chrissmas with the kids' costooms if she wants. And Mama was standing right there and Mrs. Bitner turned to her next and graced her and maybe never knew her, Mama hardly ever came to church, but Mama said later she did.

And Papa said it didn't matter, why worry about that, the point was people thought they weren't raised right, how come she let the kid show up with a costume like that, it wasn't the first time, either. We were on the way home and the horses' hooves sounded crispcrunch on the hard-packed snow of the road, and the traces jingled like bells although Papa wouldn't put brass bells on the harness like a lot of men did, he said it was frippery. And I tried to think about the Jap oranges and how they'd be when we got home and Papa let us open our bags. I had to think hard about them; to think about Elsa's drooping wing was too dangerous.

But when we got home and Papa had carried Floydie inside and us girls and Mama had our coats off and all, Elsa wouldn't even open her bag. And Mama was undressing Floydie fast asleep on the kitchen table, and Mama had one eye on Elsa sitting silent on a hard chair by the Quebec heater with her piece in her hand, and Mama looked real nice, very nice, she hardly ever dressed up.

And Papa came up behind her, his fur coat and hat still on

because he still had to go out and do the horses. And he laid his hand on Mama's shoulder and said, It's always better after church. And he showed his hard white even teeth under his silky smooth moustache, he was a very good looker always. And Mama just picked Floydie up and walked out from under his hand and said over her shoulder, Elmyra Bitner has time on her hands I hear.

And Papa turned quick to the door and stepped on the paper bag with the costumes in it, I guess I should not have left it there. And he kicked at the bag and it split and the Engelein costume got tangled in his church overshoes and he grabbed it and threw it in the corner and didn't bother putting on his barn boots because he knew he wasn't going to the barn, I guess. And he drove out the yard, the harness traces clanging no rhythm, no whatsoever rhythm, because the horses were going too hard, and it was too cold for their lungs to go hard. Like Grampa Schroeder said, Papa was not much good on horses.

And Mama came out of the bedroom and picked up the Engelein costume and said, Never mind, Grampa said you looked real pretty. And Elsa grabbed the costume out of her hands and scrunchled it all up tight and held it to her and went to the window to strain her eyes into the night to see Papa going.

And there was no moon.

And that night, before Papa got home from Elmyra Bitner's, Elsa took the key to the box stall and went in to the stallion. And Papa found her when he got home. And afterwards he would not even sell the stallion.

And when we moved to town a little later because Grampa Schroeder said so, he kept it at Elmyra Bitner's and went out from town Sundays to go to German church and ride his snow white stallion.

The words are said now. They are in order I think and it does not seem too dangerous to have them down on paper. And Elsa does not speak yet, but I somehow think, now the words are all in order, if I just sit here and do not rearrange them, and think very hard on Papa, that she will nod and go.

UNTITLED

ANNE SZUMIGALSKI

A man looked down into the handsome blue eyes of the woman he was making love to. In her left eye he was surprised to see a tiny man very much like himself. Only this one was fully dressed in trousers and a blue jacket and was sitting dejectedly on a three-legged stool. His arms were folded across his chest.

The woman blinked her eyes, and it seemed to the man that her dark lashes were the bars of the gaol cell that the tiny fellow was locked up in. "You have a prisoner in your left eye," said the man to his mistress. She didn't understand, but imagined that the remark must be some sort of compliment, for after all he *was* making love to her. And so she smiled vaguely and ecstatically up at him. "How happy I am with you," she murmured.

The man could not take his mind off the poor little captive, but still he *was* in the act of making love. And so he moaned softly to show his mistress how much pleasure she was giving him.

When the woman again opened her eyes she saw her lover leaning over her, gazing intently at her face. "Come here," he said brusquely; he took her head roughly between his hands and jerked it towards him. The woman was startled at his coldness and violence.

151

She began to weep with indignation. "Keep still you bitch," shouted the man. When at last he managed to hold down her head and turn back her left eyelid there was nothing there but a blue eye, its edges red with fury. The man had never felt so chagrined. He scrabbled about amongst the bedclothes searching desperately for the tears his mistress had just shed. For perhaps the little man, who looked so much like himself, was drowning somewhere between the crumpled sheets.

FAT

GEOFFREY URSELL

Draped on either side with immaculate white cloth, the lower torso, flat, at rest, floating on a sheen of silver metal, almost imperceptibly inflates and falls, inflates and falls. A figure, also draped in folds of cloth (immaculate and white), and masked (the mask is green), and capped (the cap is white), approaches from behind. Plastic gloves caress the long and slender fingers, which, in one hand poise, like a pen, a small, delicately-bladed knife. Which must not be a knife. For, when some other hands (plastic gloves caressing long and slender fingers), reaching in from right, deliver pale, yellow-whitish strips, the figure with the knife (not knife?), taking them, with motions graceful, swift, inserts and seals them into place within the waiting, somehow open flesh.

The torso grows, the skin begins to stretch. The knife (not knife) sliding underneath the strips, fusing cell to cell, fusing countless cells, the unseen, the frailest of capillaries joined in careful strokes. Magic! The passive torso builds, mounds, stretches smooth across the top, sags around the sides, folding down upon itself. The figure moves, always sure, precise in gestures, sealing flesh to flesh. Magic! Magic! Magic! The bellybutton lifts, rises now almost half an inch above the summit: the erect nipple of some magnificent, massive breast.

Until at last, seen from above, there just remains the cut-out shape of a waning moon, below and reaching around the nipple, thirty-six inches from tip to tip and eighteen more across the widest centre span. Open to air, the flesh there, quivering, pale, awaits the benediction of the skin.

This the figure, benevolent, provides: gathering, from hands offering them up, the three thinner arcs of moon, laying them upon the wound, the (not knife) easing them down, gently fashioning under them adhesion, blissful fusion. Then, all laid in place, secure, the not knife strokes in parallel sweeps one time, twice, a third, and, oh, a last, and skin now forms a pure and perfect veil over flesh.

The image flickered, ceased. And Dr. D., profoundly, sighed. "How beautiful," he thought, "how very, very, beautiful."

Reluctantly, he pressed a button on the control panel at the side of his lounge-recliner and the screen silently lifted itself up and out of sight, leaving a bare, cream-coloured wall at the end of the room. With a simultaneous push of three more buttons, he 1) lowered a painting — a massive Rubens oil of several women, lovely, billowing women resting near the edge of a heavy, placid stream (the trees bulging with leaves, the ponderous clouds, the thickly tufted grass an echoing backdrop for the bodies) — over the plexiglass covering of the projection booth behind him; 2) set in motion the rheostat switch that smoothly, gradually made his office light again; and 3) slid apart the pendulous, plush, dark purple velvet drapes that had been covering the wall of floor-to-ceiling windows. Through which the afternoon sun, that would have been dazzling had it not been diffused by the dark, non-reflecting, tempered glass here on the top floor of the 90-storey office tower, now flowed into his room.

Dr. D. pressed the button that tilted his lounge-recliner from a semi-prone to an upright position, and, turning to the left, slid to his feet. "Time," he promised himself, "time for something to eat." He ambled over to the alcove on the wall parallel to the windows, to the upright freezer. He opened the door, considered the assortment of frozen pies, frozen cakes, frozen rolls, fudgsicles and revels, ice cream made with real cream, finally selecting a butter cake with chocolate-cream icing and marshmallow filling. He put it in the micro-wave oven beside the freezer, turned the timing switch, pressed a button, waited. The oven clicked off, tinkled a tiny bell.

He removed the cake, its plastic tray neither warm nor cold to his touch, peeled the lid away. He licked off the icing that clung to it, tossed the lid towards the open-topped, plastic-bag-lined, teakwood wastebasket. Then, bending the tray down and away from one end of the cake, he started to eat, pushing the rich, thick mixture into his mouth. He turned back towards the windows, slowly walked in their direction. Crumbs of yellow-whitish cake and dabs of chocolate icing fell from his lips into the dark brown, deep shag rug, the crumbs leaving a trail like dandruff, the icing instantly lost to sight.

Outside, in the truly dazzling light, three flying saucers drifted. They passed from right to left, through the field of vision offered by Dr. D.'s windows, disappeared ... after a moment or two returned (from left to right), hovered. One did several flip-flops, lazily, like a cat rolling on its back, on its front, on its back, all in the same place, then stopped. Dr. D. watched them amusedly. "The damn things exist," he assured himself, "but what the hell are they *doing* here?"

The saucers were all over the place now, thousands of them everywhere. The military, he knew, had tried to shoot them down at the start, had failed. The saucers just changed colours faster for a minute or two, absorbing the energy of the laser beams in their force fields. A few times they'd somehow even reflected the beams back where they'd come from: the laser installations had been totally destroyed.

Moving closer to the windows, Dr. D. gulped down the remnants of the cake. He let the tray drop to the floor. The saucers hovered, maybe fifty feet away, oozing a red, then blue, then orange, then red again glow, so intense it blurred their entire shape. But at this range, Dr. D. could still make out without any trouble how the saucers rose from a flat, circular bottom, mounding like a marvellous, massive breast, with an erect nipple right on top. "Must be antenna or something," thought Dr. D. He blinked, and the saucers were gone.

He turned away from the windows, walked around the couch and towards the kitchen alcove. There he took a large plastic bottle of soft drink from the cooler, twisted off the top, took several lengthy gulps. He moved on to the bathroom door, and the door silently withdrew itelf, from right to left, into the wall. Dr. D. entered, went by the toilet and the handbasin, to the door of the shower stall. As he approached, the transparent door silently withdrew itself, from left to right, into the wall. He stepped into the shower room. The door resumed its place.

Dr. D. stuck his right arm out in front of him and moved towards the control console (WARM, WARM/SOAP, HOT, HOT/SOAP, WARM/SHAMPOO, HOT/SHAMPOO, etc.). He pushed the WARM/SOAP and shuffled backwards several steps until he was under the soft fall of wet froth that came out of the centre of the domed ceiling. He began caressing his flesh with the slippery liquid. The small, curly hairs that covered his body gathered in swirls as his hands passed over them. He moved back to the wall, took a soft sponge on a three-foot long teakwood handle from its hook, went back under the shower. He slid the sponge around on the underside of his belly, down and into his crotch, gently over his penis and balls, down his thighs, stopping at the knees. He raised the sponge over his head, did the top of his back, lowered the sponge along his side, bent his arm backwards, did his ass, eased the sponge into and along the deep crack.

All the while he was thinking, thinking about things for The Company, especially these days thinking about fat. "Oh, fat! ah, fat! oh! ah! fat! fat! fat! luxurious cushion of flesh! oh! FAT!" he sang in the shower.

Dr. D. had been doing a lot of thinking about fat. He loved this assignment. He had taken it to heart. The Management could not have made him happier than they did when they asked him to spend whatever time he needed to think about fat. The Company was very interested in fat. They had to be. They were in the business (among many other businesses) of insuring people's lives, and fat did not make this particular business an easy one.

There was an epidemic of fat. More and more people were getting fat. A staggering proportion of all those millions of babies born in the post-W.W. II baby-boom were now emerging into full-fledged fatdom. It seemed inevitable. And a staggering proportion of the staggering proportion had very large insurance policies. And fat was going to kill them all off early and the bill was going to come in with a vengeance. Fat was going to strip the fat from The Company. (Human fat: money fat.) "THINK ABOUT FAT," They had computer-messaged to Dr. D. He was delighted. He thought about fat; had been thinking about fat for nearly seven years now, nearly seven years to the day. He kept thinking about it while he pushed the HOT with the tip of his sponge handle.

He felt that he was getting near, very near, to putting all the pieces together. As perhaps others were too. For Dr. D. had no doubt that the Diet Division and the Fast Food Division and probably several other Divisions all had someone (in similar offices in similar buildings in similar cities all over the continent) thinking about fat, about how to get people fat and keep people fat and make people fatter. And he knew that even if he actually did discover why so many people were fat, The Company would most likely give his conclusion along with all the other conclusions to someone who thought about all these conclusions and what they might mean for The Company "In The Long Run." The profits on their multi-billion dollar sales of Fast Food, for example, might more than balance out their losses on Insurance. That was just something They had to figure out. Dr. D. didn't care — he just loved to think.

"Fat," thought Dr. D. The elementary nature of the word still fascinated him: "Fat, at, ta, ft, tf, taf, tfa, atf, aft," he said out loud. Steamy liquid streamed over him, rinsing him clean. The few remaining hairs above his ears straggled wetly down the nearly naked dome of his head.

He had thought for a while that, like bears in the fall, people were readying themselves for some sort of hibernation. But that eventually didn't seem too plausible. Then he had pursued the idea that chemicals in the food were causing a general malfunction of people's appestats (the little food thermostats inside us all that say EAT the way the thermostat on the furnace says to the furnace HEAT). But that didn't check out either.

He had studied the Clean-Plate (or Gorging) Syndrome, the Gobble Effect, the Non-Movement in the Womb Theory: all to no avail. He had investigated the question of heredity and environment: how all those chubby W.W.II baby-boomers were transforming their offspring into plump little bundles, coddling them, practically force-feeding them ("Children all over the world are *starving*! *Eat* your *dinner*! Eat it *all*! You kids just don't know how *lucky* you are!"), loading them down with a superabundance of fat cells that they would carry all through life (the cells swelling or withering, but never getting any fewer in number). Of course they got fat, but "WHY?" wondered Dr. D., "WHY? WHY? WHY?"

He shuffled over to the control console, hung up his sponge-on-a-stick, pushed off the HOT, pushed in the DRY. A whirlpool of warm air spun about him, sucking away the film of moisture from his body. "WHY? HWYHY?! WWWHWWWHY?! WWWHHYYYYYYYY??!!" He put notes to the simple words, sang a chorus of them, as a soft spray of talcum powder was swished all over his body from shoulder-high vents in the wall. Dr. D. lifted his arms, dipped his legs to open his crotch, so the powder would get everywhere it wanted to. After it did, it stopped.

Dr. D. walked out of the shower, through the vanishing-reinsinuating doors, the long tufts of the rug licking at the last dribbles of water on the soles of his feet. He eased himself down onto his couch, studied the ceiling. It was a round dome, with a circular hollow at the top where the dimmer-switch-controlled light sheltered. There were no corners to trap the ebb and surge of Dr. D.'s ideas. Only the light, only the light: illumination. He let his eyelids close.

He was at the annual HONI symposium, the Human Obesity and Nutrition Institute Proceedings. There were Doctors and Dieticians and Food Chemists everywhere. And innumerable slim, slim delegates from Overeaters Anonymous, from Weight Watchers, from Take Off Pounds Sensibly, from

Diet Guard Incorporated, from The Fat Farm Limited. There were advocates of the Last Resort (the Fast way to lose weight); of injections of HCG (humanic chorionic gonadotropin, a hormone distilled from the piss of pregnant women); of appetite-suppressant drugs; of injecting yourself with a "controlled" virus in order to make yourself too sick to eat — the Fever Diet; of swallowing a liquid, perfluoroctyl bromide, to coat your digestive tract, like putting a Teflon cover on a frying pan, in order to block the absorption of food; of pulling-water-from-the-blood drugs; of staplepuncture (in the ear-lobe); of false "fat"-message chemical substitutes; of pills to force your body to produce more heat, using up the energy that would otherwise scurry into hiding in the fat cells; of exercise — exercise, for God's sake!

Dr. D. had been open-minded, most open-minded: he had tried them all, personally. He had also tried *all* the diets — vertical (one-food only) diets: the Rice Diet, the Banana Diet, the Candy Diet, the Grapefruit Diet, the Ice Cream Diet, the Yogurt Diet; and horizontal (low-calorie, less-of-everything) diets: the Prudent Diet, the Mayo Diet (the *real* Mayo Diet, as well as many of the pirated versions). He had tried low-carbohydrate diets, high protein diets, high fat diets, and dozens of other diets — the Miracle Diet, the No Will Power Diet, the Nine-Day Wonder Diet, the Olympic Diet, the Magic-Formula-Plus Diet, the Miraculous Eggnog Diet, the Fabulous Formula Diet, the Wise Woman's Diet, the Computer Diet, the Counterweight Diet, the North Pole Slenderizing Plan, the Editor's Diet. Yes, he had tried them all. And, after longer or shorter periods of time, dismissed them all. They might work for a few, but as large-scale, practical solutions he knew that they were hopeless.

Fat people just couldn't seem to help staying fat. And Dr. D. just couldn't help sympathizing with a strenuously cheerful mob of gate-crashers from FIB (Fat Is Beautiful), carrying their Rubens posters, the women defiantly wearing bikinis — stomachs flopping down over, breasts bulging out around the scanty cloth. They were handing out information sheets with reprints of studies that showed that fat people had higher IQs than thin people, that fat people had more and better sex than thin people: no, he couldn't help but sympathize, even though he suspected that they also got their money for their really quite elaborate campaigns from the multi-billion dollar marketeers of Junk Food (i.e., The Company).

Without opening his eyes, Dr. D. reached for, found, and

deposited another handful of potato chips into his mouth from the teakwood bowl on a teakwood stand by his right side. It was his secretary's first task every morning to replenish all the teakwood bowls that were scattered in profusion throughout his room; to fill them with potato chips, cheezies, sugar-coated peanuts and raisins, cashews, chocolates (soft-centres and hard), chocolate bars, cookies (27 different varieties), cupcakes, etc. Dr. D. couldn't remember exactly when he had taken the first handful of potato chips, and he didn't want to.

Swivelling into a sitting position, he opened his eyes, grabbed both hands full with chips, lifted his arms straight out in front, rocked backwards, then forwards and down, and got his ass off the couch. He almost overbalanced and rolled forward onto his stomach, but he caught himself in time and managed to lift himself into a standing position. He made a left turn and, stuffing chips into his mouth from one hand then the other, strolled over to the wall that was dominated by the Rubens painting.

He pushed an inset and almost invisible button near the bottom-right corner of the painting, and a panel just to the right of his hand withdrew silently up into the wall and a computer terminal slid out. It was quietly humming.

"D" Dr. D. told it.

"YES" it replied.

"AGES"

"YES"

"1940 * 1950"

"YES"

"OBESE * %" (Dr. D. and the computer had long since worked out exactly what was meant by "OBESE").

"67.26 *** FRINGE * 9.87 ***TOTAL * 72.13" It had gone up a few percentage points since he had last looked two years ago.

"NU" ("NU" meant "NUMBER").

"CANADA * 7,213,479 *** USA * 57,463,963" (Both Dr. D. and the computer knew that these figures were based on actual 1989 census counts.) "PROJECTION?" the computer queried.

"SHOVE IT" Dr. D. replied.

"AND UP YOURS FELLA" the computer countered.

"DEMOGRAPHY" Dr. D. asked.

"SCREEN" said the computer.

Dr. D. turned to look at the screen which was quietly lowering itself while the Rubens lifted up behind his back. The lights dimmed, the drapes closed.

"SCALE * 1/1,000" the computer flashed onto the screen.

A map of North America (in dark purple) appeared, with a

demographic projection of the dwelling places of fat people between the ages of 39 and 49 in shades of orange — pale, pale orange in scattered dots and splotches down the centre of the continent, shading to a more intense orange in the cities, along the Great Lakes and the US coasts. Dr. D. was not at all surprised.

"SCALE * " the computer began to show, starting to zero in on the bright orange areas.

"NO" ordered Dr. D.

It stopped.

He had an impulse.

"MY NEIGHBOURHOOD" he told it.

The computer thought about that for a moment, then flashed a map of the city on the screen, scanned across it, found what it was looking for, suddenly telescoped down on the three blocks surrounding Dr. D.'s home. Bathed it in a livid orange.

"FUCK OFF" Dr. D. told the computer. It was allowed no reply to these words. The screen lifted, the painting lowered, the drapes opened, the lights brightened, the terminal retracted, the sunshine (muted) flowed in. And outside the window, swimming into Dr. D.'s field of vision, two flying saucers drifted.

Dr. D. moved to the window, placed his hands, palms pressed flat against the glass, above his head, leaned forward. His naked belly squeezed up against the chill surface of the pane, until an area some four feet across was immersed under the flesh of his stomach. He pushed his skin tight against the glass, and the air squeezed out, leaving one small, still bubble trapped in the folds of his protruding bellybutton. He shoved his nose to the window, nearly burying it within his bulging cheeks. His glasses dug into the flesh, thick, round lenses in heavy wire frames grating on the other glass. He felt a strange pull, a profound nostalgia at the sight of the saucers, pulsing quietly in the air, more than 1,000 feet above the concrete lanes of the earth. "Why do I love them so?" he asked himself.

The saucers pulsed and glowed, pulsed and glowed. And then seemed suddenly to diminish, become almost instantly small dots in the sky. They had flown away, in a direct line from Dr. D.'s vision, at some unbelievable supersonic speed. They vanished.

Dr. D. discovered that his face hurt, that he was terrified he was going to push through the window and fall, and fall, and fall, ending up a shapeless, shallow slough of human cells far, far below, unless he hit a truck, a bus, was sliced and fried by rows of power lines, of telephone wires — "Doctor, doctor, pants on fire. . . ." He wasn't wearing any pants. In fact, he wasn't wearing anything at all. Clothes interfered with the free movement of his thoughts. His secretary

160

helped him to undress every morning when he came to work, helped him to dress before he left.

He gave a hard shove with his outstretched hands, fell back onto the soft, foam-padded rug. Lay there. Looked at the ghostly print of his body left on the window by the talcum powder. Could not resolve what had happened. Felt chilled, clammy. Rolled over on his stomach, crawled to his couch, and, using its support, levered himself onto his knees. He felt desperately hungry, grabbed for the nearest teakwood bowl, took it from its stand and put it on the couch in front of his mouth, began to scoop the contents in, scarcely munching, gulping them down. They were chocolate puff cookies, with flat, circular bottoms and round tops with little chocolate dimples at their summits. Sweat dripped off his forehead, drooled down his armpits. He finished the cookies. Paused. Contemplated. "I need to take a shit," concluded Dr. D.

He got himself erect and carefully shuffled over to the bathroom, the door withdrawing before him, closing after him. He went to the toilet. The seat was waiting for him, at ass-level, tipped slightly upwards at a 35° angle to receive him. As he placed his ass upon it, it slowly subsided beneath his weight, lowering him into a shitting position. Dr. D. made a few preliminary grunts, felt his rectum opening like a time-lapse film of a flower blossom, twinging ever so slightly. He reached out his hand to a nearby teakwood bowl, gathered in some chocolate-coated raisins, brought them to his mouth. Put them in. Chewed. Straining carefully at the same time, he pushed his shit down and out. He felt the soft drift of air flowing down his body, carrying the stink out a vent behind the toilet in the floor. For once his piles were behaving.

Unhurriedly, Dr. D. thought about the supper he would consume in an hour or so. He wanted a steak, a two-pound steak, fried on their charcoal grill; with half a dozen baked potatoes slathered with butter and oozing genuine sour cream. An avocado salad, dripping with olive oil. For dessert, angel food cake buried in sugary whipped cream, mounded with the dazzling bloody drops of strawberry bodies. And big mugs of coffee, rich and sweet. Chocolates, liqueurs. Oh, and a few drinks before he ate, just to loosen him up. Paradise!

Dr. D. gave praise in his mind to the farms of his land: to the vast herds of animals burrowing their muzzles into overflowing troughs, giving milk, giving meat; to the great orchards, trees heavy with pendulous fruit; to the tracts of vegetables; to the sweep of the grain fields, filled and erect in the days of the harvest, squadrons of combines reaping them in. "Praise to the farms!" cried Dr. D. "And praise to The Company, who runs them!"

161

He heard three small plops. Satisfied, he gave a little push with his feet and a soft jet of soapy water cleansed his asshole; warm water rinsed it; warm air dried it. Then the seat elevated him again. He rose to his feet and glanced back just in time to see the three hard, dark, golf-balls of shit disappear in a swirl and suck of gurgling water.

He left the bathroom, walked over to the Rubens, pushed the button for the computer: it slid out. "ATTN PRESIDENT" he typed, "NEARING POINT OF CRITICAL MASS (Dr. D.'s last study had been of thermo-nuclear power — he had fallen in love with the terminology — and CRITICAL MASS meant the moment at which a nuclear chain reaction began) * WILL SOON BE NEEDING NEW ASSIGNMENT *** AS EVER * DR. D."

"FUCK OFF" he told the computer.

He went over to the control panel by his couch, pressed a button. The outside door (on the wall parallel to the windows, and over in the far right-hand corner, at the opposite end of the wall from the bathroom door) opened, and a young woman came in, carrying his clothes. He turned his back to the couch, stuck his arms up in the air. She dropped his sandals on the rug near his feet, went behind him, hopped up on the couch, and, lifting the bottom of his robe high, dropped it over his arms and head. The robe, billowing out around his body, settled upon his flesh. Through long practice, she had easily — holding the sleeves to the last moment — encircled his arms with the cloth.

Dr. D. shuffled his feet into his sandals, began to amble out of the room. The woman, still perched like a lank heron upon the couch, watched him go, his eight hundred and eighty-two pound body shuddering from side to side as he carefully shifted his weight so he could make his drooping, bulging calves, his bloated feet, move him along.

Dr. D. was happy with the day; he chuckled all the way down the 90 stories in his private elevator to where his car waited. He was sure he *almost* had it figured. *Almost*. The car was right there, the driver's seat, like that of the toilet, lifted and turned towards him, waiting to ease him into the car. Dr. D. sat back on the seat, and it swung and lowered him into place. He pushed the button marked HOME and stretched back, enjoying the ride.

The car moved quickly out of the depths of the building and into the bright light of late afternoon on the freeway. The traffic was nearly bumper to bumper, but it ran silently, swiftly. Dr. D. left his video screen blank, preferring to watch the animated ad screens along the road, luring people into the next QUICK-FOOD exit, for one final snack before dinner, for pizza, deep-fried chicken,

162

hamburgers (MORE THAN 229 BILLION SOLD), a couple of beer, a few cocktails.

Through the roof-glass, Dr. D. could see groups of flying saucers drifting here and there overhead. Some seemed to be playing games of tag with each other, or just showing off, zooming up into invisibility and then back again in a flash. Saucers turning flip-flops, fish-tailing, end-over-ending, all the while pulsing their gorgeous colour changes. "What a cheerful sight," thought Dr. D. He could see many of the people in the cars around him lying back and laughing at the saucers, at their impetuous frolics, just as he was doing.

Soon his car found an exit for Dr. D.'s neighbourhood and zipped off along it. Within a minute he was pulling into his driveway. The two children, Theodore D. (9) and Stephanie D. (7), were lounging around on the lawn, watching a cartoon tv program on the portable, empty packages of potato chips, empty soft drink bottles, and wrappers of ice cream bars strewn in a circle about them. "Hi, Dr. D.," they called, rippling the pudgy flesh on their faces into what Dr. D., only through long experience, recognized as smiles. Cuddles, the dog, rolled himself over from his side to his back, exposing a slack expanse of pink belly. He had waited all day on the patio near the side door, gathering his strength for this exertion born of a profound devotion.

The side door itself swung open, from left to right, and Mrs. D. edged herself through the barely passable four-foot opening. Dr. D. smiled through the windshield of his car, could see that she was smiling too. As she began to shamble her bulk towards him, in preparation for the customary kiss of greeting, Dr. D. was at first somewhat puzzled, and then suddenly shocked to see her hands reach for the centre of her robe (a match for his) between her breasts, and, with one firm pull, rip it open to the navel. She shrugged it off her shoulders, exposing massive, pendulous breasts that rode upon the top slope of the distended flesh of her stomach. Her erect nipples and her protruding bellybutton composed the points of an equilateral triangle.

Dr. D. scarcely had time to shout, "My dear! Remember the children!" before Mrs. D. had rent the garment even further, and it, once released, finding no resistance to its downward motion, plummeted to the ground. The huge folds of her sagging belly concealing her pubic area, her massive thighs shuddering as she moved, Mrs. D. shambled towards the car.

Dr. D. could not help himself: he felt, somewhere far below the drooping bulk of the centre of his body, his penis stir into a solid erection. He jabbed a thick finger at the button to open the door and

163

release him. The door flew wide, the seat, lifting and turning, brought him to his feet. "Not here!" Dr. D. shouted at his wife. "Not now!"

And yet, and yet, he felt an overpowering urge to be free of the cloth that draped his beautiful, corpulent flesh. He raised his hands. He ripped his robe, ripped it asunder from neck to crotch. It slid into a soft circle around his feet. He freed his feet from the circle, began to surge towards his wife, his penis throbbing. Saw her right foot lift, not come down again to touch the ground; saw her float into the air, feet still moving as if she were still on her way to him instead of rising slowly straight up. "Hallucination!" Dr. D. exclaimed to himself. "Effect of nearing critical mass!" He slapped himself hard with both hands on both bulging cheeks. Mrs. D. continued to float upwards, was now more than 5 feet in the air, her wriggling, puffy toes at Dr. D.'s eye level. And, in the view now cleared by the removal of her bulk, Dr. D. saw the dog also afloat, belly up, tongue lolling, waiting to be scratched.

"What? What? What? What?" Dr. D.'s mind asked itself again and again. He glanced around at the children. They too, stripped naked, were in the process of leisurely ascent, still consuming ice cream bars. The pudgy flesh on their faces was rippling into what Dr. D., only through long experience, recognized as amazement, as delight. He turned to watch his wife once more, found himself gazing at the centre of the equilateral triangle formed by her nipples and bellybutton. "She's coming down! She's coming down! Thank God!" thought Dr. D.

He held his eyes steadily on her: her neck appeared, her lips, her nose, her eyes, her hair. He could see over her now, over the ten-foot fence into the back yard of their neighbours. "Over the fence!?" He looked down at his toes, saw twelve feet of air between them and the earth. His feet began to churn involuntarily, clawing for solid footing: his arms flapped at his sides, palms up, trying to fly himself back down. His bowels loosened marvellously, releasing a thin stream of watery debris.

Calming down, Dr. D. scanned his neighbourhood from this novel perspective. And discovered family after family gently ascending, mother-naked, into the sky. Some were pawing the air with their feet, waving their arms, stubby little appendages stuck on great globes of bodies.

Dr. D.'s mind washed his vision with a flare of brilliant orange. Then the film of the operation began a frenzied instant-replay in his head, rolling *forward* this time, not backwards as he so loved to view it, the body becoming fat in a few dreamlike moments. No. Rolling forward now, the surgeon stripping the fat away, relentlessly slicing

164

it out from the strangely bloodless, moonlike pit. "Deliciously flat tummy needn't be merely a pleasant memory. Those fatty deposits can be *removed!*"

The replay speeded up, the frames beginning to jump out of control. The film caught, held on the image of the not knife, on the KNIFE! Burned up.

And Dr. D. raised his eyes reluctantly, knowing he had never even come close to guessing, knowing very well what he was going to see: the undersides of the flying saucers, now very close, circular holes gaping open in the centre of their bases, quietly hovering, pulsing their beautiful colours. And the first of the wonderful harvest of fat lifting and easing inside.

DANCING BEAR

GUY VANDERHAEGHE

The old man lay sleeping on the taut red rubber sheet as if he were some specimen mounted and pinned there to dry. His housekeeper, the widowed Mrs. Hax, paused in the doorway and then walked heavily to the bedside window, where she abruptly freed the blind and sent it up, whirring and clattering.

She studied the sky. Far away, to the east, and high above the bursting green of the elms that lined the street, greasy black clouds rolled languidly, their swollen underbellies lit by the occasional shudder of lightning that popped in the distance. After each flash she counted aloud to herself until she heard the faint, muttering accompaniment of thunder. Finally satisfied, she turned away from the window to find Dieter Bethge awake and watching her cautiously from his bed.

"It's going to rain," she said, moving about the room and grunting softly as she stooped to gather up his clothes and pile them on a chair.

"Oh," he answered, feigning some kind of interest. He picked a flake of dried skin from his big toe and lifted it tenderly to the light like a jeweller, intently examining its whorled grain and yellow translucence.

Forlornly, Mrs. Hax smoothed the creases of his carelessly discarded trousers with a soft, fat palm and draped them over the back of a chair. The old bugger makes more work than a whole tribe of kids, she thought.

She glanced over her shoulder and saw him fingering the bit of skin between thumb and forefinger. "Leave that be," she said curtly. "It's time we were up. Quit dawdling."

He looked up, his pale blue eyes surprised. "What?"

"Time to get up."

"No," he said. "Not yet."

"It's reveille. No malingering. Won't have it," she said, fixing an unconvincing smile on her broad face. "Come on now, up and at 'em. We've slept long enough."

"That rubber thing kept me awake last night," he said plaintively. "Every time I move, it squeaks and pulls at my skin. There's no give to it."

"Complainers' noses fall off," Mrs. Hax said absent-mindedly as she held a shirt up to her own wrinkled nose. She sniffed. It wasn't exactly fresh, but she decided it would do, and tossed it back on the chair.

The old man, now, as whenever he was thwarted or ignored, felt his face burn with humiliation. "I want that damn thing off my bed!" he yelled. "This is my bed! This is my house! Get it off!"

Mrs. Hax truculently folded her arms across her large, loose breasts and stared down at him. For a moment he defiantly met her gaze, but then he averted his eyes and his trembling jaw confirmed his confusion.

"I am not moved by childish tempers," she announced. "You haven't learned that yet?" Mrs. Hax paused. "It's about time you did. One thing about Mrs. Hax," she declared in a piping falsetto that betrayed her anger, "is that when someone pushes her, she pushes back twice as hard. I am ruthless." She assumed a stance that she imagined an illustration of ruthlessness, her flaccid arms akimbo. A burlesque of violence. "So let me make this perfectly, crystal clear. That rubber sheet is staying on that bed until you forget your lazy, dirty habits and stop them accidents. A grown man," she said disparagingly, shaking her head. "I just got sick and tired of hauling one mattress off the bed to dry and hauling another one on. Just remember I'm not getting any younger either. I'm not up to heavy work like that. So if you want that rubber *thing* off, you try and remember not to pee the bed."

The old man turned on his side and hid his face.

"No sulking allowed," she said sternly. "Breakfast is ready and I have plenty to do today. I can't keep it waiting forever."

Dieter turned on to his back and fixed his eyes on the ceiling. Mrs. Hax shook her head in exasperation. It was going to be one of those days. What went on in the old bastard's head, if anything? What made him so peculiar, so difficult at times like these?

She walked over to the bed and took him firmly by the wrist. "Upsie daysie!" she cried brightly, planting her feet solidly apart and jerking him upright. She skidded him to the edge of the bed, the rubber sheet whining a muffled complaint, and his hands, in startled protest and ineffectual rebellion, pawing at the front of her dress. Mrs. Hax propped him upright while his head wobbled feebly from side to side and his tongue flickered angrily, darting and questing like a snake's.

"There," she said, patting his head, "that's better. Now let's let bygones be bygones. A fresh start. I'll say, 'Good morning, Mr. Bethge!' and you answer, 'Good morning, Mrs. Hax!' "

He gave no sign of agreement. Mrs. Hax hopefully cocked her head to one side and, like some huge, querulous bird, chirped, "Good morning, Mr. Bethge!" The old man stubbornly disregarded her, smiling sweetly and vacantly into space.

"Well," she said, patting her dress down around her wide hips and heavy haunches, "it's no skin off my teeth, mister."

She stumped to the door, stopped, and looked back. The old man sat perched precariously on the edge of the bed, his white hair ruffled, tufted and crested like some angry heron. A pale shadow fell across the lower half of his face and threw his eyes into relief, so that they shone with the dull, glazed intensity of the most devout of worshippers.

Mrs. Hax often saw him like this, mute and still, lost in reverie; and she liked to suppose, that somehow, he was moved by a dim apprehension of mortality and loss. Perhaps he was even overcome with memories of his wife, and felt the same vast yearning she felt for her own dead Albert.

She mustered a smile and offered it. "Five minutes, dear," she said, and then closed the door softly behind her.

Bethge made no response. He was thinking — trying to pry those memories out of the soft beds in which they had so comfortably settled, sinking deeper and deeper with the weight of all the years, growing more somnolent and lazy, less easily stirred from sleep. He could no longer make his head crackle with the sudden, decisive leap of quick thought, hurtling from synapse to synapse; chemistry subsumed, disguised by consciousness. Instead, memories had now to be pricked and prodded, and sometimes, if he were lucky, they came in revelatory flashes. Yet it was only old, old thoughts and things that came to him. Only they had any real clarity — and the sharpness to wound.

And now it was something about a bear. What?

Bethge, with jerky, tremulous movement, swiped at the spittle on his chin with the back of his hand. In his agitation he crossed and re-crossed his thin legs; the marbly, polished legs of a very old man.

Bear? He rubbed the bridge of his nose; somehow, it was important. He began to rock himself gently, his long, curving nose slicing, like a scythe, back and forth, reaping the dim air of his stale little room. And as he swayed, it all began to come to him, and he began to run, swiftly, surely, silently back into time.

In the dark barn that smells of brittle straw, and sharply of horse dung, the knife is making little greedy, tearing noises. It is not sharp enough. Then he hears the hoarse, dragging whisper of steel on whetstone. Although he is afraid that the bear his father is skinning may suddenly rear to life and hunt, he climbs over the wall of the box stall and steps into the manger and crouches down. He is only five, so the manger is a nice, tight, comforting fit.

What a bear! A killer, a marauder who had left two sows tangled in their guts with single blows from his needle-sharp claws.

The smell of the bear makes him think of gun metal — oily, smoky. Each hair bristles like polished black wire, and when the sun catches the pelt it shines vividly, electrically blue.

The curved blade of the knife, now sharpened, slices through the bear's fat like butter — relentlessly peeling back the coat and exposing long, flat, pink muscles. As his father's busy, bloody hands work, Dieter feels a growing uneasiness. The strong hands tug and tear, wrestling with the heavy, inert body as if they were frantically searching for something. Like clay under a sculptor's hand, the bear begins to change. Each stroke of the knife renders him less bear-like and more like something else. He senses this and crouches lower in the manger in anticipation.

His father begins to raise the skin off the back, his forearms hidden as the knife moles upward toward the neck. At last he grunts and stands. Reaches for the axe. In two sharp snapping blows the head is severed from the trunk and the grinning mask flung into a corner. He gathers up the skin and carries it out to salt it and peg it down in the yard. Dieter hears the chickens clamouring to pick it clean.

He stares down into the pit of the shadowy stall. This is no bear. Stripped of its rich, glossy fur — naked, it is no bear. Two arms, two legs, a raw pink skin. A man. Under all that lank, black hair a man was hiding, lurking in disguise.

He feels the spiralling terror of an unwilling accomplice to murder. He begins to cry and call for his father, who suddenly appears in the doorway covered in grease and blood, a murderer.

From far away, he heard someone call him. "Mr. Bethge! Mr. Bethge!" The last syllable of his name was drawn out and held like a note, so that it quivered in the air and urged him on with its stridency.

He realized he had been crying, that his eyes were filled with those unexpected tears that came so suddenly they constantly surprised and embarrassed him.

For a bear? But this wasn't all of it. There had been another bear; he was sure of it. A bear who had lived in shame and impotence.

He edged himself off the bed and painfully on to his knobbed, arthritic feet. Breakfast.

At breakfast they quarrel in the dreary, passionless manner of master and charge. He wants what she has, bacon and eggs. He tells her he hates porridge.

"Look," Mrs. Hax said, "I can't give you bacon and eggs. Doctor's orders."

"What doctor?"

"The doctor we saw last month. You remember."

"No." It was true. He couldn't remember any doctor.

"Yes you do. Come on now. We took a ride downtown in a cab. Remember now?"

"No."

"And we stopped by Woolworth's and bought a big bag of that sticky candy you like so much. Remember?"

"No."

"That's fine," she said irritably. "You don't want to remember, there's nothing I can do. It doesn't matter, because you're not getting bacon and eggs."

"I don't want porridge," he said tiredly.

"Eat it."

"Give me some corn flakes."

"Look at my plate," she said, pointing with her knife. "I'm getting cold grease scum all over everything. Fight, fight. When do I get a moment's peace to eat?"

"I want corn flakes," he said with a little self-satisfied tuck to the corners of his mouth.

"You can't have corn flakes," she said. "Corn flakes bung you up. That's why you eat hot cereal — to keep you regular. Just like stewed prunes. Now, which you want," she asked slyly, "Sunny Boy or stewed prunes?"

"I want corn flakes." He smiled up happily at the ceiling.

"Like a stuck record." She folded her hands on the table and leaned conspiratorially toward him. "You don't even care if you eat or not, do you? You're just trying to get under my skin, aren't you?"

"I want corn flakes," he said definitely and happily.

"I could kill that man," she told her plate. "Just kill him." Then, abruptly, she asked, "Where's your glasses? No, not there, in the other pocket. O.K., put them on. Now take a good long look at that porridge."

The old man peered intently down into his bowl.

"That's fine. Take it easy. It's not a goddamn wishing well. You see them little brown specks?"

He nodded.

"That's what this whole fight's about? Something as tiny as that? You know what that is. It's flax. And flax keeps you regular. So eat it."

"I'm not eating it. What do I want with flax?" he asked quizzically.

"Sure you're crazy," she said. "Crazy like a fox."

"I want some coffee."

Mrs. Hax slammed down her fork and knife, snatched up his cup, and marched to the kitchen counter. While she poured the coffee, Bethge's hand crept across the table and stole several strips of bacon from her plate. He crammed these clumsily into his mouth, leaving a grease shine on his chin.

Mrs. Hax set his cup down in front of him. "Be careful," she said. "Don't spill."

Bethge giggled. In a glance, Mrs. Hax took in his grease-daubed chin and her plate. "Well, well, look at the cat who swallowed the canary. Grinning from ear lobe to ear lobe with a pound of feathers bristling from his trap."

"So?" he said defiantly.

"You think I enjoy the idea of you pawing through my food?" Mrs. Hax carried her plate to the garbage and scraped it with a flourish. "Given all your dirty little habits, who's to know where your hands been?" she asked wickedly. "But go ahead and laugh. Because he who laughs last, laughs best. Chew this around for a bit and seè how she tastes. You're not getting one, single, solitary cigarette today, my friend."

Startled, he demanded his cigarettes.

"We're singing a different tune now, aren't we?" She paused. "N O spells no. Put that in your pipe and smoke it."

"You give them. They're mine."

"Not since you set the chesterfield on fire. Not since then. Your son told me I was to give them out one at a time so's I could watch you and avoid 'regrettable accidents.' Thank God, there's some sense in the family. How he came by it I'm sure I don't know."

The old man hoisted himself out of his chair. "Don't you dare talk to me like that. I want my cigarettes — and I want them now."

Mrs. Hax crossed her arms and set her jaw. "No."

"You're fired!" he shouted. "Get out!" He flapped his arms awkwardly in an attempt to startle her into motion.

"Oh ho!" she said, rubbing her large red hands together in delight. "Fired, am I? On whose say so? Them that hires is them that fires. He who pays the piper calls the tune. And you don't do neither. Not a bit. Your son hired me, and your son pays me. I don't budge a step unless I get the word straight from the horse's mouth."

"Get out!"

"Save your breath."

He is beaten and he knows it. This large, stubborn woman cannot, will not be moved.

"I want to talk to my son."

"If you got information you feel your son should have, write him a letter."

He knows this would never do. He would forget; she would steal the letter, conveniently forgetting to mail it. Justice demands immediate action. The iron is hot and fit for striking. He feels the ground beneath his feet is treacherous; he cannot become confused, or be led astray. One thing at a time. He must talk to his son.

"Get him on the telephone."

"Your son, if you *remember*," Mrs. Hax said, "got a little upset about all those long distance phone calls — *collect*. And his words to me were, 'Mrs. Hax, I think it best if my father phone only on important matters, at your *discretion*.' At *my* discretion, mind you. And my discretion informs me that this isn't one of those times. I've got a responsibility to my employer."

"I'll phone him myself."

"That I've got to see."

"I will."

"Yes, like the last time. Half the time you can't remember the city John lives in, let alone his street. The last time you tried to phone him you got the operator so balled up you would have been talking to a Chinaman in Shanghai if I hadn't stepped in and saved your bacon."

"I'll phone. I can do it."

"Sure you will. Where does John live?"

"I know."

"Uh huh, then tell me. Where does he live?"

"I know."

"Jesus, he could be living in the basement and you wouldn't realize it."

This makes him cry. He realizes she is right. But minutes ago he *had known* where his son lived. How could he have forgotten? In the sudden twistings and turnings of the conversation he has lost his way, and now he hears himself making a wretched, disgusting noise — but cannot stop.

Mrs. Hax feels she has gone too far. She goes over to him and puts an arm around his shoulders. "Now see what's happened. You went and got yourself all upset over a silly old bowl of porridge. Doctor says you have to watch that with your blood pressure. It's no laughing matter." She boosts him out of his chair. "I think you better lie down on the chesterfield for a bit."

Mrs. Hax led him into the living room and made him comfortable on the chesterfield. She wondered how an old bugger like him could make so much water: if he wasn't peeing, he was crying.

"You want a kleenex?" she asked.

He shook his head and, ashamed, covered his face with his forearm.

"No harm in crying," she said bleakly. "We all do some-time."

"Leave me be."

"I suppose it's best," she sighed. "I'll be in the kitchen clearing up if you need me."

Dieter lay on the chesterfield trying to stifle his tears. It was not an easy job because even the sound of Mrs. Hax unconcernedly clacking the breakfast dishes reminded him of her monstrous carelessness with everything. His plates, his feelings. He filled with anger at the notion that he would never be nimble enough to evade her commands, or even her wishes. That he cannot outwit her or even flee her.

The living room gradually darkens as the low scudding rain clouds blot out the sun. He wishes it were a fine sunny day. The kind of day which tricks you into believing you are young and carefree as you once were. Like in Rumania before his family emigrated. Market days almost always felt that way. People bathed in sun and noise, their wits honed to a fine edge for trading and bartering. Every kind of people. The Jews with their curling side-locks, the timid Italian tenant farmers, the Rumanians, and people like himself, German colonists. Even a gypsy or two. Then you had a sense of life, of living. Every good thing the earth offers or man's hand fashions could be found there. Gaily painted wagons, piles of potatoes with the wet clay still clinging to them; chickens, ducks and geese; tethered pigs tugging their backlegs and squealing; horses with hooves as black and shining as basalt, and eyes that were as large and liquid-purple as plums.

Nothing but a sheet of sky above and good smells below: pickled herring and leather, paprika and the faint scent of little hard sweet apples.

Innocence. Innocence. But then again on the other hand — yes, well sometimes cruelty too. Right in the market.

A stranger arrived with a dancing bear once. Yes, the other bear, the one he had forgotten. He led him by a ring through the nose. When a crowd gathered, the man unsnapped the chain from the bear's nose and began to play a violin. It was a sad, languorous tune. For a moment, the bear tossed his head from side to side and snuffled in the dirt. This, for him, was a kind of freedom.

But the man spoke to him sharply. The bear lifted his head and then mournfully raised himself up on to his hind legs. His arms opened in a wide, charitable manner, as if he were offering an embrace. His mouth grinned, exposing black-speckled gums and sharp teeth. He danced, slowly, ponderously, tiredly.

The music changed tempo. It became gay and lively. The bear began to prance unsteadily; the hot sun beat down on him. A long, glittering thread of saliva fell from his panting mouth on to the cinnamon coloured fur of his chest.

Dieter, fascinated, tugged and pushed himself through the crowd. The bear hopped heavily from leg to leg. It was pathetic and comic. The pink tip of his penis jiggled up and down in the long hair of his loins. There was a wave of confused sniggering.

The trainer played faster and faster. The bear pirouetted wildly. He whirled and whirled, raising a small cloud of dust. The crowd began to clap. The bear spun and spun, his head lolling from side to side, his body tense with the effort of maintaining this human posture. And then he lost his balance and fell, blindly, with a bone-wrenching thump on to his back.

The scraping of the violin bow stopped. The bear turned lazily on to his feet and bit savagely at his fleas.

"Up, Bruno," the man said.

The bear whined and sat down. People began to laugh; some hooted and insulted the bear's master. He flourished the bear's nose lead and shouted, but the bear refused to budge. In the end, however, he could do nothing except attempt to save face; he bowed deeply, signifying an end to the performance. A few coins, a very few, bounced and bounced at his feet. He scooped them up quickly, as if he were afraid they might be reclaimed.

The audience began to disperse. Some hurried away to protect their wares. But Dieter had nothing to protect and nowhere to go, and so he stayed.

The sight of so many fleeing backs seemed to pique the bear. He got to his feet and began, once again, to dance. He mocked them. Or so it seemed. Of course, there had been no music, but the bear danced much more daintily and elegantly than before, to a tune only he could perceive. And he had grinned, hugely, sardonically.

But his trainer had reached up, caught his nose ring and yanked him down on all fours. He swore and cursed, and the bear breathed high, squeaking protests, feigning innocence.

This was unacceptable. This was rebellion. This was treason to the man who fed him, cared for him, taught him.

"Hairy bastard. Play the fool, will you?" the stranger muttered, wrenching and twisting the nose ring while the bear squealed with pain. The man punched his head, kicked him in the belly, shook him by the ears. "Traitor. Ingrate."

Dieter had held his breath. His mind's eye had seen the bear suddenly strike, revenge himself. Yet nothing happened. Nothing; except the bear was beaten and battered, humiliated, even spat upon.

What shame he had felt witnessing such an indignity, such complete indifference to the pride which should be a bear's. Such flaunting of the respect owed him for his size and, in theory, his power. Couldn't the man realize what he did? He wanted to shout out the secret. To warn him that appearances deceive. That a bear is a man in masquerade. Perhaps even a judge, but at the very least a brother.

But he couldn't. He ran away instead.

The house is still. He hears her footsteps, knows that she is watching him from the doorway. As always she is judging him, calculating her words and responses, planning. Her plots deny him even the illusion of freedom. He decides he will not turn to look at her. But perhaps she knows this will be his reaction? Petulant, childish.

"I want to be left in peace." He surprises himself. This giving voice to thought without weighing the consequences is dangerous. But she doesn't catch it. "What?"

"I don't chew my words twice," he says.

She comes to the side of the chesterfield. "Feeling better now?"

175

"Yes."

"Truth?"

He nods.

"Now mind, you got to be sure. I'm going down to the store. You need the bathroom?"

"No."

"All right then. I'll just be a few minutes. That's all. You'll be O.K.?"

He is trying to think. All this talk, these interruptions annoy him. He burns with impatience. "Fine. That's fine. Good." Suddenly, he feels happy. He *can* steal a little peace. He'll do it.

"I must be careful," he tells himself aloud. How do these things slip out?

But Mrs. Hax doesn't understand. "With your blood pressure, I should say so."

His luck, his good fortune, make him feel strong and cunning. Following her to the front door he almost pities this fat woman. He watches her start down the street. It is lined with old and substantial homes, most of them painted modestly white, and their yards flourish tall, rough-barked elms. On this street, Mrs. Hax, in her fluorescent orange rain slicker, appears ridiculous and inappropriate. Like a bird of paradise in an English garden. He waits until he loses sight of her at the first turning of the street.

He hurries to his business. His hands fumble with the chain on the front door; at last it is fastened. His excitement leaves him breathless, but he shuffles to the back door and draws the bolt. Safe. Mrs. Hax is banished, exiled.

At first he thinks the noise is caused by the blood pulsing in his temples. But it fades to an insistent, whispering rush. Dieter goes to the window to look out. The rain is falling in a gleaming, thick curtain that obscures the outlines of the nearest house; striking the roadway, it throws up fine silvery plumes of spray. He decides to wait for Mrs. Hax at the front door. He stands there and smells the cocoa matting, the dust and rubber boots. Somehow, he has forgotten they smell this way, a scent that can be peculiarly comforting when you are dry and warm, with a cold rain slashing against the windows.

And here is Mrs. Hax, trotting stiff-legged up the street with a shredding brown paper bag huddled to her body. She flees up the walk, past the beaten and dripping caraganas, and around back to the kitchen door. He hears her bumping and rattling it.

Here she comes again, scurrying along, head bent purposefully, rain glancing off her plastic cap. But as she begins to climb the front steps he withdraws and hides himself in the coat closet. Her key rasps in the chamber, the spring lock snaps free. The door opens several inches but then meets the resistance of the chain and sticks. She grumbles and curses; some fat, disembodied fingers curl through the gap and pluck at the chain. For a moment he is tempted to slam the door shut on those fingers, but he resists the impulse. The fingers are replaced by a slice of face, an eye and a mouth.

"Mr. Bethge! Mr. Bethge! Open up!"

Bethge stumbles out of the closet and lays his face along the door jamb, eye to eye with Mrs. Hax. They stare at each other. At last she breaks the spell.

"Well, open this door," she says irritably. "I feel like a drowned cat."

"Go away. You're not wanted here."

"What!"

"Go away."

Her one eye winks suspiciously. "You do know who I am? This is Mrs. Hax, your housekeeper. Open up."

"I know who you are. I don't want any part of you. So go away."

She shows him the soggy paper bag. "I bought you a Jersey Milk."

"Pass it through."

Her one eye opens wide in blue disbelief. "You open this door."

"No."

"It's the cigarettes, I suppose? All right, I give up. You can have your damn cigarettes."

"Go away."

"I'm losing my patience," she says, lowering her voice. "Now open this door, you senile old fart."

"Old fart yourself. Old fat fart."

"You wait until I get in there. There'll be hell to pay."

He realizes his legs are tired from standing. There is a nagging pain in the small of his back. "I've got to go now," he says. "Goodbye," and closes the door in her face.

He is suddenly very light-headed and tired but, nevertheless, exultant. He decides he will have a nap. But the woman has begun to hammer at the door.

"Stop it," he shouts. He makes his way to his bedroom on unsteady legs; in fact, one is trailing and he must support himself by leaning against the wall. What is this?

The bedroom lies in half-light, but he can see the red rubber sheet. It must go. He tugs at it and it resists him like some living thing, like a limpet clinging to a rock. He feels a great weakness spreading like a stain down his left side. His leg crumples, his mouth falls open in surprise as he falls. He lands loosely like a bundle of sticks, his legs and arms splayed wide, but feels nothing but a prickling sensation in his bladder. No pain, nothing. There are shadows everywhere in the room; they seem to float, and hover, and quiver. He realizes the front of his pants are wet. He tries to get up, but the strength ebbs out of his limbs and is replaced by a sensation of dizzying heaviness. He decides he will rest a minute and then get up.

But he doesn't. He sleeps.

Mrs. Hax waited under the eaves for the rain to abate. It fell for an hour with sodden fury, and then began to slacken into a dispirited drizzle. When it did, she picked her way carefully through the puddles in the garden to where the hoe lay. With it, she broke a basement window and methodically trimmed the glass out of the frame. Then she settled herself on to her haunches, and gasping, wriggled into the opening. She closed her eyes, committed her injuries to his head, and then let herself drop. She landed on one leg, which buckled, and sent her headlong against the gas furnace, which set every heat vent and duct in the building vibrating with a deep atonal ringing. Uninjured, she picked herself up from the floor. Her dignity bruised, her authority wounded, she began to edge her way through the basement clutter toward the stairs.

Dieter Bethge woke with a start. Some noise had broken into his dream. It had been a good and happy dream. The dancing bear had been performing for him under no compulsion, a free gift given in freedom. It had been a perfect, graceful dance, performed without a hint of the foppishness or studied concentration that mars the dance of humans. As the bear had danced he had seemed to grow, as if fed by the pure clear notes of the music. He had grown larger and larger, but Dieter had watched this with a feeling of great peace rather than alarm.

The sun glinted on his cinnamon fur and burnished his coat with red, winking light. And when the music stopped, the bear had opened his arms very wide in a gesture of friendship and welcome. His mouth had opened as if he were about to speak. And that was exactly what Dieter had expected all along. That the bear would confide in him the something that only Dieter had recognized.

But then something had broken the spell of the dream.

He was confused. Where was he? His hand reached out and touched something smooth and hard and resisting. He gave a startled grunt. This was wrong. His mind slipped backward and forward, easily and smoothly, from dream to the sharp, troubling present.

He tried to get up. He rose trembling, swayed, felt the floor shift, and fell, striking his head on a chest of drawers. His mouth filled with something warm and salty. He could hear something moving in the house, and then the sound was lost in the tumult of the blood singing in his veins. His pulse beat dimly in his eyelids, his ears, his neck and fingertips.

He managed to struggle to his feet and beat his way into the roar of the shadows, that slipped by like surf, and out into the hallway.

And then he saw a form in the muted light, patiently waiting. It was the bear.

"Bear?" he asked, shuffling forward, trailing his leg.

The bear said something he did not understand. He was waiting.

Dieter lifted his arms for the expected embrace, the embrace that would fold him into the fragrant, brilliant fur; but, curiously, one arm would not rise. It dangled limply like a rag. Dieter felt something strike the side of his face — a numbing blow. His left eyelid fell like a shutter. He tried to speak but his tongue felt swollen and could only batter noiselessly against his teeth. He felt himself fall but the bear reached out and caught him in the warm embrace he desired above all.

And so, Dieter Bethge, dead of a stroke, fell gently, gently, like a leaf, into the waiting arms of Mrs. Hax.

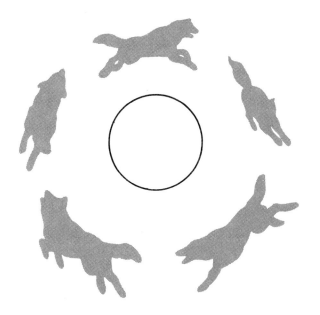

NOTES ON THE CONTRIBUTORS

EDNA ALFORD is from Livelong. Her stories have appeared in periodicals such as *Fiddlehead*, *Prism International*, and *Branching Out*. Her first collection of stories will be published in 1981 by Oolichan Press.

BYRNA BARCLAY of Regina has had poems and stories in periodicals and anthologies, including *Salt*, *NeWest ReView*, *Northward Journal*, and *Smoke Signals*. Her novel, *Summer of the Hungry Pup*, is to be published by NeWest Press.

MICK BURRS lives in Regina, where he organized "Warm Poets for Cold Nights", a series of winter poetry readings which, since 1975, has featured more than 40 poets. He has several chapbooks to his credit and many periodical publications, as well as two books, *Moving in from Paradise* (Coteau Books) and *Children on the Edge of Space* (Blue Mountain Books).

ANNE CAMPBELL is from Regina, but is now working in Calgary as Communications Co-ordinator for Heritage Park. Her poems have appeared in such journals as *Grain*, *Dandelion*, and *NeWest ReView*, and on CBC radio.

ROBERT CURRIE lives in Moose Jaw. He founded the literary magazine *Salt*, and edited it for eight years. Besides numerous periodical publications and several chapbooks, he has two books of poetry published by Oberon Press: *Diving into Fire* and *Yarrow*. A suite of poems from the latter book won a prize in the 1980 CBC literary competition.

KRISTJANA GUNNARS was born in Iceland, but has lived in Regina for several years. Her book, *Settlement Poems*, was published by Turnstone Press, and three more are soon to appear, including *One-Eyed Moon Maps* (Press Porcepic) and *Wake-Pick Poems* (Anansi).

TERRENCE HEATH lives near Saskatoon, where he is Executive Director of Saskatchewan's Western Development Museums. He also works as a freelance art curator, and writes critical articles about art. Besides numerous publications in journals and anthologies, he has two books, *The Truth and Other Stories* (Anansi) and *Interstices of Night* (Turnstone Press).

JOHN V. HICKS lives in Prince Albert, where he is organist of St. Alban's Cathedral. During 1978, he was named Writer-In-Residence by the City of Prince Albert. His poems have been widely published in magazines and anthologies in Canada and the United States. His first book, *Now is a Far Country*, was published by Thistledown Press, who will soon release his second collection, *Winter Your Sleep*.

WILLIAM J. KLEBECK lives in Saskatoon, where he is studying law. His work has appeared in such western periodicals as *Grain* and *The Chelsea Journal*. He is President of the Saskatchewan Writers Guild.

FREDA KORBER lives in Saskatoon, where she attends university as a "perennial undergraduate". Two of her stories were read recently on CBC radio. "Writing beats doing housework," she says, "but — on some days — not by much."

PAT KRAUSE lives in Regina. She has been a freelance broadcaster and story editor with the CBC, where she learned to swear. She has worked for several summers as co-ordinator of the creative writing classes at the Saskatchewan School of the Arts. Her short story collection, *Freshie*, which won a prize in the 1979 Department of Culture and Youth literary competition, is being published by Potlatch Publishing.

KEN MITCHELL of Regina is a prolific writer of novels, stories, poetry, and drama. He is also a performer, teacher, and editor. His novels include *Wandering Rafferty* (Macmillan) and *The Con Man* (Talonbooks). Some recent plays are *Cruel Tears* (written with Humphrey and the Dumptrucks), *The Shipbuilder*, and *The Great Cultural Revolution*. His original screenplay, *The Hounds of Notre Dame*, has been made into a feature film. He edited the important anthology of prairie writing, *Horizon*, for Oxford University Press. His critical study of the works of Sinclair Ross will be published in 1981 by Coteau Books.

BRENDA RICHES of Saskatoon is a past President of the Saskatchewan Writers Guild. She has had work published in literary journals, including *Grain*, *Fiddlehead*, and *Dandelion*. Her first book, *Dry Media*, will be published by Turnstone Press.

WILMA RILEY teaches in Regina, and writes stories, plays, and poems. Her stories or poems have appeared in *Journal of Canadian Fiction*, *This Magazine*, and on CBC radio. She is taking a year's leave of absence in Montreal to work on her writing.

BARBARA SAPERGIA lives in Regina. She has published poems and stories in periodicals and anthologies, and three of her radio dramas have been produced by CBC. Her poetry collection, *Dirt Hills Mirage*, will be published by Thistledown Press.

REG SILVESTER is from North Battleford, and now lives in temporary exile in Edmonton, where he works as a freelance writer and editor. His stories have appeared in *Grain*, *Fiddlehead*, *Dandelion*, and *NeWest ReView*.

LOIS SIMMIE of Saskatoon teaches creative writing at the Saskatchewan School of the Arts and is a former associate editor of *Grain* magazine. Her poems and stories have appeared in journals and anthologies. Her first novel will be published in 1981 by Macmillan-NAL.

GLEN SORESTAD of Saskatoon teaches high school English, and writes poems and stories, which have appeared in journals and anthologies, and on CBC radio. His books of poetry include *Pear Seeds in My Mouth* (Sesame Press), and *Prairie Pub Poems* and *Ancestral Dances* (both Thistledown Press). He is also co-editor of three short story anthologies, including *Tigers of the Snow*, a collection of Canadian stories.

EUGENE STICKLAND of Regina writes stories and plays. His one-act play, *Revelations*, was produced by Regina's Noon Stage, and a story has been read on CBC radio. He is studying playwriting at York University.

GERTRUDE STORY lives in Vanscoy, and works as a freelance writer and broadcaster, as well as attending the University of Saskatchewan. She writes stories, poems, and radio dramas, which she has sold to numerous magazines and to CBC radio.

ANNE SZUMIGALSKI lives in Saskatoon. She has taught at the Saskatchewan School of the Arts and has served as an associate editor of *Grain* magazine. She has three books of poetry, *Woman Reading in Bath* (Doubleday), *Wild Man's Butte*, written in collaboration with Terrence Heath (Coteau Books), and *A Game of Angels* (Turnstone Press).

GEOFFREY URSELL lives in Regina. His poems, stories, and songs have appeared in many periodicals and anthologies, and his play, *The Running of the Deer*, won a national playwriting award, the Clifford E. Lee award, in 1977. His songs for *Number One Hard*, a play about the grain industry, have been released on a long-play album, and he is co-author (with Rex Deverell) of *Superwheel*, a musical play for high schools, published by Coteau Books.

GUY VANDERHAEGHE of Saskatoon has had stories published in various literary magazines and anthologies, including *Grain*, *Quarry*, and the *Malahat Review*, and in Doubleday's *Aurora* anthologies.

ROBERT KROETSCH, winner of the Governor-General's award for fiction, was born in Alberta, and now lives in Winnipeg, where he teaches at the University of Manitoba. His novels include *But We Are Exiles*, *The Studhorse Man*, *Badlands*, and most recently, *What The Crow Said* (General Publishing). He has also developed an increasing interest in poetry, and has become a leading exponent of the longpoem. His poetry books are *Stone Hammer Poems* (Oolichan Press), *The Ledger* (Applegarth Follies), *Seed Catalogue* (Turnstone Press), and *The Sad Phoenician* (Coach House Press). He is well loved by the many writers, from Saskatchewan and elsewhere, who have worked with him in creative writing classes at the Saskatchewan School of the Arts near Fort Qu'Appelle.

WILLIAM JOHNSON, the designer of *Sundogs*, is a freelance illustrator and book designer, artist, and poet. He has designed many books for Coteau Books, including *Moving in from Paradise* and *Ghost House*, and also provided the delightful drawings for *Odpoems &* and *Superwheel*. He has done design and illustration work for Black Moss Press, and other presses.

ACKNOWLEDGMENTS

Some of the stories included in *Sundogs* have appeared previously (or will appear) in the following places, and are used by permission of the authors. Mick Burrs: *Smoke Signals*; Robert Currie: *NeWest ReView*; Kristjana Gunnars: *NeWest ReView*; Terrence Heath: *Canadian Fiction Magazine*; John V. Hicks: *Smoke Signals*; Brenda Riches: *event*; Reg Silvester: *Grain*; Lois Simmie: *Smoke Signals*; Glen Sorestad: *Northward Journal*; Gertrude Story: *Grain*; Anne Szumigalski; *Writers News Manitoba*; Guy Vanderhaeghe: *The Chelsea Journal*.

The THUNDER CREEK CO-OP is a production co-operative registered with the Saskatchewan Department of Co-operation and Co-operative Development. It was formed to publish prairie writing — poetry, prose, songs, and plays.

PUBLICATIONS

SUNDOGS, an anthology of the best in Saskatchewan short stories, edited by Robert Kroetsch, $7.95.

WILD MAN'S BUTTE, a dramatic poem set in Saskatchewan's Big Muddy, by Terrence Heath and Anne Szumigalski, $3.00.

SUPERWHEEL, the musical play about automobiles, with script by Rex Deverell and music and lyrics by Geoffrey Ursell, $5.00.

NUMBER ONE HARD, an L.P. of the songs by Geoffrey Ursell from the original Globe Theatre production, "an investigative documentary about the prairie grain industry," $6.00.

NUMBER ONE NORTHERN, an anthology of Saskatchewan poetry. Winner of the 1978 Saskatchewan Publishing Prize, $7.00.

EYE OF A STRANGER, poems by Garry Raddysh, $4.00.

ODPOEMS &, poems by E. F. Dyck, $4.00.

GHOST HOUSE, stories and poems by Lois Simmie, $3.00.

MOVING IN FROM PARADISE, poems by Mick Burrs, $3.00.

HOME STREET, poems by Gary Hyland, $2.00.

MOVING OUT, poems by Robert Currie, $2.00.

PRAIRIE GRASS, PRAIRIE SKY, an L.P. with songs by Rob Bryanton, Bob Evans, Glenn Koudelka, Connie Kaldor, and Geoffrey Ursell, $7.00.

All of the above may be ordered from

THUNDER CREEK CO-OP
Box 239, SUB #1
Moose Jaw, Saskatchewan
S6H 5V0

coteau books